PRAISE FOR *Seekers of the Wild Realm*

"Ott's fast-paced fantasy highlights the importance of persistence, especially with regard to changing society's (rather set) ways."
—*Kirkus Reviews*

"Recommended for all collections. A lovely story of friendship, empowerment, and the effectiveness of people working together." —*SLJ*

"This well-executed story offers a wonderfully imaginative world for young fantasy fans to dive into." —*Booklist*

ALSO BY ALEXANDRA OTT

Rules for Thieves
The Shadow Thieves
Seekers of the Wild Realm

SEEKERS
OF THE WILD REALM

Legend of the Realm

ALEXANDRA OTT

ALADDIN
New York London Toronto Sydney New Delhi

ALADDIN

An imprint of Simon & Schuster Children's Publishing Division
1230 Avenue of the Americas, New York, New York 10020
First Aladdin hardcover edition June 2021
Text copyright © 2021 by Alexandra Ott
Jacket illustration copyright © 2021 by Cathleen McAllister
All rights reserved, including the right of reproduction in whole or in part in any form.
ALADDIN and related logo are registered trademarks of Simon & Schuster, Inc.
For information about special discounts for bulk purchases, please contact
Simon & Schuster Special Sales at 1-866-506-1949 or business@simonandschuster.com.
The Simon & Schuster Speakers Bureau can bring authors to your live event.
For more information or to book an event contact the Simon & Schuster Speakers Bureau
at 1-866-248-3049 or visit our website at www.simonspeakers.com.
Jacket designed by Heather Palisi
The text of this book was set in Bembo Std.
Manufactured in the United States of America 0521 FFG
2 4 6 8 10 9 7 5 3 1
Library of Congress Cataloging-in-Publication Data
Names: Ott, Alexandra, author.
Title: Legend of the Realm / by Alexandra Ott.
Description: First Aladdin hardcover edition. | New York : Aladdin, 2021. |
Series: Seekers of the Wild Realm | Audience: Ages 8–12. |
Summary: Bryn, Ari, and their dragon Lilja discover a sick baby gyrpuff
and join the rest of the Seekers in trying to determine if
a dreadful plague has returned—and if human forces brought it back.
Identifiers: LCCN 2020049089 |
ISBN 9781534438613 (hardcover) | ISBN 9781534438637 (ebook)
Subjects: CYAC: Dragons—Fiction. | Magic—Fiction. | Plague—Fiction. |
Sex role—Fiction. | Adventure and adventurers—Fiction. | Fantasy.
Classification: LCC PZ7.1.O88 Leg 2021 | DDC [Fic]—dc23
LC record available at https://lccn.loc.gov/2020049089

FOR MOM, DAD,
AND KATIE

ONE

It's finally time to see the dragons.

The moment the sun peeks through the window of our hut, I leap out of bed and rush to help Mama prepare breakfast, skipping through the kitchen with excitement.

"What's wrong with you?" Elisa asks, giving me a suspicious look as she sits at the table. Her dark, braided hair is messy from sleep. "What are you so happy about?"

"It's dragon day!" I announce, ladling oatmeal into her bowl so enthusiastically that it sloshes over the side.

"Mama, Bryn's spilling breakfast!" Elisa yells instantly. She has recently entered the tattletale stage of being six years old. And, of course, her favorite target is her older sister—me.

"Careful, Brynja," Mama says without looking up. She's preparing a cup of tea steeped in starflower leaves for Elisa, who drinks it every morning to keep her coughing fits away.

Papa's uneven footsteps suddenly fill the room as he enters

the small kitchen. "Well, someone's up early this morning," he says cheerfully. "What's the occasion, Bryn?"

"Dragon day!" I announce, grinning up at him. Papa, a former Seeker himself, is the only person in this hut besides me who properly appreciates dragons. Elisa goes through different phases of fascination with magical creatures, but I think she's back to unicorns at the moment.

"Ah, that's right," he says, leaning his cane against the wall and settling into his seat. "They're giving you the whole tour, eh?"

"Don't you ride on a dragon, like, every day?" Elisa asks. "What's so special?"

"I'm going to meet *all* the dragons today," I say proudly. "The Seekers have finally given me and Ari permission to go into the Valley of Ash, where the dragons live. I've been *dying* to see it."

"Oh." Elisa ponders this for only a moment. "Finally," she declares. "You've been a Seeker for *forever*."

Actually, it's been only a month, but I don't disagree with her sentiment. After Ari and I were appointed Seekers, I thought we'd begin the job right away and start entering the Realm frequently—but that hasn't exactly been the case.

The other three Seekers on the Council, who have all been doing the job for ages, have insisted that Ari and I need more training before we're allowed to enter the Realm on our own. Which is ridiculous, because I thought the whole point of the Seeker competition was to train us *before* we started the job.

Of course, I have a sneaking suspicion that I know why the Seekers are doing it. I didn't exactly win the job in the most conventional way. In fact, I didn't have any formal training at all, the way Ari did. But you'd think that defeating our oldest enemies, the Vondur, and driving them off the island would've been proof enough that I can handle things. It's particularly absurd given the fact that I'd been in the Realm by myself before becoming a Seeker, but it didn't seem wise to mention that to the Council, since I was definitely breaking the rules at the time.

So far Ari and I have seen only bits and pieces of the Realm, as the Seekers have given us a gradual tour, insisting that one of the older Seekers accompanies us at all times to show us the ropes. But we've encountered only the tamer creatures so far—until today.

Mama sets the cup of starflower tea down in front of Elisa and glances at me. "Bring back some more flowers when you get a chance, Brynja. We need more tea."

I sigh. "I can only go when the Seekers give me permission."

"But you *are* a Seeker," Elisa says, slurping her tea.

I couldn't agree with her more. I thought being a Seeker meant being able to go into the Realm whenever I wanted—not having to wait for one of the older Seekers to tell me it's okay. They claim this training period is only temporary, but they also haven't said anything about when it will end.

Surely it must be soon, though. Once they've introduced

us to dragons, which are the most dangerous creatures in the entire Realm, then what else is there for us to learn?

Papa senses my dejection and gives me a pat on the shoulder. "Have patience, Seeker Bryn. Your time will come soon enough."

I sigh again. I hate patience.

I hate it so much, in fact, that I rush through the rest of breakfast, say quick goodbyes to my family, and hurry out the door before Mama can insist I help with the dishes. Outside, the air is crisp and cool, a breeze from the sea stirring the leaves of the garden. I tug my official Seeker cloak over my shoulders and set off down the path toward the village.

Even though it's early, the village square is already bustling with activity. The fishermen are heading down to the docks, the shopkeepers are opening their doors, and many of the children are gathering at the wells to collect water for cooking breakfast. Few people look up as I walk through the crowd, my cloak flapping in the breeze.

A shopkeeper bumps me as I pass and mumbles, "Morning, Brynja," before quickly moving away. He's supposed to say *Seeker* in front of my name now, but none of the villagers do. No one else even bothers to greet me.

I hold back a sigh. I've lived in this village my whole life, yet everyone treats me differently since I was appointed Seeker—and not in the way I thought they would. Since I'm the first girl to be appointed Seeker, and since I got the job in an unusual way, some of the villagers seem openly resentful of me now, and the rest acknowledge me grudgingly. But once I start bringing more magical artifacts from the Realm into the village to trade, things will get better. They'll want to talk to me once I have briarwood to repair their buildings and phoenix feathers to heal their ailments. I just need the other Seekers to actually let me into the Realm first.

"Morning, Seeker!" someone calls brightly, and I spin around to see who's greeted me—only to find Ari instead. He waves to the villager who spoke to him, a little shyly, and fastens a loose button on his Seeker cloak.

"Hey, Bryn," he says, smiling as the wind ruffles his curly hair. Like me and everyone else in the village, Ari has light-brown skin and dark-brown eyes, but his curls are more corkscrew than mine, which are always messy. "Excited for dragon day?" he asks.

"Of course. I can't wait to—"

"Good morning, Seeker Ari!" another villager says cheerfully as they pass him.

I hold back a groan, and Ari glances at me, frowning. As an empath, he can magically sense my emotions, an ability that is sometimes cool but also sometimes annoying if you're the person whose emotions he reads all the time.

"Why so frustrated?" he asks.

"Don't worry about it. Let's get going so we can meet some dragons!"

We rush up the path to Dragon's Point, the sunlight warming our backs as we ascend. The land surrounding the village to the north slopes gradually upward, giving way to hills, plateaus, and eventually towering mountain peaks that ring the Realm and create a natural boundary. The only way to cross the mountains is to fly over them on the back of a dragon, which is why Seekers have to use this means of transport every day.

Dragon's Point, the large plateau, which serves as the most natural landing spot for dragons close to the village, is deserted when we arrive.

"Guess we got here a little too early," Ari says, wrapping his cloak more tightly around his shoulders as the wind picks up. Jokingly, he adds, "I'm going to have a word with the other Seekers about this whole early-morning thing."

I snort. Since Ari and I became Seekers a month ago, he's barely said two words to any of the other Seekers. We're both still a little intimidated by them, I guess. We're not only new to the job but also only twelve, while the others are adults who've been Seekers for ages. But since I grew up knowing them as Papa's friends, they seem less scary to me. One of the perks of being a Seeker's daughter, I suppose, is realizing that Seekers are ordinary people first and foremost. Which is probably why I believed I could become one. Good thing I was right.

"Do you think this will be the last day of our completely unnecessary training?" I ask. "Surely dragons have to be the final lesson, right?"

Ari shrugs. "I wouldn't say *completely* unnecessary. It was helpful when Seeker Larus showed us how to find saellons and when Seeker Freyr taught us how to check sea wolves for injuries without getting bit, and—"

"True, but they could've also let us explore the Realm a bit on our own. I mean, we raised a baby dragon by ourselves! Do we really need all this supervision?"

Ari's eyes widen. "Someone's coming up!" he whispers.

I turn and glance down the path. Sure enough, another figure cloaked in green is making his way to the top of the plateau. Hopefully he's still too far away to have heard me complaining.

"Ah, our young Seekers are here bright and early! Excellent!" calls a cheerful voice that can belong only to Seeker Ludvik.

"Good morning, Seeker Ludvik," Ari and I call.

Seeker Ludvik huffs a little as he reaches us, then claps his hands together brightly. "So, who can tell me what we'll be seeing today as we journey into the Valley of Ash?"

"The valley is at the foot of the Realm's largest volcano," I say immediately. "It's covered in a layer of hardened lava from multiple eruptions, and it's the place where dragons are born."

"Where dragons build their dens," Ari adds.

Seeker Ludvik smiles. "Correct, Seeker Ari! We'll be visiting the dragon dens today and meeting the Realm's largest occupants!"

I frown. Both Ari and I were correct, yet Seeker Ludvik only said Ari's name. Did I say something wrong?

"What are we waiting for!" I declare, perhaps louder than necessary. But Seeker Ludvik is always enthusiastic, so I should be too if I want to impress him. "Let's get going!"

Seeker Ludvik chuckles. "That's the spirit!"

Ari and I whistle for our dragon, Lilja, and Seeker Ludvik does the same for his dragon, who is a big brown adult named Snorri. Snorri arrives first, with Lilja following close behind and looking very excited to see another dragon here. Her pearlescent silver scales glimmer in the sunlight as she lands, her thin, batlike wings folding at her sides. She greets us by tapping our shoulders with the end of her massive snout. She's going to have to stop doing that, though, because pretty soon she'll be big enough to knock us over. She's still a baby, but she'll be full grown in no time.

Seeker Ludvik leads the way as we fly the dragons directly toward the valley. Mountains rise on all sides, their jagged gray peaks disappearing into the clouds. As we pass over them, the varied landscapes of the Realm come into view: sprawling forests, winding rivers, flower-laden meadows. Glacier peaks and sheets of ice lie to the north, jagged cliffs span the coastline to the south, and a rough line of ashen volcanoes runs diagonally through the middle. We aim for the large valley in the center of the volcanoes and land on a layer of hardened rock, ash flying into the air as the dragons settle onto the ground.

"Now," Seeker Ludvik says, turning on Snorri to face us, "you're both quite familiar with dragons, of course, so I don't think we need to go over general dragon behavior. But every dragon, like every human, is an individual, and each of them has traits that you need to be aware of. Take Snorri, for instance." He gives the brown dragon a pat on the neck. "Snorri here absolutely loves to be rubbed right on the ears." He demonstrates, scratching the tips of Snorri's ears, and the dragon slaps his tail to the ground happily. "But *do not* try this anywhere near his mouth. Most dragons love being scratched along the jaw, but Snorri will bite off the hand of anyone who tries it!" He states this cheerfully, like it's a fun fact instead of a warning, but I suspect he's being serious about Snorri's bite. "That's why, for your first trip into the valley, we wanted to introduce you to each of our resident dragons and share some of the traits you need to be aware of when interacting with them. I'll also show you each of the dens, so you know how to find them when you need them. Sound good?"

Ari and I nod fervently. Lilja perks up her ears.

"Excellent," Seeker Ludvik says. "Let's begin the tour!"

First we fly to one of the largest dens at the far end of the valley. We peer inside, only to see a golden dragon curled in the corner, fast asleep.

"You already know Gulldrik, of course," says Seeker Ludvik. "He's been Seeker Larus's chosen flight companion for many years now. He shares this large den with his mate, Groa, and his sister, Helena."

"Is that common?" Ari asks. "Do dragons usually share dens with family members?"

"Sometimes," Seeker Ludvik says. "Dragons are very social creatures and will often choose to share space with at least one other." He glances at Lilja, then leans forward and whispers conspiratorially, "I suspect that Lilja may be related to this particular family of dragons. None of them are silver, but metallic hues seem to run in this line. Alas, we can never know for certain which nest Lilja's egg was taken from, but I'd guess this is the home of her blood relatives."

Ari's eyes widen. "Has she interacted with them at all? Do they get along?"

"Yes, and yes, as well as can be expected," Seeker Ludvik says. "Keep in mind that, because Lilja was away from the Realm for so long, she's still a bit of an outsider here—they don't know that her egg originated in this valley, since she was born outside of it. It will take some time for Lilja to be fully integrated into the group. But the other dragons have reacted tolerably to her, if not warmly, which is a promising first step."

I give Lilja a pat. "Don't worry," I whisper to her. "The other dragons will love you in no time."

"Now," Seeker Ludvik says, "let's work clockwise, shall we? The next den is just over here. . . ."

The next few minutes pass in a blur as Seeker Ludvik introduces us to dozens of dragons in a wide variety of hues. He shares random facts about each one and clearly knows them all well. There's a berry-red one whose fiery breath "reaches farther than any other," a soft-yellow dragon with a whiplike tail and a "weakness for chocolate," and a plum-colored dragon Ludvik says is nearsighted.

"Well," he says finally as he pats the side of a rusty-orange adolescent dragon. "There's only one dragon left to meet."

"Seeker," I say carefully. I've been wanting to ask this, and Seeker Ludvik seems more approachable than the others, but . . . I'm afraid of the answer. "When do you think Ari and I will be able to enter the Realm on our own?"

I might be imagining it, but I think Seeker Ludvik's smile falls slightly. "Let's speak about that at the next Seeker meeting with the others, all right? We'll let the whole Council decide when the best moment is."

"But, Seeker, how long does it normally take for new Seekers to be fully trained?"

"Well, we've had some, er, unusual circumstances, and there are two of you this time, so fewer Seekers to help train you, so I'm not sure I can say. . . ."

"That's why I think Ari and I should begin real Seeker duties," I say quickly. "You and Seeker Larus and Seeker Freyr must be so overworked, handling all the duties of the Realm with just the three of you, plus all the extra boundary spells you've been setting because of the Vondur. . . . I just think Ari and I really need to help."

He shakes his head slowly. "Don't you worry, Bryn." He lays a hand on my shoulder as if to comfort me. "I've put a lot of work into maintaining the boundary over these last few months, and I can assure you that the Vondur won't be able to break through. There's no need to worry yourself. Just stay focused on your training instead, eh?"

He smiles as he passes me, returning to his dragon, but I don't. It feels like he's treating me like a baby, essentially telling me to let the grown-ups handle it. Seeker Ludvik seems nice enough, but I don't think he sees me as a Seeker yet. Aren't I supposed to be his equal now, not his student?

I open my mouth, about to say something else, but Ari shakes his head at me, climbing onto Lilja's back to follow Seeker Ludvik. I know what Ari's thinking—he doesn't want to cause a scene, doesn't want any of the Seekers to be upset with us. He wants to make a good impression, but I don't think sitting quietly and letting them treat us like babies is the best way to do that.

With a sigh, I hop back onto Lilja, and we take off for the final den. This one is small, tucked into an almost-forgotten corner away from the others.

"Now," Seeker Ludvik says as we land, "I'd like you to be particularly cautious here. This dragon is our newest arrival, and we're still developing trust with him."

"Newest?" Ari asks, hopping off Lilja's back. "You mean the red one? The one that came with the Vondur?"

Seeker Ludvik nods. "The very same."

Ari and I exchange glances. When the dark magicians from the mainland came onto our island a month ago, they planned to fly into the Realm on a stolen dragon—a baby red one they'd been keeping in chains ever since a former Seeker,

Agnar, stole its egg from the Realm. It was injured and mis-treated by the Vondur, so I don't doubt that it's mistrustful of humans. I'm a bit ashamed to realize I'd completely forgotten about it. I didn't think to wonder how this dragon's been doing now that the Vondur have been exiled and it's been returned to the Realm.

"Let's keep Lilja and Snorri outside," Seeker Ludvik says as he and I dismount. "Wouldn't want to scare the poor thing."

"Does he have a name?" I ask as Ari and I give Lilja the signal to stay put, and we proceed into the darkened cave after Seeker Ludvik.

"Not yet," Seeker Ludvik says. "Larus and Freyr and I have all been visiting this little fellow regularly, but not too often. We don't want to overwhelm him."

A low growl issues from ahead of us, and Ari freezes. "He heard us," Ari says, "and he's afraid."

I shiver as the dragon lets out a fierce, echoing roar.

TWO

The dragon's growls echo around us as we stop just outside the den. Seeker Ludvik issues a soft, three-note whistle that pierces through the darkness. "We've been using that signal to approach him," he explains, "so that he knows who's coming before he sees us. It seems to help."

"It did," Ari says, his empathy gift swirling around his hands. "He just calmed down a bit."

Seeker Ludvik beams. "Excellent work, Seeker Ari. Now, he usually likes to sleep just around the next bend. Let's approach slowly. I'll go first, with the two of you directly behind me, so he can see us clearly. All right?"

We do as he suggested and round the bend. The red dragon glares at us as we enter, his yellow eyes bright. He's smaller than Lilja, and skinnier, but he looks healthier than the last time I saw him—his wound has healed, and it looks like he's been eating more.

"Will he grow to full size?" Ari whispers as we stop walking, letting the dragon study us.

"We're not sure," Seeker Ludvik says. "It's possible that being underfed has stunted his growth. But he's also quite young, so he may yet have a growth spurt."

"Hey, buddy," I whisper. "Seeker Ludvik, may I use my gift?"

"Go ahead," Seeker Ludvik says.

Magic wells up within me as I summon my gift, and green light bursts from my fingertips. It swirls toward the red dragon, seeking out his life source. It's huge and bright, just like Lilja's, but I approach carefully, not wanting to scare him. His yellow eyes snap toward me—he can sense my magic reaching for him.

"Hi, dragon," I say softly, letting my gift linger in the air near him without pushing forward. "How are you doing?"

He snorts, looking wary, but his spikes aren't raised.

Beside me, Ari's hands are lost in a whirl of yellow light as he uses his gift. "You can go closer," he murmurs, confirming my guess.

Ever so slowly, I reach toward the dragon with my magic and let my gift brush softly against his energy. His eyes widen at the unexpected contact and his ears pull back, but his spines are still relaxed, which means he's more startled than afraid. I linger there for a moment, letting him sense me. His energy brightens around mine, like he's exploring my gift, wanting to see more of it. I push a little more magic toward him.

"Not too much, Bryn," Seeker Ludvik whispers, and I

pull back. The violet light of Seeker Ludvik's gift is merely a wisp around his hands, like he's barely using it at all, yet he seems to be able to sense what I'm doing anyway. "Excellent work, Seeker Ari."

I glance toward Ari in confusion. Was he using his gift differently than me? I'm not sure what I did wrong.

"Has he let anyone ride him?" Ari asks quietly, watching the red dragon.

"Not since we brought him here," Seeker Ludvik says. "But I suspect that the two of you might be just the Seekers for the job."

My eyes widen. "Really? You mean we can ride him?"

"Let's take it one step at a time," Seeker Ludvik says quickly. "How about we see if we can get him to follow us out of the den first, and take things from there."

I grin and reach into my pocket, where I have a whole bag of bilberries for Lilja. "I think I know how we can coax him out."

Sure enough, the red dragon is *very* interested in the bilberries. He sniffs the first one hesitantly, unsure if it's safe, but after the first bite, his eyes go wide and he takes a step toward me, looking for more. I toss him another, then a third, and within moments he's following the three of us out of the den, sniffing loudly as I hold up a handful of berries.

"Good job!" I shout as he emerges from the den and stretches his wings. I toss the handful of berries, and his wide jaws scoop them up in one big gulp.

Then he notices Lilja and Snorri, and he stops moving, ears pulled back, and his spikes rise.

Ari's gift dances around him immediately, sending out calming waves. "It's okay," he says. "They're not going to bother you."

Slowly, the red dragon's spikes sink back down, but he still looks wary.

"Perhaps one of you would like to hop on Lilja's back and demonstrate for him?" Seeker Ludvik suggests. "It might be helpful for him to watch you with other dragons and know what to expect."

Ari and I glance at each other. Who wants to take the risk of trying to ride this dragon?

I do.

Ari nods once, sensing what I'm feeling. "I'll take Lilja this time," he says.

I grin. I can't help it—training dragons is so much *fun*. "Okay," I reply, turning back to the red dragon. "We really need to give you a name so I can call you something."

He blinks back at me, yellow eyes bright.

"How about . . ." I pause, studying his shimmering scales. They're a dusty red, like scorched earth, or the sky right before sunset. But I can't think of a name related to his color that fits. I turn to Seeker Ludvik. "What's he like when he flies? What's unique about him? Have you noticed anything?"

"Well, he's certainly fast," Seeker Ludvik says. "We

noticed his speed when we first brought him here. And he seems to love flying, though he hasn't yet taken a rider."

"Hmm." What are words related to flying? Maybe I should pick a word from the old language, like Lilja's name, which means "lily." I turn back to Seeker Ludvik. "What's the word for 'wind' in the old language?"

"Vin," he replies, smiling.

"Vin," I repeat, studying the dragon again. "I think it suits him, don't you? Because he flies like the wind?"

Seeker Ludvik beams at me. "I think you're right. And, come to think of it, the word 'vin' could also mean 'friend.'"

"Perfect!" I say. "Because we're friends now, aren't we, Vin?" I wave my gift to draw his attention to me. "Are you ready?"

He snorts.

Slowly, I take a step toward him, then another, my gift filling the air. "That's a good dragon," I murmur when he doesn't move. "Just let me come a little closer. . . ."

Vin snorts when I step within a foot of him, but he doesn't move. "Great job," I say, tossing him a bilberry. He snaps it up, and the ground trembles as his tail slaps down.

"Over here," Ari calls calmly, and Vin turns to look. Ari climbs onto Lilja's back more slowly than usual, letting Vin see how it's done. Once he's situated, Lilja snaps her wings wide, preparing for takeoff. Vin tilts his head, watching with confusion.

"What do you think?" I murmur to him. "Want to give it a try?"

I coax him with my gift, encouraging him to lower his body so that I can climb up. He resists at first, but after a few more bilberries, he lowers himself to the ground.

A few cautious steps later, I stroke his scales with my hand, letting him get used to being touched. When he doesn't react, I climb carefully onto his back.

For a moment we're all completely silent, holding our breath, waiting to see how Vin will react. I let my gift swirl around him, getting him comfortable with my presence. Ari watches from Lilja's back, and Seeker Ludvik stands nearby.

Vin snorts, then quickly rises to his feet. I grab hold of one of his spikes just in time as he lurches upward. "Whoa, go slower, boy. Slower—"

His wings snap wide, and Seeker Ludvik looks concerned. "Ari, see if you can calm—" he starts, but he doesn't get the chance to finish.

Without any coaxing at all, Vin suddenly leaps forward and takes off, heading for the sky. It's all I can do not to lose my grip on him as we launch forward.

"Whoa, Vin," I shout, "slow down!"

The wind rushes in my face as his wings beat faster, faster, faster—

I try to use my gift to slow him, but he's not used to taking directions and completely ignores me. He swoops through the air, circling the valley, his tail lashing back and forth. He's *fast*, even faster than Lilja, and I have to lower my head behind his neck to keep the wind from whipping into my face.

"Bryn!" Ari calls, his voice surprisingly close. "You okay?"

I glance up just enough to see the silver gleam of Lilja's scales approaching us, Ari atop her back.

"Fine," I shout back, "but can you slow him down?"

Ari's gift reaches toward Vin, swirling around us, and I back off with mine, not wanting to interfere with whatever Ari's doing. Vin seems to respond better this time. After a moment, he's calmer, and his speed gradually slows. He and Lilja fly side by side, and he lets out a happy snort, apparently enjoying the company.

"He's a natural," Ari remarks, watching the beat of his wings. "I think he's enjoying this!"

"He's enjoying it too much!" I shout back.

Ari grins. "Think you can get him to follow Lilja around? Let's show him some moves."

I summon my gift again as Ari steers Lilja into a turn. With a little nudge from me, Vin imitates her, turning sharply. "Not bad," I say to him. "Let's try a smoother one."

Ari leads us through a couple more turns, then banks slowly, losing altitude. Vin copies Lilja, following her every move. As we practice, he starts responding more quickly to my gift as I steer him, and within moments we're circling, diving, and climbing, pulling off a dozen tricks in the air. Vin *is* a natural, and he takes on every move eagerly, like he's been waiting his whole life for this.

I throw my head back and laugh, relishing the feeling of

the wind in my face and the sound of wingbeats in the air. *This* is what being a Seeker is all about.

"Um, Bryn?" Ari calls suddenly, sounding worried. "Do you think you can land him?"

My heart jumps in my chest. I have a sudden memory of Lilja's first landing, when we crashed into a lake and I nearly drowned.

"Um," I say. "Guess it's time to find out!"

Ari leads the way, guiding Lilja into a slow descent. Vin goes along with it perfectly at first, following Lilja down, but when he realizes we're landing, he suddenly pulls up, trying to climb into the air again.

"I know you love flying," I say gently, letting him circle around the valley again, "but I don't want you to get too tired, okay? We'll do this again later."

Vin huffs, a spark flying from his nose, and climbs higher into the air.

I give him a more forceful nudge with my gift, steering him back toward Lilja. "Don't you want to go say hi to Lil, your dragon friend? She's not up here anymore."

His wings beat faster, more frantically. I'm losing control.

"Okay, okay," I say soothingly, pulling my gift back a little. "Everything's fine. Don't panic."

He doesn't speed up, but he doesn't slow down, either. He turns, now facing Lilja again, but doesn't descend.

Ari shouts something, but from up here I can't hear it. "What?" I yell back.

"Berries! *Berries!*"

It takes me a moment to understand, but then my eyes widen. I reach into my pocket and yank out a handful of berries. Quickly, I toss one over Vin's head, hoping it catches his attention. He doesn't see it. I toss another.

This time he lurches forward, clearly following the berry, and his jaws snap as he catches it. I toss another and another. Again he descends slightly as he tries to catch them. I fling a handful, watching them fall. Vin is forced to fly lower and lower to catch them all.

We're close enough to Ari and Lilja to see them now, and Ari holds up his own handful of berries. "Here, Vin!" he calls. "Come get them!"

Finally, Vin seems to understand. He slows down and lands shakily, thudding to the earth. I cling to his back, expecting to be tossed around, but aside from a momentary scramble with his claws, the landing is smooth. He runs toward Ari, who tosses more berries to him. "Good job, Vin!" Ari says.

"Good job," I repeat breathlessly, loosening my grip. My legs have turned to jelly. "Good job."

From behind me, someone applauds.

I slide from Vin's back and turn to Seeker Ludvik, who's clapping and smiling. "Excellent work!"

"Thanks, Seeker," I say, willing my legs not to tremble at their sudden return to the earth.

But Seeker Ludvik isn't looking at me. "Fantastic job,

Seeker Ari, using your gift to guide Lilja and luring with the berries! Smart thinking."

I wait for him to say something to me, but he just gives Ari a pat on the shoulder. Ari blushes but doesn't speak, and I bristle. Sure, Ari did a great job, but *I* was the one flying on an untrained dragon and risking my life.

"Any training suggestions for me, Seeker Ludvik?" I say loudly.

He turns, looking startled, like he'd forgotten I was there for a moment. "Well, good flying, of course," he says. "Though *ideally* we could have slowed him down before he took off so quickly. But nice work under the circumstances."

Under the circumstances? What does he mean by that?

I try to brush off the ugly feeling rising within me. It doesn't matter, I remind myself. This is no longer a competition. Both Ari and I are Seekers, and we don't have to beat each other anymore. We both did well, and that's what matters. I *know* I did well, even if Seeker Ludvik doesn't say so.

But I can't stop the anger that fills my chest as Seeker Ludvik shakes Ari's hand vigorously, beaming at him.

"Seeker," Ari asks, looking up at Seeker Ludvik, "is it common for baby dragons to lose teeth?"

"Why, yes," Seeker Ludvik says with a nod. "They have sharp baby teeth that fall out around a month or two of age, to make room for the larger adult teeth that grow in."

"Do they look like that?" Ari asks, pointing. Ludvik and I

follow his gaze and catch sight of a white, fang-shaped tooth lying just outside Vin's den.

"Well spotted!" Seeker Ludvik cries. He approaches the tooth and studies it for a moment. "Dragon teeth are quite strong," he explains. "I imagine this will fetch quite a good trading price in the village. Ari, you spotted it first, so it's yours."

The anger fills my chest again as Ludvik continues congratulating Ari on the find. *I'm* usually the one who collects the most magical objects from the Realm. How could I have missed the dragon tooth? Probably because I was on Vin's back and fearing for my life as we left the cave. Which is completely unfair.

I take a deep breath as Ari approaches me, trying to hide my resentment. He gives me an odd look as he passes, probably sensing it with his gift. I sigh. I know I should be happy when Ari does well, but that's hard when the other Seekers treat me like I'm still a contestant in training instead of a full Seeker. I just flew on an untamed dragon, for crying out loud, and it wasn't enough to get a decent compliment from Seeker Ludvik.

How can I prove that I'm a real Seeker when nobody's even paying attention?

Seeker Ludvik soon ends our training session, as he has more work to do in the Realm, and instructs us to fly back to Dragon's Point. Lilja seems reluctant to leave, and I feel the same way. There's so much of the Realm to see and so much time left in the day to explore it. If only the other Seekers would just trust us enough . . .

A tiny seed of an idea sprouts in my mind as Ari and I hop onto Lilja's back and use our gifts to coax her into the air. The only way we're ever going to prove ourselves is by *proving ourselves*. And if the Seekers aren't going to give us the opportunity to do that, then we need to create one. Maybe, just maybe, we can make this happen ourselves.

"Ari," I say slowly, hardly daring to give voice to my thoughts. "Don't you think we should do something else?"

"What?" he calls over the roar of the wind as Lilja picks up speed. His curls fly wildly in front of his eyes. "Something else?" he repeats.

"Why should we go back to the village now? We're Seekers! We should go out into the Realm and *do something*!"

Ari frowns, and I suspect he's picking up more from my emotions than from my words. "But we can't. The other Seekers—"

"We're Seekers too," I say. "Don't you want to prove it?"

Ari's eyes widen. "I don't think this is a good idea—"

But his protest comes too late. I steer Lilja into a landing, using my gift to nudge her in the right direction. Lilja is thrilled by this turn of events—she'd much rather explore the Realm than drop us off at the Point—and responds to my magic immediately, swooping into a low dive. Before Ari can say another word of protest, Lilja aims for a clearing at the top of a cliff and lands, shaking her wings and running to a stop.

We're on our own in the Wild Realm.

THREE

What were you thinking?" Ari shouts as soon as he catches his breath. "Where are we?"

"No idea!" I say brightly. "Let's go explore and find out!"

"Bryn, we're going to get in so much trouble. The other Seekers already told us not to—"

I slide off Lilja's back, my boots landing in soft grass. All around us, the cliffside is rocky and studded with clumps of late-summer junipers and rosewood. The grass is impossibly green and full of life, just like everywhere else in the Realm.

I look back at Ari. "What are they going to do? Not let us come into the Realm? They're already doing that. Besides, we're Seekers too. This is our job. We've been respectful of all their training so far, but at a certain point, we just have to start doing our jobs."

"Um, what happens if they decide not to let us be Seekers anymore? The Council does everything by vote, and the older Seekers outnumber us. We might not have this job for long if they vote us out!"

"That's not going to happen," I say. "The Seekers rarely vote anyone out. They only did it to Agnar because he was a literal traitor selling magical objects to the Vondur and helping them take over the island. They're not going to exile us just because we broke some arbitrary rules."

"They also rarely appoint Seekers who didn't win the competition," Ari counters, "and they've never picked a girl before, either. They already broke precedent by giving you the job, so who's to say they won't decide to take it away?"

Admittedly, I hadn't thought things through that far, but I still don't think it's likely to happen. "Well, then we'd better make this a successful outing so they won't have any reason to kick us out, right?"

"Successful how? What's the point of being here? We don't even know where we are!"

"We're Seekers, Ari. The point is to *seek* something. Let's see if we can find some magical creatures and collect some items. Maybe we'll find some sea-wolf fur or phoenix feathers or—" I spin around, suddenly realizing exactly where we should go. "Or gyrpuff nests!"

"What?" Ari asks, sliding down from Lilja's back.

"Look, we're on one of the southern cliffs! See how it drops off on the side there? This is exactly the kind of spot where gyrpuffs tend to make their nests. Imagine if we brought a whole gyrpuff egg back to the other Seekers! Then they'd see that we know what we're doing."

Ari gazes skeptically at the cliffside. "How do we know for sure we'll find a nest? Seems awfully risky, Bryn."

"What risk? Gyrpuffs are completely harmless, and one of the easiest creatures in the Realm to deal with. We could hardly get into any trouble tracking them. And if we don't find anything, we'll just go back to the village and the other Seekers won't even know we were here. But if we *do* find something, then it'll be proof that we're ready to go out into the Realm on our own. No more training sessions or unnecessary supervision. Just us and the Realm!"

"And what happens if we fall off the cliff and die?"

I wave away his concern. "You worry too much. This is going to be great!"

I stand at the top of the cliff, certain death waiting below.

From a distance, the cliff didn't seem nearly so scary. But standing at its edge, I'm starting to think Ari might have been right. At my feet, the ground drops away, revealing the sea churning far below, its white-capped waves frothing up as if threatening to consume anyone who dares to cling to the cliffside, which is so steep and rocky that I can't imagine anyone has ever descended it before.

But that's exactly what Ari and I are about to do.

It turns out that finding gyrpuff nests might be harder than I thought.

"Well," Ari says from beside me, peering down at the sea below, "this looks tricky." The wind blows a tuft of his wild curls back from his face.

"My thoughts exactly," I mutter. Behind us, Lilja snorts loudly. She seemed interested in the landscape at first, just like she always is when we fly someplace new in the Realm, but it's been only a few minutes since we landed here and she's already lost interest. Any landscape that does not contain food for her is one that doesn't hold her attention for long.

These rock walls are peppered with tiny ledges, crevasses, and pockets, perfect for the small gyrpuff birds to make their nests. The cliffs are so high that only creatures with wings can reach them, but the caves are so small that dragons like Lilja couldn't possibly get to them. The only predators that stand a chance of accessing their nests are humans. Which is precisely what Ari and I plan to do, assuming we don't fall hundreds of feet to our deaths.

We could, of course, just have Lilja fly level with the sides of the cliffs and try to reach them that way. But, aside from the tricky maneuvering required to get from her back to the smallest of rock ledges, Lilja's presence would scare the gyrpuffs. Since they have the ability to disappear and reappear in another location (within a limited range), they'd just pop themselves and their nests deeper into the crevasses of the rock where we can't possibly find them.

There's only one way for a good Seeker to reach a gyrpuff nest: climbing straight down the side of the cliff.

"This is ridiculous," Ari says, echoing my thoughts as we stand at the edge and look down. "This has to be the stupidest thing I've ever done."

"You just flew hundreds of feet into the air on a dragon's back," I remind him.

"That's different. Lilja has wings. We don't."

"Oh, come on. You're just scared I'm going to beat you to the nests, and then all the good eggs will be mine."

"No, I just have a perfectly reasonable fear of plunging to my death."

"A *real* Seeker wouldn't be afraid."

He sighs deeply. "I really hope I live long enough to regret this."

With nothing left to say, we descend.

The jaggedness of the rock gives us plenty of handholds and footholds to work with as we cling to the side of the cliff and make our way down. But it's also wet with sea spray and much more slippery than I would've liked. At one point I make the mistake of looking down, and the sea is so far below us that it makes me a little bit dizzy.

"You all right?" Ari calls as I stop for a moment, waiting for the world to quit spinning.

"Fine," I say. "My eyes just decided to protest this height for a minute."

"I have to agree with them," Ari mutters, looking down at the raging sea. "Do you think Lilja will catch us if we fall?"

I glance at the top of the cliff, where Lilja is chomping

nonchalantly on what looks like a clump of dandelions. "I wouldn't count on it," I say. "Just try not to die."

"Working on it."

Thanks to my dizziness, it's Ari who finds a safe place to stand first. He lands carefully on a small ledge that's only a few feet wide, and I scramble to follow him. As soon as my feet hit the stone, I look around the ledge for any sign of gyrpuffs.

"See anything?" Ari whispers.

"Not yet. Let's walk a little farther," I whisper back.

"Sure hope you're right about there being gyrpuff nests here," Ari mutters.

I roll my eyes. "Have I ever been wrong?"

Ari mutters something too low for me to hear.

We walk single file along the ledge, carefully placing one foot in front of the other and clinging to the rocks with our hands. "What are the three things we're supposed to look for when tracking gyrpuffs?" I ask Ari, even though I know the answer. The other Seekers have been quizzing us so much that it's become a habit.

"Any loose feathers, of course," Ari says. "And three-pronged claw marks along the rocks. And . . . their poop."

"Ew. If we see anything that looks like poop, I'm not stopping to examine it."

Ari laughs. "All part of the glamorous life of being a Seeker." He stops suddenly, bending down to study something on the ground. "Hey, do you think this looks like a claw—"

He takes a step closer, and abruptly the rocks shift underneath him, and he loses his footing. His feet slide off the ledge, and I leap forward, grabbing his arm. His other hand clings to the rock wall, but his feet are dangling off the side of the cliff.

"I've got you!" I shout. "Don't move!"

Ari looks up at me, his eyes wide. I'm now precariously perched on the ledge, near the same spot where the loose rocks sent him tumbling. One wrong step, and I'll be headed over the side of the cliff too. But I can't haul Ari up by myself; I'm not strong enough to lift him.

"I'll pull you up," I lie, to calm his panic. "Just don't make any sudden movements."

"I can tell when you're lying, you know," he says, his voice coming out in a shaky croak. "Empath, remember?"

"Yeah, well, I'm really wishing you were a warrior right about now. Then you could just move the rock and push yourself up."

"But I'm not one, so I hope you've got a better idea."

"I'm working on it!" My arms are straining to hold him, and his other hand is barely clinging to the rock. I have to think fast.

On instinct, I reach for my magic, letting it flow into the air, searching for something, for *anything*. But we're surrounded by stone, and there's nothing for me to latch on to. . . .

There. Below Ari, and slightly to the right, I definitely feel something. There's another ledge, or some kind of protrusion, and a bright spark of life is perched on it. Something small, but its energy is strong enough that it's obviously magical. Which means . . .

"Ari," I say slowly, "I'm going to have to let you drop."

"What!"

"But first you need to move, like, a couple of inches to the right."

"If this is some kind of joke, Bryn, it's *not* the best time."

"Listen. There's a gyrpuff nest down there. I bet you can sense it with your gift. It should be plushy enough to land in, and it's not that far down. You just have to aim for it."

"How am I supposed to do that? I'm falling off the side of a cliff, Bryn!"

I take a deep breath, trying to ignore his panic. My arm is shaking. "I'm going to move a little bit to the right," I say, "and pull you in that direction. Then, on three, you need to let go of the rock. Okay?"

He shakes his head, looking down at the drop below.

"Ari. Use your gift. You can feel where the gyrpuff is. That's what we're aiming for. You feel it?"

"No!"

"Remember that thing you taught me? About finding the rhythm of things to sense them? You need to do that now. Close your eyes. Stop looking down."

Mutely, he shuts his eyes. I wish I could give him more time, but my strength is gone. In a second, I'm going to drop him whether I want to or not.

"Okay," I say, "I'm moving now." I take a careful half step to the right. The rock shifts under my feet, but it holds. I move my other foot and pull on Ari's arm, dragging him over.

"We're letting go on three," I say. "One."

Ari opens his eyes.

"Two."

He opens his mouth, but no words come out.

"Three."

We both let go at the same time.

Ari plummets, and I squeeze my eyes shut, sensing his landing with my gift instead of my eyes. For a second his magic is everywhere, flying through the air all around, and then—

He lands. His life force is right next to the smaller one that I sensed just below me.

He made it.

I peer carefully over the side of the ledge, but I can't see that far down in the shadows. "Ari?" I call.

Silence.

"Ari!"

"I'm here!" he croaks, and I exhale. "Bryn, you've got to see this! Just jump down."

Jump. Right.

"Um, maybe I'll look for a safer way. I'd really rather climb." But as I examine the rocks surrounding me, it's clear that our weight has disturbed them too much. The ledge under my feet is still trembling as I shift my footing, and I'm not sure if it will hold me much longer.

Jumping would be faster than climbing.

I don't give myself more time to think it through. I step toward the edge, trying to position myself directly over the two life forces below. I don't make the mistake of looking down again, keeping my eyes pressed tightly closed.

One. Two. Three.

I jump.

My heart hammers in my chest as the wind whooshes past me, my gift flying off in all directions, and—

I hit something soft with a little *thump*. It feels like a pillowy cushion is below me. I open my eyes.

"What took you so long?" Ari says with a grin.

I try to respond, but the fall has knocked all the air out of my lungs. "Ugh," I moan.

But as far as falls go, this one wasn't so bad. I am surrounded by super-soft black-and-white feathers, and the impact didn't hurt much at all. I sit up, brushing the feathers off my arms. Ari has a whole clump of them sticking out of his hair, but he doesn't notice. He's looking around in awe.

The nest is larger than I'd imagined, made of thick twigs and lined with softer grasses and fairy clovers as well as the feathers. And inside the nest with us sits what is unmistakably a gyrpuff. It's just under a foot tall, with a short orange beak and little webbed feet. Its primary feathers are jet-black, but there's a tuft of white on its belly that gleams in the soft sunlight. Its tiny wings are tucked in at its sides, and it regards us with inquisitive black eyes.

One of a gyrpuff's magical characteristics, aside from relocating in the blink of an eye, is the ability to imitate any sound they hear. It's an impressive skill, but, given that they're not the Realm's most intelligent creatures, they mostly just use it to be annoying. They generally emit squawks, squeaks, and chirps of varying pitch and intensity with no real pattern and for no real reason. Unless, that is, they're trying to scare predators away from their nests, at which point they can make any number of high-pitched screams, shrieks, or other horrible noises.

Which is exactly what happens to us now.

The gyrpuff begins to make a terrible, tremendously loud rumble, like a crash of thunder. Ari jumps at the unexpected sound, but when it doesn't deter us, the gyrpuff changes tack. The boom of thunder is replaced with a high-pitched, horrifying shriek that sounds like an animal in pain. Ari and I both cover our ears, cringing away from the noise. The gyrpuff only gets louder, taking a little hop forward and aiming its awful screech right at us.

With our hands covering our ears, we can't direct our gifts, so I reluctantly lower mine, exposing my ears and bracing myself against the onslaught of sound. I send my gift toward the gyrpuff as quickly as possible, reaching for its life force much less gently than usual. The gyrpuff stops abruptly, trying to figure out what the sensation of my gift is. It tilts its head curiously, the last echo of its shriek fading away.

"I think my ears are bleeding," Ari mutters.

"Don't be such a baby," I say. "If you hadn't been too busy cowering, you could've used your empathy gift to make it stop."

"I—" Ari starts, but I ignore him, climbing to my feet and taking a step closer to the bird.

"Hello there, pretty gyrpuff," I say, winding my gift around its life source so that it will feel more comfortable. "Don't mind us. Just go about your business."

Ari snorts.

"You want to lend me a hand here?" I say. Too loudly. The gyrpuff startles, and in the blink of an eye, it vanishes.

"Oops," Ari says.

"Well, at least it didn't take its nest with it. There are eggs here—look."

Ari and I crouch over the nest and examine our bounty. The gyrpuff feathers, of course, are a prize all on their own. They're extra soft and insulating, and often used to make clothes and blankets that repel cold. But all the feathers in the world aren't worth as much as the other objects lying in the nest. Two shiny eggs, both the size of my palm, are nestled in its center. And both of them have thick eggshells made of solid gold.

"How do we know if we can take them?" Ari whispers.

Much like chickens, gyrpuffs often lay eggs that don't actually have babies inside. Seekers can take the empty eggs to trade but must never take an egg that actually contains a baby gyrpuff.

"With your gift, of course," I reply. Even as I say it, I reach out with my own, searching for a life spark within each golden sphere.

The egg closest to me has a spark, albeit a small and feeble one. There's definitely something inside. But the one closer to Ari is hollow, with no spark at all.

"Guess this is it," Ari says. He unties the satchel from around his shoulder and carefully tucks the hollow egg inside.

"We should look around some more," I say. I don't know if it will be enough to impress the other Seekers if we return from our great gyrpuff-tracking mission with only one egg, especially considering how many of their rules we're breaking. Besides, it took a lot of effort to get all the way down this cliff. We need something more to show for it.

Ari glances around, the yellow glow of his gift dancing around his fingertips and providing illumination to the darker corners of this crevasse. "Is it just me," he says after a moment, "or is that another nest back there?"

I follow his gaze and call on my gift, feeling it rushing in my veins and flowing through me. Green sparks dance around my hands as I step closer to Ari. Sure enough, the twigs of a second nest are tucked on a rocky ledge about a foot over our heads, barely visible in the recesses of the rock.

"More climbing," Ari says with a sigh, but I'm already in motion. I latch on to a jagged edge and haul myself up, my boots finding traction against the rough stone. Within moments, I'm scrambling into the small nest, Ari right behind me.

"Careful," I say. "These twigs are pretty loose."

Ari's foot nearly slips as he steps into the nest, and he grimaces. "Noted."

"How many times am I going to have to save you from falling today?" I ask with a grin.

"Depends. How many more cliffs are you planning on climbing?"

I start to reply, but then a flicker of movement catches my eye, and I freeze. "Did you see that?" I whisper.

"Is that . . . ?" Ari doesn't finish his sentence. He doesn't need to.

As we both step forward, our gifts alight on a huddled figure at the back of the nest. It's a tiny gyrpuff, lying alone, and I know immediately that something is wrong.

Gyrpuffs usually sleep curled up in little balls, but this one is stretched on its side, and it's barely responding at all as Ari and I approach. One of its wings flickers feebly, and I exhale in relief—at least that means it's alive.

"Maybe it's injured?" Ari asks softly.

I kneel hesitantly, not wanting to scare the little bird, but it barely responds to my presence. I carefully reach out with my gift, the soft green light enveloping the gyrpuff and brushing against its energy. Gyrpuff life sparks are small, of course, given their size, but they're usually vibrant, since they're such magical creatures. But this gyrpuff's spark is feeble, flickering softly. I'm tempted to give it more energy immediately, to share my gift with it, but I shouldn't do that until I've figured out what's wrong. The cure will be much more effective once I know exactly what I'm curing.

"Do you see any injuries?" I ask Ari, who's kneeling on the other side of the bird. His gift shimmers in the darkness. Upon closer examination, this gyrpuff is slightly larger than the one we saw in the nest, which means it's probably male.

"No," Ari replies. "And I don't feel any, either. It's not like he's in pain, exactly. It's an illness."

Unlike my nature gift, Ari's empathy allows him to sense different things than I do—emotions, namely. He's as quick to detect illness as any healer, so I'm sure he's right.

I try to remember the protocol the Seekers shared with us for finding sick creatures. We've never actually encountered one during our first month as Seekers. "Well, we can't touch him, then," I say. "Might be something contagious that we could spread to other creatures."

"Right," Ari says. "Let's see if we can figure out his symptoms and identify the illness, and then we'll know whether we can heal him ourselves, or whether we need to get Seeker Larus or Seeker Freyr."

We probably *should* contact one of the other Seekers, since they have healing gifts and way more experience than we do. But this is the first serious challenge Ari and I have faced since officially becoming Seekers, and we have to prove that we can handle ourselves. Otherwise they'll *never* let us out here on our own again.

"His pulse is steady but weak," I say, feeling it with my gift. "His breathing isn't labored. He's low on energy, but I'm not sensing a source."

"Me neither," Ari agrees, closing his eyes to concentrate. "Nothing wrong with him physically, oddly enough, other than the fact that he's so lethargic. I can't really pinpoint anything."

I examine the little gyrpuff again. "Something's wrong with his feathers. They're not shiny like they should be, and it looks like he's got some bald patches. They're falling out."

"That could be a symptom of a lot of things," Ari says.

"True." I move a little closer to his head. "His beak looks normal."

As I shine my gift over him, his eyes twitch open, and I gasp. Ari flinches.

"Is he . . . ? Are they . . . ?" I start, but I can't finish.

Gyrpuffs naturally have big, bright-orange irises that take up most of their eye. It's one of their most distinguishable features.

But this bird's eyes are entirely black. Like his pupil has swallowed up his whole eye.

"Have you ever heard of anything like this?" I ask. "Black eyes?"

Ari shakes his head. "Gyrpuffs can go blind, but that usually makes their pupils look white."

"Well, I guess we should ask the other Seekers," I say reluctantly. "It's such an unusual symptom that they should be able to identify what it is."

Ari nods. "I'm trying to soothe him a little. I'm giving him some happier emotions to make him feel better. But I don't want to overdo it. If we give him too much energy, he won't be aware that his body is sick and needs to rest."

"Good thinking. Maybe you can just get him into a peaceful sleep while we ask the other Seekers about it?"

Ari nods, his eyes closed as he works with his gift. The gyrpuff's life spark brightens a little, so whatever Ari's doing must be working.

After a moment, Ari opens his eyes again. "All right," he says. "That's all I can do for now."

"Do you think one of us should stay with him?" I ask. "I hate to just leave him here all alone."

"The Seekers are already going to be furious with us for coming out here together. Imagine how much worse it will be if one of us stays out here alone."

"Will they really care about those rules in an emergency?" I ask.

"I'm pretty sure emergencies are when the rules are *most* important," Ari says, and I sigh.

"Fine. We'll go together for help. Do you think we can find this nest again? We need to remember exactly where it is."

"We've got the ribbons," Ari reminds me, reaching for his satchel.

"Oh. Right." The Seekers gave us a small bag of supplies, but I keep forgetting everything we have, since they've never actually given us any opportunities to use it. They did say something about using ribbons to mark locations we need to return to, now that I think about it.

We climb down from the nest carefully, reentering the slightly bigger one, where the mama gyrpuff we scared away still hasn't returned. Ari digs a bright-blue ribbon from his satchel and looks around for a place to tie it. Finally, we spot a large enough branch on a cliffside bush, and Ari makes quick work of knotting the ribbon around the end of it.

"Um, Ari . . . ," I say, glancing up the side of the cliff, "how were we planning to get back up?"

Ari's eyes widen. "Um . . ."

"You think Lilja could . . . ?"

We try attracting Lilja's attention with our gifts, but our dragon is apparently uninterested in helping out. Which leaves us stuck in a gyrpuff's nest on the side of a cliff, trying to figure out what to do.

Eventually, we manage to identify a couple of spots that will serve as handholds and footholds to get us up to the next ledge over. We climb the whole painstaking way up like this. At the top, Lilja is taking a nap. She cracks one eye open when we approach and gives us a look as if to ask what took so long.

"You are the laziest dragon in history," Ari says to her.

Lilja closes her eye again.

It takes several minutes of nudging her with our gifts before Lilja reluctantly wakes up, spreads her wings, and lets us climb onto her back. A minute later, we're in the air.

As we soar away from the cliffs, I glance back over my shoulder, as if I could somehow see the blue ribbon fluttering in the air, beckoning us to the poor creature who needs our help.

Hang on, little gyrpuff, I think. *We're going to save you.*

FOUR

It's midafternoon by the time Ari and I reach Dragon's Point, where Lilja drops us off. It's too early for the other Seekers to have left the Realm yet. "Who's off duty today?" I ask Ari as we land.

"Seeker Freyr, I think."

I groan. Out of the current Council, Seeker Freyr is my least favorite. Ari and I beat his son Tomas during the Seeker competition, and he definitely still holds a grudge. But at the moment, he'll be the only Seeker not currently busy in the Realm. We could go back to the Valley of Ash to see if Seeker Ludvik is still there, but he's probably moved on by now.

"Guess we'd better find Freyr," Ari says, sounding as reluctant as I feel. "At least he's one of the healers," he adds. "I'm sure he'll know what to do for the gyrpuff."

He's probably right, but I still wish we could speak to Seeker Larus instead. He's the head of the Council, since he's the most experienced Seeker, *and* he's a healer, so he'd be an even bigger help. Plus, he doesn't hate us, unlike Seeker Freyr.

Ari and I wave goodbye to Lilja as she flies back into the Realm—probably going to resume her nap—before making our way down the side of the rocky slope and following the path back to the center of the village. Seeker Freyr's hut is located just off the main square, so it doesn't take us long to reach it. Ari raps twice on the front door, fidgeting nervously with the clasp of his cloak.

Unfortunately, it's Tomas who opens the door.

He scowls the minute he sees us, and I'm pretty sure my expression mirrors his. "Oh," he mutters, "it's you."

Ari draws himself up, as if trying to look more official. "We need to speak with Seeker Freyr," he says. "It's urgent."

Tomas rolls his eyes. "Duh. Why else would you be here?"

"Is he awake?" I cut in.

"No. Come back later. Or never, preferably."

"This can't wait," Ari says. "Wake him up."

Tomas sneers. "You'd better have a good excuse for this," he says, "or he'll be furious."

"Just do it," I say.

Tomas slams the door in our faces.

Ari and I glance at each other. "Think he's waking him?" I ask.

"No idea."

A minute passes, then two. I'm about to suggest we try

breaking the door down when suddenly it swings open again. A rather disheveled-looking Seeker Freyr stands in the doorway, a cloak haphazardly wrapped around his shoulders. He blinks at us with bleary eyes and a scowl. "What is it?"

Ari has to open and close his mouth a couple of times before managing to speak. "Emergency," he croaks.

I quickly take over. "We found a sick gyrpuff in the Realm," I say. "He's lethargic and unresponsive, and his energy is very weak. We couldn't identify the illness, but he needs a healer now."

Immediately Seeker Freyr looks a little more awake, though he hasn't stopped scowling. "You were alone in the Realm? Just the two of you?"

Ari and I exchange glances. "We were with Seeker Ludvik for dragon training today," I say finally. "We were on our way out of the Realm when we found the gyrpuff."

I don't think for a moment that Seeker Freyr has missed the glaring omissions in that story, but he doesn't take the time to question it right now. "And you checked all of its symptoms like we've taught you?"

"Yes," I say impatiently. "He's breathing steadily, and his pulse is fine. But he's losing his feathers, he hardly responded to us at all, and his eyes have gone completely black."

Seeker Freyr freezes, his gaze locked on to me. "What did you say?"

"His eyes," Ari echoes. "They were black."

"*Completely* black," I add.

For a few heartbeats, Seeker Freyr doesn't say anything. "That can't be right," he says finally. "You must be mistaken."

Ari and I glance at each other.

"With all due respect, Seeker," I say, "we're not mistaken. We both saw it. We thought you'd know what it is."

"What it *is*," Seeker Freyr repeats, "is impossible. We eradicated that long ago."

I hold back a sigh. It's clear he doesn't believe us, but I don't know why we expected him to. "Come see for yourself," I say. "If we're wrong, then I'm sure it's something else that you can cure. And if we're right . . ."

"For the sake of the Realm," Seeker Freyr says gravely, "you'd best hope you're *not* right. Wait here a moment." With that, he closes the door in our faces again.

Ari looks at me. "*That* was ominous," he says.

I shrug. "He's probably just being dramatic."

But whatever the problem is, Seeker Freyr is certainly in a rush. He returns only a moment later, fully dressed in his Seeker cloak and throwing a satchel over his shoulder. "Seeker Ari," he says, "do you remember where you saw this gyrpuff?"

"Yes, Seeker," Ari says. "We were tracking along the southern cliffs. We flagged the spot with a blue ribbon."

"Good. I need you to take me to this gyrpuff immediately. And you—" He turns to me. "Find the bellmaster and have the highest bell rung, right now. Then go to Dragon's Point and wait for Larus and Ludvik. When they land, tell them we're assembling a meeting immediately."

"A meeting? Right now?" I ask, but Seeker Freyr is already rushing past me, hurrying down the steps and onto the street. Ari hastens to follow him.

"Right now, Seeker. Do it," Seeker Freyr calls over his shoulder as he rushes away.

In moments, he and Ari have disappeared down the street.

"Well," I say to no one, "all right, then."

I don't know what the rush is, but it must be important if it's got Seeker Freyr calling for a Council meeting while the other Seekers are in the Realm. The highest bell in the tower is used only to call the Seekers from the Realm in case of emergency. I can't remember the last time it was used.

I run through the village and up the hill to the chapel, which is dwarfed by the bell tower rising above it. There are three village bells, all controlled by our bellmaster, Elder Armann. The larger ones are rung at dawn and dusk, and on particular holidays or special occasions. They're just ordinary village bells. But the smallest, highest one of the trio is imbued with magic, allegedly cast in the fires of a Realm volcano, and its signal will carry to anyone on the island, even if they're within the depths of the Realm itself.

I scurry into the chapel and spot Elder Armann polishing the candles under the small stone archway.

"Good afternoon, Seeker Bryn," he says brightly as I approach. "What can I do for you?"

"I need you to ring the highest bell," I say, and he freezes.

"Is something wrong? Have the Vondur returned? Are we under attack?"

"No," I say quickly, "nothing like that. But there is a Seeker-related emergency, and Seeker Freyr has asked me to ring the bell at once."

"Of course," he says. "Of course." He drops his cleaning rag and hastens toward the steps of the bell tower. "Right away, Seeker."

His words give me a surge of confidence, and I straighten my spine. Not all of the villagers are so quick to recognize me as a Seeker just yet. But I *am* a real Seeker, and this is my first big job. I've got to handle it exactly right.

I leave the tower and rush up the path to Dragon's Point, which is deserted when I arrive. I sit down in the grass just as the high, clear notes of the bell ring across the landscape.

Ding. Ding. Ding. Ding.

I don't know exactly where in the Realm the others are now. Seeker Ludvik and Seeker Larus have been pretty focused on strengthening the boundary spells ever since the Vondurs' almost-successful attack a month ago. They've been traveling all over the length of the Realm to work on the spells, so there's no telling where they've ended up.

Fortunately, their dragons are fast, so I don't have long to wait. In less than five minutes, the familiar shape of a dragon emerges from the clouds. As it nears, the sunlight glints off its golden scales. It's Gulldrik, Seeker Larus's dragon, whom we met in the valley this morning. Seeker

Larus must've entered the Realm sometime after that.

Within moments, Gulldrik lands, and Seeker Larus slips gracefully off his back. "Seeker Bryn?" he asks, concern in his voice. "What's happened?"

I realize, abruptly, that I haven't even thought about how I'm going to explain this to the other Seekers. "Um, Seeker Freyr asked me to ring the bells and call a Council meeting," I say. "Ari and I found a sick gyrpuff at the southern cliffs. We couldn't identify the illness, so we went to Seeker Freyr, and when he heard its symptoms, he rushed off with Ari to find it and told me to wait for you here."

Seeker Larus frowns. "Why would a sick gyrpuff require a meeting?" he asks.

"I'm not sure exactly," I say. "Seeker Freyr seemed very concerned about it when we told him the gyrpuff has black eyes."

I don't remember ever seeing Seeker Larus look startled, but he looks that way now. He blinks, and for a moment he says nothing. "Black eyes?" he asks finally. "Are you *certain*?"

"Yes. Both Ari and I saw it."

Seeker Larus looks over his shoulder, in the direction of the Realm. "It can't be. . . ."

"Seeker?" I ask hesitantly. "What do the black eyes mean? Why is everyone so concerned?"

Seeker Larus twists around sharply, like he forgot for a moment that I'm here. "We'll discuss it at the meeting," he says finally. "I must ask Seeker Freyr what he thinks after he's had a moment to examine the gyrpuff. Where did you find it?"

"A nest at the southern cliffs," I say. "We flagged the spot with ribbon so that we could find it again."

"Good thinking," Seeker Larus says with an approving nod. "Regardless of whether this turns out to be as serious as I fear it is, you and Seeker Ari have done excellent work, bringing this to our attention."

Before I can respond, the sound of beating wings echoes above us as a second dragon emerges from the clouds. It's Snorri, and Seeker Ludvik is perched atop his back. "What's wrong, Larus?" he calls before the dragon has even finished landing. "I heard the bells!"

Seeker Larus glances at me before he speaks. "We need to hold a meeting immediately," he says. "I'll fill you in on the way."

After they send their dragons back into the Realm, we walk down the path to the village together, and Seeker Larus quickly repeats the story to Seeker Ludvik, whose mouth falls open in shock when Seeker Larus mentions the black eyes. "If it's true . . . ," Seeker Ludvik says, "if it's come back . . ."

"I know," Seeker Larus says gravely. "We must take precautions immediately. We can't allow it to spread like last time."

"Spread?" I repeat. "You mean the illness?"

They both glance at me and turn quickly away, and I can barely contain my frustration. I know they still see me as a twelve-year-old girl, but I'm a Seeker now, and I'm supposed to know what's going on. "Tell me," I say. "What are we dealing with?"

"It's best if we wait until we're sure," Seeker Larus says finally. "Once Seeker Freyr returns, we'll explain everything to you and Seeker Ari."

That's hardly an answer, but it seems to be the best I'm going to get.

Before becoming a Seeker, I assumed that private Council meetings took place somewhere grand and formal. Which is silly, now that I think about it, because there isn't a single grand or formal building anywhere on the island. Instead, the designated meeting place is the tiny front room in Seeker Larus's hut, which is stuffed full of comfy furniture. After we arrive, I sink into a plush armchair across from Seeker Ludvik while Seeker Larus bustles about in the kitchen, making us a pot of tea.

Papa says Seeker Larus has chosen to devote his entire life to the well-being of the Realm, and that's abundantly clear from his small hut. Aside from the basic furniture, the hut holds almost no possessions. Seeker Larus doesn't actually spend very much time here. When he isn't eating or sleeping or hosting Council meetings, he's busy with Seeker duties.

The few objects he *does* possess are entirely from the Realm. A single shelf attached to the wall above the stove holds some of the most priceless treasures I've ever seen: a sarvalur tooth, a phoenix claw, an entire jar of unicorn hairs.

Seeker Larus, more than anyone else, knows their value, but he displays them almost casually, in the same way other people would position their sugar bowls or cooking pots.

Seeker Larus has just finished distributing tea to me and Seeker Ludvik when a quick rap sounds at the door, and Seeker Freyr strides in without waiting for a response. His dark hair is windswept, and his satchel is missing. Ari is right on his heels, his eyes wide with an expression I've never seen on him before. Whatever Seeker Freyr said, or whatever emotion Ari's picking up from him with his empathy gift, it isn't good.

"Well?" Seeker Ludvik asks without preamble as Seeker Larus sits beside him.

"It should be impossible," Seeker Freyr says gravely, "but it's true. The dark plague has returned."

I catch Ari's eye. *Dark plague?* I mouth silently at him, but he shrugs, looking as confused as I feel.

"Surely that can't be possible," says Seeker Ludvik. "We eradicated it completely—I'm certain."

"I didn't want to believe it either," says Seeker Freyr, "but I saw it for myself. The gyrpuff Seeker Ari found today has all the symptoms, and the eyes are completely black. It resists my healing in all forms, and it . . . well. You know what it does when one tries to heal it."

Considering I was the one who actually made us try to find the gyrpuff in the first place, I'm not sure why Seeker Freyr left me out. So I say loudly, "Excuse me, but we don't all know, actually. Could someone please explain to me and Seeker Ari what's going on?"

Seeker Freyr scowls at the interruption, but Seeker Larus nods. "Of course, Seeker Bryn," he says. "It's unsurprising that you and Seeker Ari are unfamiliar with this plague, given that it happened several decades ago. We were young Seekers ourselves then—Seeker Freyr had only just joined the Council, and your papa was not yet a member. It was Seeker Oskar who led us back then, and who first discovered the plague."

"What plague?" I ask.

"It causes many symptoms, across many different kinds of creatures within the Realm," Seeker Larus says. "But its most telltale sign is that it turns an infected creature's eyes completely black, just like the gyrpuff you saw today. This plague acts slowly, but it is always deadly in the end—infected creatures don't survive unless they are cured. But there are several reasons why we fear this plague above all others. It is the worst that we have seen during our time as Seekers.

"First, it is highly contagious and affects all magical species. During the original outbreak, every known type of magical creature in the Realm contracted it at some point, and it spread rapidly. Half the Realm was infected before we had fully realized what we were dealing with."

"Half?" Ari asks, and I gulp. That must be hundreds of creatures, if not thousands. "How did you stop it?"

"Well, I'm getting to that. The second thing that makes the plague so deadly is that there is no known cure, and it seems to be resistant to all types of healing. You see, what's unique about this illness is that it . . . well, it *drains* energy. In fact, it seems to feed on magic. The more magical a creature is, the faster the illness seems to affect them—it feeds on their very life force, on the magic that gives them their power. And when we tried, with healing gifts, to cure the creatures, we found that our gifts merely provided fuel for the plague. It fed on the energy of our healing."

"How is that possible?" Ari asks. "Something like that . . . How did anything survive?"

The Seekers exchange glances. "Unfortunately," Seeker Larus says softly, "we never found a cure. When we realized how rapidly it was spreading and how little we could do to stop it, we made a difficult decision. We used boundary spells to create quarantine zones in areas of the Realm—spells that none of the Realm's creatures could cross. We confined the sick creatures within the boundaries, separate from the healthy ones. This way, the plague stopped spreading, and the creatures who had not yet contracted it were spared."

"But what about the creatures who had the plague when you created the quarantine? How did you cure them?" I ask.

A heavy silence fills the room. It's Seeker Ludvik who finally breaks it. "We . . . didn't," he says softly.

"Didn't?" I repeat.

"They died, Bryn," Seeker Larus says quietly. "The creatures who were infected did not survive the plague. It was all we could do to keep it from spreading to the rest of the Realm."

"Wait," I say. "You're telling me that *half of the Realm* was wiped out in a plague a few decades ago? Why have I never heard about this?"

"We decided to keep the extent of the damage a secret from the villagers," Seeker Larus explains. "We didn't want to cause a panic until we had found a solution, and in the aftermath . . . Well, it didn't seem necessary to reveal what had happened."

"But my papa never mentioned it," I say. "Did he know?"

"The Seekers who have joined our ranks since were told about the plague at one point or another," Seeker Larus says, "though, again, we did not disclose all of the details. There seemed to be little point in doing so, since the plague had disappeared."

Ari looks at Seeker Larus. "Did you ever find out what caused it? Was there a source?"

"No," responds Seeker Freyr. "We were never able to trace its origin. But after the creatures in the quarantine zone had passed, we carefully inspected every inch of those areas to ensure that there were no remaining signs of contamination. We let the creatures back into those areas slowly at first, one at a time, to ensure that the plague was truly gone. When they did not catch it, we concluded that the plague had been eradicated."

I'm not sure I believe what I'm hearing. "You just sealed half the Realm off and left the creatures to die?"

"It wasn't quite so simple," protests Seeker Freyr sharply.

"We were working to find a cure, I can assure you. But we never managed it—not in time to save them. And once the plague was gone, we no longer had any way to test a cure. But we truly believed that it had died out—perhaps one of the Realm's dragons or sea wolves contracted the illness from the sea and spread it to the other creatures. We have seen no sign of the plague in the Realm since . . . until today."

"How would a gyrpuff get it, then?" I ask. "Gyrpuffs don't travel very far from the island, even when they're on the water."

Seeker Larus glances at Seeker Ludvik, but neither of them speaks.

"We don't know what has caused this," Seeker Larus says finally, "but that is hardly the most pressing concern at the moment. To prevent the same kind of tragedy we witnessed before, we must act swiftly. Seeker Freyr, did you secure the gyrpuff?"

"Yes," Seeker Freyr responds. "Seeker Ari and I placed a boundary around the cliff. But I would appreciate your help in strengthening it, Ludvik."

Seeker Ludvik nods. As the only one of us with a defender gift, he's the expert at boundary spells.

"But what about—" I start.

Seeker Larus doesn't hear me. "We will just have to hope that this gyrpuff is the only one," he says, "and that the plague hasn't spread too far yet. We will keep the quarantine zone small for now, and expand if necessary."

"Wait," I say, louder so they won't ignore me again. "Are you saying you're just going to leave that gyrpuff there, with a deadly and *highly contagious* illness, and quarantine the whole cliff? What about the other gyrpuffs that live there? It was right next to another nest where we found an egg with a hatchling inside and a mama gyrpuff. They'll catch the plague if we don't do something."

There's another beat of silence. "It's likely that they already *have* been exposed, Bryn," Seeker Larus says softly. "And we can't move the infected gyrpuff without risking further spread of the illness. Our only hope is to prevent any other creatures from entering that area and to prevent the potentially infected ones from leaving. It's the only way to stop the spread of the plague before it's too late."

"But that means we're just leaving all those healthy gyrpuffs in the quarantine zone to die," I say. "Can't we save them?"

Seeker Freyr shakes his head sharply. "The plague is a slow death, and it takes time for the symptoms to develop. Some of the creatures who seem healthy now might already be carrying it and could spread it to others. For now, we can't allow any creatures to travel to and from that cliff. We will also have to begin monitoring the surrounding cliffsides. If the illness has already spread there, we will have to quarantine them as well."

It makes sense, but I still can't believe that this is our only option. "So that's it, then? That's all we can do?"

"Of course, we will also try to find a cure for the plague," Seeker Larus says. "But containing it must be our first priority."

"If it hasn't spread to the other cliffs," Seeker Freyr adds, "then the gyrpuff population will bounce back quickly. There are many more nests along the southern coast."

"The Realm's creatures are adept at recovering from events like this," Seeker Ludvik adds. "We saw that last time. Despite losing so many creatures, the populations replenished themselves within a few generations."

"But what about *this* generation?" I say. "We're Seekers. Protecting these creatures is supposed to be our job. Why doesn't anyone else have a problem with just abandoning those gyrpuffs to die?"

"Bryn," Seeker Freyr says sharply, "I find it odd that you are choosing this moment to argue, given how flagrantly you broke the rules this morning. Just because we have more pressing matters to discuss does not mean we've overlooked the fact that you and Seeker Ari found this gyrpuff while exploring the Realm by yourselves and ignoring our clear instructions not to do so. Clearly, you are not ready to enter the Realm on your own; nor are you equipped to help us handle this crisis."

I can't hold back my anger. "But if it weren't for us, you wouldn't even know about the illness. You're going to punish us for alerting you to the plague?"

"No," Seeker Freyr says, "but I think any Seeker who

cannot be trusted alone in the Realm should not be allowed in it. Your trial period should be extended."

"What?" I say.

"You knew the rules," Seeker Freyr says firmly, "and you chose to break them. Until you can be trusted to conduct yourself more maturely, I don't think you should enter the Realm again, unless under direct supervision."

I look helplessly to Seeker Larus. As the most senior member on the Council, surely he'll decide to overrule Seeker Freyr—

Seeker Larus shakes his head. "I understand that you have been eager to assume your full Seeker duties, Bryn, but Seeker Freyr is correct; you broke the rules that we asked you to abide by, for your own safety and that of the Realm. For that reason, I think we need to extend your training period. Shall we have a vote?"

Seeker Freyr nods curtly. After a moment, so does Seeker Ludvik.

Larus continues. "All in favor of extending the training period for Seekers Ari and Bryn and restricting their access to the Realm during that period?"

Seeker Larus and Seeker Freyr both raise their hands. Seeker Ludvik seems a little reluctant, but then he raises his hand too.

Seeker Larus nods once. "Motion passed," he says. "Now, let's return to the emergency at hand. Seeker Freyr, please show Seeker Ludvik where the gyrpuff is located so that he can begin setting the boundaries. I'll monitor the other cliffs and then join you."

Seeker Freyr nods once. "Ludvik, are you ready? I will show you." The two of them rise and exit the hut quickly, and just like that, the meeting is adjourned.

"Seeker Larus?" Ari asks quietly. It's the first time he's spoken up in ages. "I have a question about this illness."

"Of course," Seeker Larus says, nodding.

"Can it be passed to humans? Or can humans pass it to others? Is there a chance Bryn and I might get sick after being exposed to the gyrpuff? Is there a chance we could spread it to our families, or to our dragon?"

"Oh, not to worry," Seeker Larus says. "We determined last time that the illness doesn't seem to affect humans; nor do we seem to transmit it. It appears that this illness is one that feeds off magical energy. The creatures of the Realm are vulnerable because they have so much magic. And while we all have our gifts, they are nothing in comparison to the magical energy of the Realm's creatures. Humans simply don't seem to have enough magic for the illness to feed off. If this is the same plague we faced before, we have nothing to worry about on that front."

Ari nods. "Thank you, Seeker. Is there anything Bryn and I can do to help from here, while you're in the Realm?"

"I suggest the two of you spend this time resting up," says Seeker Larus. "If the illness has spread farther than we're aware of, there will be a lot of work for all of us in the coming days. You've done very well in alerting us."

I open my mouth to make a sharp retort, anger building in my chest, but Ari places a hand on my shoulder. "Thank you, Seeker Larus," he says. "Please keep us informed if you find any more infected creatures."

"Of course," Seeker Larus says. "And please, don't say anything about the plague to any of the villagers—not now. We don't want to cause any sort of panic, and we don't know yet what we're facing."

"We won't," Ari promises.

I open my mouth again, but Ari gives my arm a sharp tug. He can sense exactly how I'm feeling, and he knows I'm about to explode. "Good day, Seeker Larus," Ari says, and he hauls me out of the hut.

The minute we're out of Seeker Larus's hearing, I explode with rage.

"Did you *hear* them?" I fume. "I cannot *believe* this."

"I know you're upset," Ari says. "But . . ."

"Aren't *you* upset? They're banning us from the Realm! In the middle of an emergency!"

"I told you we shouldn't have broken the rules," Ari says. "We'll just have to go along for now, to prove that we're not going to be reckless."

"But there's no time for that. There's a whole cliffside full of gyrpuffs who might be infected. There must be a hundred! And the other Seekers don't know how to save them. They're not even trying!"

"But what can we do?" Ari asks. "If the illness doesn't have a cure—"

"I should've known," I say with a huff. "Should've known you'd take their side over mine."

"What are you talking about? There are no sides, Bryn. We're all just trying to do what's best."

"But they didn't even listen to me," I say. "Didn't you notice? It's like this every time."

Ari frowns, brushing a stray curl from his forehead. "It's like *what* every time?"

I point back to Seeker Larus's hut. "Nobody listens to me in there. Every time I say something, they dismiss me or talk over me or ignore me. It's been happening since the very first meeting. And haven't you noticed how they talk to me? They don't compliment my work like they do yours. And they call me 'Bryn' instead of 'Seeker.' Even Seeker Larus did it just now. They don't take me seriously."

"We're both still getting used to being Seekers," Ari says calmly. "I'm sure it's an adjustment for everyone to remember to call us that."

"But they never forget to call *you* Seeker."

"Well . . ."

"And they don't listen to me. We're being sidelined when we could be helping! We have to find a cure, some way to heal them, or—"

"Bryn," Ari says gently, "are you sure *you* were listening to *them*? There's no cure. How do we cure something that feeds off healing energy? If we try to heal them, we'll make it worse. The other Seekers have seen this plague before. We should trust their judgment."

"What about our own judgment?" I cross my arms over my chest. "Is that what *you* think we should do? If it were just me and you, would you decide the same thing?"

"Well . . . ," Ari says again, hesitating.

"You and I are official Seekers now. That means we get just as much of a say on the Council as they do. They shouldn't be able to just *decide* without taking everyone's opinions into consideration. They can't just ban us from the Realm like this. They're not treating us like Council members."

"But we've only been Council members for, what, four weeks?" Ari says. "They have, like, a decade of experience *each*. We should be taking their advice and learning from them."

"Maybe so." I glare back at Seeker Larus's hut. "But that doesn't mean we should just sit back and do nothing. I'm right about this. I *know* I'm right about this. A Seeker's job is to protect the creatures of the Realm. We have to do that, even if they don't want us to."

"All right," Ari says, throwing his hands up in defeat. "All right. We'll bring it up again at the next meeting. I'm sure everyone's a little on edge right now, finding out about this plague. When everyone's calmer, we can discuss our options rationally."

I roll my eyes. "Right, just like they've listened to my

opinions *rationally* in any other meeting. You really don't see it, do you?"

Ari just looks at me, and I sigh. "Whatever. Let's just go."

As Ari and I head down the path, I glance back at Seeker Larus's hut.

They might have experience with this plague, but that doesn't mean they're always right.

If they won't do anything to save the gyrpuffs, then I'll just have to do it myself. Even if it means going into the Realm in secret.

FIVE

I return home that evening with a plan.

Elisa greets me as I walk up the garden path. Ever since I became a Seeker, she's started pestering me with all kinds of questions. I haven't had the heart to explain to her that I haven't been allowed to see much of the Realm yet.

"What did you see today?" she asks. "Were there firecats or unicorns or—"

"Gyrpuffs," I tell her, trying to muster some fake enthusiasm. Elisa jumps up and down in excitement. She's still learning all about the creatures of the Realm, and they excite her just as much as Papa's stories excited me when I first heard them.

"Did they disappear right in front of you? Did they make any sounds?"

"Yes," I say, but I don't really have it in me for this conversation right now. "Does Mama need help cooking?"

Elisa follows me into the hut, where we find Mama

chopping vegetables at the table. "Just in time," Mama says. "The chicken stew needs to be stirred, Brynja. Elisabet, your tea is ready."

"Hi, Mama," I say with a grin. Giving orders is Mama's usual form of greeting. But the chicken stew means she's in a good mood. Now that I'm a Seeker and going to start trading things I find in the Realm, we can afford nicer ingredients for meals, and Mama's even been splurging on the chicken sometimes. Of course, I haven't actually gotten very much from the Realm to trade yet, so I'd better start finding more things soon.

Elisa sits at the table before a steaming mug of her starflower tea. "Bryn saw gyrpuffs in the Realm today!" she begins excitedly.

"Is that so?" Mama says, chopping briskly. "Bryn, make sure that stew thickens up right."

"Yes, Mama." I head to the pot over the fire and begin to stir. For a few minutes, I close my eyes and enjoy the familiar sounds of home—Elisa's chatter, Mama's footsteps, the bubbling stew. Before I became a Seeker, all I wanted was to get out of this hut every day. But now that I spend so much time at Seeker meetings and training sessions, it's nice to come home to something familiar.

Dinner is nearly ready by the time Papa strides through the door, setting down his walking stick and shrugging out of his coat. Elisa starts babbling to him right away, luckily, so I'm saved from having to answer any questions about what happened in the Realm.

It doesn't last long, though. As we sit down at the table and begin to eat, Papa turns immediately to me. "I heard the bells," he says. "What happened?"

Of course. As a former Seeker, Papa knows exactly what that signal means.

"The bells were pretty," Elisa chimes in, splashing her spoon around in her bowl of stew.

"Manners, Elisabet," Mama says, placing her hand over Elisa's.

For a moment I hope Papa's been distracted enough to forget the question, but he looks expectantly at me. "Well, Bryn?"

"Ari and I found a sick gyrpuff in the Realm," I explain. "We couldn't heal it ourselves, so we asked Seeker Freyr, and then he rang the bells to call in the other Seekers."

Papa immediately homes in on the missing information in this story. "Seeker Freyr wasn't able to heal the gyrpuff either?"

"He said it was some kind of . . . plague," I say carefully. "One that the Seekers have seen before."

Papa freezes, his spoon halfway to his mouth. "I see," he says carefully. "Well, I'm sure you'll get it all straightened out."

I frown. Papa's forehead is creased in concern, and I suspect he knows exactly what kind of plague I'm talking about. But instead of asking any more questions, he changes the subject and starts telling Mama about how some of the garden vegetables are doing. No one asks me anything else for the rest of the meal.

But after dinner, Papa takes me aside. While Mama does the dishes and Elisa runs behind the clothesline to our bedroom, Papa leads me into the garden.

"Was it the black eyes?" he asks me immediately, and I nod. He sighs, running a hand over his beard. "I was afraid so. I can't believe it's come back."

"It was before you became a Seeker, right?" I ask.

"Yes. But I saw the devastation it wrought. I became a Seeker while the Realm's population was still recovering from the loss."

"The other Seekers have decided to quarantine the area where we found the gyrpuff. The whole cliff. They say there's nothing we can do except to stop the plague from spreading."

"They may be right," Papa says. "They've seen this before. And we certainly wouldn't want the plague to reach other portions of the Realm."

I stare at him. I can't believe Papa, of all people, would be in favor of this plan. "But what about the gyrpuffs? We can't just leave them all there to die. We have to find a way to save them."

"And I'm sure you will," Papa says. "Perhaps this time you'll all be able to find a cure. But don't take any chances with this, Bryn. It could endanger the entire Realm."

"I understand," I say. "I just think there's got to be something more I can do."

"Well, this is why a little new blood on the Council is always a good thing. You and Ari will bring optimism and new ideas, and perhaps that's what you need to find the solution."

"Yeah," I say. "Except the other Seekers aren't really letting me and Ari do anything. They still don't let us into the Realm unsupervised." I leave out the part about how I broke the rules today and got us into more trouble. Papa doesn't need to know about that.

"This must be quite upsetting for them," Papa says. "Seeker Freyr lost his first dragon to the plague. It must have been devastating."

"I didn't know that," I say, and for a moment I actually do feel a pang of sympathy for Seeker Freyr. I can't imagine what it would be like to lose Lilja.

"I'm sure they'll come around." Papa gives me a pat on the shoulder. "Everyone's emotions are just running high."

"Yeah," I say. "I guess."

He gives me another pat. "You'll all figure it out, Bryn. Protecting the Realm is what the rest of the Council has been doing for decades, and I'm sure you and Seeker Ari are more than up to the task."

Papa returns to the hut a minute later, but I sit outside on the garden bench to think. He's right about finding a solution, but I don't think the Seekers are ever going to listen to me about it, not when they still see me as an inexperienced little girl. I'm going to have to enact this plan myself. I'll make sure that the Realm stays safe. I'll find a cure for the plague. And when I do, the other Seekers will finally have to start taking me seriously.

Luckily, I know just the person who can help me.

By the time I arrive at Runa's farm, the sun has set, and only a few slivers of moonlight illuminate the path leading to her hut. Her family will likely already be in bed, but I walk up to the door anyway. One of the perks of being a Seeker.

Runa's mama opens the door. "Good evening, Seeker Bryn," she says. "We were just heading to bed."

"Sorry to disturb you," I say quickly. "I need to speak with Runa for a minute. It's about a Seeker matter."

"I see." She studies me a moment, then nods. "I'll get her."

Runa appears a moment later, wearing a loose nightgown embroidered with flowers, her black hair neatly braided. "What's wrong?"

I pull Runa into the garden, out of earshot of her parents. "I need to tell you something about the Realm," I say. "But this has to be a secret, okay? We're not supposed to tell anyone."

"Okay," she says, looking concerned. "You know I can keep a secret."

I quickly recount what happened today. By the time I finish, Runa's eyes are wide.

"I can't believe that there was a plague like that in the Realm and no one ever knew," she says.

"I know. But now that it's back, we have to figure out how to save all the infected creatures. The other Seekers think it's enough to establish a quarantine for the gyrpuffs and leave them there to die, so that the plague dies out too. But I don't think that's right. There's got to be a cure that will save the gyrpuffs. There's got to be a way."

"Maybe," Runa says slowly, "but if the Seekers couldn't find a solution before . . ."

"That was ages ago." I wave one hand dismissively. "We know a lot more about magical healing than we used to. And I'm sure the best young healer in the village can figure it out."

Runa immediately shakes her head. "No way. I'm not nearly experienced enough to handle some kind of death plague, Bryn. I'm not even a real healer!"

"But you know more about healing than anyone."

"You should be asking the doctor or the other Seekers or—"

"They're not going to listen to me. But you will. I know you can do this."

"I don't—"

"Just think about it, okay? It's a plague that drains healing energy. If you encountered something like that, what would your first instinct be?"

As I suspected, Runa can't resist the challenge of trying to figure it out. Her eyes light up as she tilts her head to the side, pondering the question. "Well, using healing magic directly on the creatures won't work, then," she says. "It'll just feed the plague. But direct healing isn't the only form of medicine. I'd try a potion or a tonic. There might be some kind of ingredient that would kill the plague without feeding it any energy."

"That's perfect!" I say. "See, I knew you were a genius."

"But I haven't come up with anything." She shakes her head again. "I have no idea what kind of ingredient would stop this plague. There could be thousands of possibilities."

"But it's a start. Creating a potion is exactly what we need to do. We just have to figure out the right ingredients. What about starflowers or fairy clovers or something else from the Realm?"

"I don't know," Runa says. "The only way to figure it out would be to start making potions and testing them."

"Then that's exactly what we'll do. Runa, I can bring you any ingredients from the Realm that you need to start brewing the right potions. And one of your cures could work!"

"But I don't even know where to start," Runa protests. "I don't know anything about this plague or what it might be resistant to. We need to narrow down the possibilities."

She makes a fair point, but I won't let that temper my enthusiasm. We *have* to figure this out. The gyrpuffs are counting on us. "Okay, how about this," I say. "I'll talk to the other Seekers and ask more questions about the plague. I'll find out all of its symptoms and ask if they've ever tried any kind of potion or tonic before. I'll tell you everything I learn, and we'll go from there."

"All right," Runa says skeptically. "It's really a long shot, Bryn."

"I know," I say. "But it's either this or do nothing, and I won't do nothing. We have to try. If the other Seekers won't do it, then we will."

Runa sighs loudly. "What have I gotten myself into?"

I grin. "Aren't you glad we're best friends?"

"I'd never find trouble if it weren't for you," she grumbles, but she smiles as she says it.

I leave Runa's farm with a spring in my step, following the trail of moonlight toward home. If anyone can figure this out, it's Runa. I just know it.

We're going to find the cure and save the Realm, no matter what.

SIX

I wake bright and early the next morning, unable to sleep. After helping Mama with breakfast and completing my chores, I bid my family goodbye and take off for Seeker Larus's hut.

He looks flustered as he opens the door, blinking in the early-morning sunlight. "Seeker Bryn," he says. "What an unexpected surprise."

"Sorry it's so early," I say quickly. "But with the . . . with everything that happened yesterday, we don't have any time to waste."

He nods. "Of course. Come in."

I settle into the living area as Seeker Larus brews a pot of tea, and we make small talk for a moment before finally getting down to business.

"What can I do for you?" he asks.

"I wanted to ask you a few questions," I say. "About what

happened with the plague before. Ari and I can help come up with solutions, but we need to know what we're up against."

Seeker Larus nods, which I take as a signal to continue.

"Can you tell me all the symptoms of this plague?" I ask. "I want to know exactly what it does."

"Extreme lethargy, loss of feathers and fur, dullness of coat, low life sparks . . . and the black eyes, of course."

"I see," I say slowly. This sounds bad, but I forge ahead. Any information I get will be helpful to Runa. "So . . . what did you try last time, to find a cure for it? You said it feeds on energy?"

"Yes," Seeker Larus says. "Any attempt we made to use healing gifts on the sick creatures only made the illness worse. The magical energy seemed to feed the plague instead of curing it."

"What about, say . . . ?" I pause, as if the idea just occurred to me. "What about a potion or a tonic or something? What if you didn't try to heal with a gift directly?"

Seeker Larus nods. "That's the conclusion we reached as well," he says, and I deflate a little. I was hoping the idea was new. "We tried a few different things, but none seemed to work."

"What did you try, specifically? Maybe we just need the right ingredients."

Seeker Larus rattles off a list, and my head spins trying to keep up. "Starflower tonic, a potion made from fairy clovers and aven roots and poppy seeds, a tonic made from snowpetals and arctic thyme . . ."

"And none of them worked? Did they affect the plague at all?"

"We got closest with a potion made from starflower petals, mountain avens, figrose roots, and bilberry juice," he says. "A few of the creatures who were given a potion with that combination seemed to show signs of improvement. But they didn't improve quickly enough. We were still missing something."

"A missing ingredient," I say slowly. "Something that would speed up the healing? Or take out the plague more directly?"

"Right. But by that point, we didn't have time to try every possible ingredient to perfect the potion. The Realm was dying. We had no choice but to establish the quarantine, and none of the infected creatures survived long enough for us to continue experimenting."

"But that gives us somewhere to start," I say. "This time we can figure it out faster."

Seeker Larus smiles. "I admire your optimism, Bryn. Perhaps you're right."

"So what can Ari and I do right now that would be helpful?"

"I'd like you to accompany Seeker Freyr today," he says. "We've decided to check all the largest populations of the Realm to see if any other creatures have signs of infection. Seeker Freyr is going to check the phoenix nests, and he could use some assistance. The nests tend to be scattered about, so the additional sets of eyes will be useful."

I nod slowly. I suppose it *is* a way to help, and at least they're letting us into the Realm, though I doubt Seeker Freyr will be thrilled about it.

After a few more minutes of discussion, I bid Seeker Larus goodbye, lost in thought. I fetch Ari from his family's hut and repeat Seeker Larus's instructions, and we head up to Dragon's Point to meet Seeker Freyr. While we wait for him to arrive, I tell Ari about my conversations with Runa and Larus. Ari is skeptical, to say the least.

"The missing ingredient could be *anything*," he says. "Or nothing at all. Maybe there's nothing that works."

"We have to try. Don't you want to help the gyrpuffs?"

"Of course I do."

"Well, then, we don't have a choice."

"But Seeker Larus said they've already tried to find a cure."

I roll my eyes. "Seeker Larus doesn't know everything."

"He pretty much does," Ari mumbles.

"So you won't help me? Is that what you're saying?"

"I didn't say that. I just think there are other ways to help. We need to make sure the boundaries around the quarantine stay strong, we need to make sure no other creatures in the Realm are sick, and we need to try to figure out what's causing this plague in the first place. Where did it even come from?"

My eyes widen. "Ari, that's brilliant," I say. "If we know what's causing this plague, we might be able to figure out how to cure it *and* stop it from ever coming back!"

"Right, but how do we do that?"

I bite my lip, considering. "We need to make sure that there are no other infected creatures in the Realm first. If this plague has only affected those gyrpuff caves so far, then it must be coming from there. That will help us narrow it down."

Ari nods. "All right. But technically our assignment is to check on the phoenix nests."

"Of course. We'll just make the suggestion to Seeker Freyr. Maybe he'll let us go over to the caves after we check the phoenixes." I don't believe for a second that Seeker Freyr will let us do anything at all, but that doesn't mean I can't do it on my own later. Ari doesn't need to know that.

Besides, it will be good to check on the phoenixes anyway. Phoenix feathers are pretty powerful magical items. Maybe that could be just the ingredient Runa needs to create a healing potion that will work.

Ari starts to say something else, but he's cut off by the arrival of Seeker Freyr, who nods at Ari and ignores me entirely. "Call your dragon and we'll head to the phoenix nests," he says, looking at Ari and not me.

With a somewhat-apologetic glance at me, Ari whistles the three-note melody that we taught Lilja. Seeker Freyr then whistles a series of sharp notes to call his own dragon. Within a few moments, both dragons appear on the horizon.

Lilja soars through the sky, her silvery scales glinting in the sun. She's already grown so much since I first met her a few weeks ago, but she's still smaller than the adult dragons. Even so, Ari and I have to take a few steps back to leave her plenty of space as she swings in for a landing, her batlike wings outstretched. Her feet thud against the ground, and I duck as her right wing arcs toward me.

"Good morning, Lilja," Ari says, already reaching into his pocket for some bilberries. Lilja spins eagerly toward him, and he tosses a few berries into her waiting jaws.

"Spoiled dragon," I mutter. "We've got to stop feeding you so many treats."

She huffs at me, then lowers her snout toward Ari, seeking out more of the delicious fruit.

We finally manage to distract her from berries long enough to hop onto her back, and we use our gifts to guide Lilja into the air and direct her to follow Seeker Freyr's dragon. By now she's used to this routine, and she flies straight over the mountains and into the Realm without much coaxing.

The phoenix nests are in the volcanic area, not far from the Valley of Ash. But we aim instead for the low valleys at the southernmost tip of the region, where the warmest climate in the Realm suits phoenixes just fine.

Seeker Freyr lands in the ashy fields, and Lilja follows suit, snuffing contentedly at the ground. The volcanic region is home turf for a dragon, even if they don't usually wander this far south.

Seeker Freyr surveys the landscape surrounding us. "We'll begin here," he says, and leads the way across the ash-covered ground.

The tricky thing about tracking phoenixes is . . . Well, everything about tracking them is tricky. They don't like company, and they build their nests in secluded crevasses of these volcanic valleys, where the heat is trapped between the rocks and they can pile the ash into their nests. They don't leave many traces of their presence behind, so they're hard to spot unless you know where to look.

"Where are we headed, Seeker?" I ask, having to jog to keep up with his long strides.

"South," he says without looking at me. "To the Mount Hekla colony."

"Good idea," I say. It's the biggest group of phoenixes, and the easiest to find. If the plague has entered this region at all, we'll probably see it there.

Seeker Freyr doesn't respond.

The mountains rise higher on every side as we trudge through the valley, ash caking under our boots. The south-facing side of Mount Hekla is the most likely place to find phoenix nests—it's got dozens of little pockets and craters along its edges that make perfect nesting places.

"Should we split up?" I ask. "We have a lot of nests to check."

Seeker Freyr considers for a moment, then nods. "You may check for nests individually, but do not go too far. We'll work our way around the base of the mountain and meet back here. Do *not* wander. Understood?"

We nod.

"And keep your dragon here," he says, with a curt nod to Lilja, who's snuffling at the ground behind Ari. "If any of the phoenixes are already ill, you don't want to expose her."

I have to admit, I didn't think about that. I suppose there are *some* benefits to having an experienced Seeker with us. We give Lilja the signal to stay put—which she usually obeys, if she feels like it—and then take separate paths around the base of the mountain, looking for telltale signs of nests.

I spot the first one after only a minute or two, the briarwood twigs poking out of a tiny gap between the rocks. I peek in and find an empty nest. No eggs, no phoenixes.

Which seems . . . odd. Summer is hatching season, so I'd expect to find the phoenix parents here with their chicks, guarding over them and storing up supplies for the winter hibernation. Maybe this is just an older nest, though.

I trudge on and find a second nest tucked into a crevasse below my feet. Getting down on my hands and knees, I peek in, only to see another empty nest. No eggs here, either. I *do* find a stray phoenix feather stuck on one of the branches and tuck it into my pocket immediately, but there are no other signs that the phoenixes have recently been here.

I check another nest, and another, and another. The same

thing happens—they're all empty. Aside from the occasional stray feather, there's no sign that they were here at all.

I meet up with Ari at the spot where we started, and one look at his face tells me that he saw exactly the same thing.

"They're gone," I say. "It's like they just . . . disappeared."

"Maybe the colony moved?" he asks. "Found a different place to prep for hibernation?"

I frown. "I didn't think phoenixes migrated like that."

Ari nods. "Or maybe something about the climate here changed? Or there's a new predator hunting them in the area?"

"I don't know. This doesn't sound like how they usually behave."

At that moment, Seeker Freyr reappears, trudging toward us. "Did either of you find anything?"

"No," I say.

"They have moved," he says heavily. He glances up at the sky, as if hoping the answer will be written there. After a moment, he turns back to us, and at the sight of the sorrow on his face, I swallow back all of my questions.

"We must warn the others," he says.

In heavy silence, we return to the dragons and leave the Realm.

The Council of Seekers usually meets only once a week, but given the circumstances, I'm not surprised to find that the others are already sitting in Seeker Larus's hut when Ari and I arrive, having left Lilja at Dragon's Point.

"I checked the central forests," Seeker Larus begins, offering all of us tea. "No sign of the plague there."

Seeker Ludvik nods. "I reinforced all of the boundaries surrounding the quarantined area. I believe it will hold, for a time. No creatures will be getting in or out."

Seeker Larus glances at Freyr. "And the phoenixes?" he asks.

"They're gone," I blurt. "We found dozens of nests where the Hekla colony used to be, but aside from a few feathers, there's no sign of them. No chicks in the nests, no food stores, nothing. It's like they've disappeared."

The older Seekers glance sharply at each other, and for a moment no one speaks.

"Do you know what that means?" I ask. "What happened to them?"

"It's rare for an entire colony of phoenixes to relocate into new nests," Seeker Larus says quietly. "When it happens, it means they've sensed some kind of threat. I've known it to happen only once before."

"The plague," Ari says, and Seeker Larus nods.

"They kept moving north last time," Seeker Ludvik explains, "until they could go no farther, due to the climate. We managed to keep most of the phoenixes safe during the quarantine, because they relocated themselves."

"It's like they knew," Seeker Freyr says quietly. "And if they've done it again . . ."

"The plague may not be as contained as we thought," Seeker Larus says gravely.

"Could they be sensing the presence of the plague by the cliffs?" Ari asks. "They're not that far apart."

"It's possible," Seeker Larus says, but he doesn't sound convinced.

Seeker Freyr nods. "We'll need to locate them. Make sure none of the birds have been infected yet."

"They've likely moved north," Seeker Ludvik replies. "I remember where they went last time. I will go now and check it out."

"I'll go with you," Seeker Larus says, rising from his seat.

"What can we do?" I ask, leaping up.

"You've done good work today," Seeker Larus says. "I suggest you rest up. We'll need to continue checking on all of the Realm's creatures to make sure that none have been infected. Perhaps you can accompany one of us again tomorrow."

They continue discussing strategy for a couple of minutes, but it's almost as if Ari and I aren't even in the room.

By the time the meeting ends and Ari and I head home, I'm fuming again.

"They just keep telling us where to go, but they don't tell us anything significant, and they don't ask us for our opinions," I say irritably.

"I did notice it more this time," Ari admits. "But I'm sure they're just . . . . stressed."

"We all are," I say. "That's no excuse for ignoring us. We're Seekers too."

"Well, at least they let us look for the phoenixes."

"It isn't enough," I say. "Tonight I'm going to talk to Runa again. We can't forget about the gyrpuffs who are sick right now."

"Bryn," Ari says. He stops walking, forcing me to look him in the eye. "Don't tell me you're planning to sneak into the Realm again."

"I'll be fine on my own, and—"

He shakes his head, his curls flying. "Don't. You've already gotten us in enough trouble by breaking the rules the first time."

"I—"

"Promise," he insists.

I study him for a moment. He's not going to budge on this.

But neither am I.

"Fine," I say stiffly. "I promise."

Ari doesn't need his empathy gift to know it's a lie.

SEVEN

I planned to talk to Runa about the potion tonight, but Mama ruins everything.

"Absolutely not," she says when I start to leave the hut after dinner. "This wandering about at all hours is unacceptable. An emergency is one thing, but two nights in a row? I don't think so."

"But, Mama, it's—"

"Don't argue with me, Brynja."

"*Mama*," I protest, "I'm a Seeker now! And this is about the Realm, and it's important. I promise!"

She puts her hands on her hips, which means I'm about to get lectured. "Seeker or not," she says, "the rules haven't changed. You're still a child, and your papa and I will decide what's best for you. I've been lenient with some of this Seeker business, but no twelve-year-old daughter of mine will go gallivanting around the village at all hours of the night, no matter how 'important' she thinks she is."

There's absolutely no arguing with Mama when she's in one of these moods. "Papa," I call, trying to get his attention. Surely he'll be on my side, at least.

"Listen to your mama, Bryn," Papa calls from the bedroom.

"But that isn't fair! The other Seekers don't have to get approval from *their* mothers to do their jobs."

Mama's eyebrows rise. Another bad sign. "I am quite certain that Seeker Ari's mother makes him obey her rules," she says. "And the other Seekers may be fully grown adults now, but I'm sure they listened to their mothers when they were younger. Now come help with the dishes."

"But it's Elisa's turn!"

"Would you like to do tomorrow's breakfast dishes too? Keep arguing and see where that gets you."

I sigh.

After I do all of the dinner dishes, help Mama fold the laundry, and promise five times that I'll return home before dark, Mama *finally* gives me permission to leave. I rush out of the hut before she comes up with any more chores for me.

Runa doesn't look surprised by my arrival. She's finishing her chores in the stable, tending to her horse, Starlight.

"Please tell me you changed your mind," she says as I walk in, the smell of hay filling my nose.

"When have I ever changed my mind about anything?"

"True. I knew you'd stick with this ridiculous plan. I was

just hoping maybe Ari talked you out of it or came up with something better."

I raise my eyebrows indignantly. "You think *Ari* is the one who comes up with the good plans?"

"Well, it definitely isn't you. Every plan you've ever come up with has been dangerous or reckless or—"

"Okay, okay. Not *all* of my decision-making has been successful in the past," I concede, giving Starlight a pet. "But the other Seekers are refusing to come up with any alternatives, so we've got to do this. But I have good news!"

Runa looks skeptical.

Quickly I tell her what Seeker Larus said about the potion they concocted before, and how close it came to working. As I talk, Runa starts to look slightly more hopeful.

"That's a start, at least," she says finally. "But it could be missing *several* ingredients, not just one. Who knows what the right combination is to fight off this mystery plague."

"But it's already so close, according to Seeker Larus," I say. "I'm sure you can figure it out in no time."

Runa bites her lip. "But I don't have any of those ingredients, Bryn. Where am I going to get them?"

"I already have some starflowers, and I can find figroses in the Realm. Why not just ask the herbalist for the rest?"

"Mountain avens are expensive," Runa protests. "I don't have anything I could trade that would get as many as we'd need to experiment properly."

"But Elder Ingvar loves you," I point out, rubbing Starlight's nose. "Why don't you ask him if you can help out in his shop in exchange for whatever you need?"

"But how will I explain why I need it? You said the plague has to be a secret. I can't tell anyone what we're doing or why."

I brush a loose curl behind my ear, giving it some thought. "You still want to be a doctor, right?"

Runa shrugs. "What's that got to do with anything?"

"Tell Elder Ingvar that! Tell him you want to convince the doctor to take you on as an apprentice, and you're trying to prove how much you know about healing by coming up with new cures. He should be thrilled, since it will benefit his business too."

Runa brushes a stalk of hay off her skirt, considering. "I'll talk to him," she says finally. "But that's all I can promise. I don't know when or if I'll be able to make this potion—and that's not considering that we have no idea what else to put in it."

"Actually, I had a thought about that." I slide a phoenix feather from my pocket and hold it up. "Got this from the Realm today. Think it'll do?"

Runa's eyes widen. "Of course!" she says. "Phoenixes are regenerative. It's some of the most powerful healing magic in the world! Surely *that* could . . ." She trails off, her eyes sparkling.

I grin and hand her the feather. "Let's try it and see if it works. Make the potion as soon as you can, and let me know when it's done."

Runa sighs again. "Sure, boss."

My smile widens. "Did I mention you're the best?"

She rolls her eyes. "I'm well aware."

A figure waits for me in the garden when I return home.

I expect it to be Mama, scolding me for returning after dark, or Papa, wanting to tell me something. But it's a yellow light that illuminates the garden bench.

Ari.

His gift sinks back into his fingers as I approach, the yellow glow fading. "I've been thinking," he says without preamble.

"What are you doing here?" I whisper.

"Don't worry. Your parents know I'm here. I already asked them if I could wait for you," he says.

My eyebrows lift. Mama doesn't usually let me have visitors after dark. I guess she takes *Ari* seriously as a Seeker, at least.

"So what were you thinking about?" I ask, settling onto the bench beside him. His dark-brown eyes are barely visible in the fading light.

"I've been thinking about what you said, about finding potion ingredients."

"Right . . ."

"Well, you know what lives in the northern forests that could be really useful to us."

It takes me a moment too long to catch on. "You mean icefoxes?" I say, my mouth falling open.

"Of course. If we're going to need an ingredient for the potion, who better to help us find it than icefoxes?"

He's right, and I can't believe I didn't think of this before. One of an icefox's magical characteristics is that they have a perfect sense of direction and can guide someone to any place they've ever been. When Seekers have difficulty locating a rare plant or creature in the northern forests, they often use icefoxes as guides. Some even venture far enough south to provide direction through some of the Realm's other territories.

"But what should we ask the icefox to help us find?" I ask.

"Whatever we want," Ari says. "Have any ideas about what might cure this plague? Something rare that the Seekers wouldn't have tried the first time?"

"No idea," I say. "I already thought about using phoenix feathers in a potion, since they're such good healers."

"That's a great idea!" Ari says. "Did you tell Seeker Larus?"

I shake my head. "He doesn't listen to me, Ari. None of them do."

"So what's your plan? Don't tell me you're still thinking of making the potion yourself and going into the Realm alone."

"Of course not." It isn't entirely a lie—I'm planning to have *Runa* make the potion. But Ari picks up on the deception anyway, his eyes narrowing. Stupid empathy gift.

"I'm just going to have Runa help me," I say quickly.

"Once that's done, we'll take the potion to Seeker Larus and talk to the Council about how to safely test it."

Ari considers this for a moment, then nods.

"And your idea is good too," I say. "Let's both try to think of some other ingredients that might work for the potion, and then we can find an icefox who can lead us to them."

"Tall order," Ari says. "These things are *rare* for a reason. We don't even know if we can find an icefox, let alone one who can guide us to what we want."

"But it's worth a try," I say. "Anything's worth a try if it will stop this plague."

Ari nods. "All right."

"So . . . Do you want to go tonight?"

Ari's eyes widen. "We're not supposed to—"

"I know what we're not *supposed* to do. But the Seekers will never let us do it ourselves, and besides, we don't have any time to waste. Why not go tonight?"

Ari bites his lip. "I don't know."

"If you don't come with me, I'll just go by myself. At least we could work together, right?"

At that moment, Mama's voice calls from the window of the hut. "Brynja! It's late!"

I sigh. "Come on, Ari. Don't you remember the training we used to do together? It'll be just like old times."

"Yeah, and we got in trouble for breaking the rules then, too," he says. But he smiles a little, and I know I've convinced him.

"Meet me at the Point in a few hours, after my family's asleep," I say, and after a moment of hesitation, Ari nods.

He heads back up the path to the village, and I trudge inside. Mama doesn't even pretend not to have been standing at the window spying on us the whole time. "What did that boy want?"

"*Seeker* Ari," I say, putting emphasis on the title, "just needed to talk to me about something we're going to do in the Realm tomorrow."

"At this time of night? Surely it could wait for the morning," Mama says, drawing the curtain over the window.

"It was important," I grumble. Just when I thought Mama was starting to take my job seriously.

She doesn't think of me as a real Seeker, and neither does anyone else.

I'm just going to have to show them I know what I'm doing. I'll cure the plague myself, and then everyone will know that I didn't get this job by chance. I earned this position, and I'm going to prove it.

EIGHT

There you are," Ari says as I walk up to Dragon's Point a few hours later. "What took you so long?"

"What does it look like?" I gesture toward the ridiculous outfit I have assembled in preparation for tracking icefoxes. My own coat is a simple wool one that's fine for winters in the village but will never hold up under the arctic temperatures of the Realm's glaciers and ice forests. So I had to improvise. Over my coat, I've thrown a heavy wool blanket across my shoulders and fastened it with pins from the clothesline. And over *that*, I've added one of Papa's thickest coats. We traded away his heaviest winter gear when he had to retire as a Seeker, unfortunately, but this coat is still thicker than mine, with a nice double layer of lining on the inside that Mama stitched in for his birthday. It's way too long on me, though, so I had to roll the ends up and tuck them into a pair of Papa's pants, which I am wearing over my own, and then tuck the ends of the pants into my snow boots and fasten one of Papa's belts over the whole thing to keep it all in place.

Ari takes one look at my outfit and laughs.

"Go ahead and tease me," I grumble. "I haven't had time to trade for new winter gear yet."

Ari whistles three clear notes to signal Lilja, and we wait for her to appear.

"So what do you know about icefoxes?" Ari asks as we wait. We haven't encountered one in the Realm yet, so this will be new for both of us.

"A few things," I say. I've seen drawings of icefoxes in Papa's journals. While they look a lot like the ordinary red foxes that lurk in the woods around the village, icefoxes have solid white fur that magically grows ice crystals. The crystals don't bother the foxes, who are impervious to cold anyway, and serve as a defense mechanism, since they can shape them into icy spikes that will wound predators and even shoot ice daggers at potential threats.

More importantly, the crystals have a lot of other properties that are useful for humans. They're as hard as diamonds and can be used to make tools like blades and saws, but they can also be easily melted down for use in potions and tonics that the village herbalist claims have all sorts of useful properties. And most important of all, icefox crystals are often set in stone to form jewelry that many people believe can ward off dark magic. Not many villagers actually wear icefox crystals like that, but apparently icefox jewelry is a big trend on the mainland, and their traders will give away a small fortune in other goods for the finest of icefox crystals, even if they're small. Papa once gave Mama a necklace made of the crystals as a wedding present, and it's her most prized possession.

The good news is that icefox crystals are fairly easy to collect: the foxes are generally friendly and will socialize with humans as long as they're not made to feel threatened, and they shed the crystals easily.

The bad news is that icefoxes live in the remotest parts of the Realm and aren't easy to find. They're clever and skilled at hiding themselves, so it takes a talented Seeker to track them down.

I try to run through everything Papa's ever told me about them as Lilja arrives. She tilts her head to the side when she sees me, probably trying to figure out why I look so funny. We climb onto her back and soar over the mountains and into the Realm. Ari and I use our gifts to steer her north, toward the glacier fields. Luckily, they're easy to spot even in the dark: a wide expanse of glittering white ice, gleaming under the light of the moon.

The Realm is so beautiful, and from all the way up here I can truly get a sense of its expanse, of its wide and varying landscapes. There's the dark, jagged line of the volcanoes surrounded by lava fields, home to dragons and firecats and phoenixes; there are the thick forests to both the west and east of the lava fields, where the most magical plants like starflowers and creatures like unicorns live and flourish; there are the coastal cliffs dotted with gyrpuff nests and sleeping saellons; the cool glacial lakes hiding vatnaveras in their depths; and all of it surrounded by the thundering sea, where the sea wolves hunt and the sarvalurs fill the waves with their song.

There's so much to see, so much to do, so much to explore. I want to travel every inch of it.

But first things first: it's time to find some icefoxes.

The glaciers loom before us, and the air turns frigid, causing Lilja to swoop lower and reduce her speed. She's reluctant to fly here, and I can't blame her. Dragons are creatures of fire, and sensitive to cold. Plus, there are boundary spells set by the Seekers to keep them out of this territory. Though I doubt we've reached the boundary yet, there may be some Seeker magic in the air discouraging Lilja from traveling in this direction.

"We need to land her soon," Ari says loudly, echoing my thoughts. "We're about to hit a border."

I nod and give Lilja a nudge with my gift, encouraging her to descend. We guide her into a landing at the edge of a forest, about a mile or so from the glacier fields. It'll be a long walk for us, but I'm not sure how much farther she can go, and she'll be warmer here anyway.

The wind whips my face as Lilja descends, and I'm realizing too late that my makeshift outfit isn't going to be warm enough. As Lilja thuds into a landing, jostling us, our breath creates fog in the air. I reach into the pocket of Papa's coat and pull out the ugly knitted hat Mama made him one year, which is far from appealing but does have flaps that hang down and cover my ears. I shove on my only pair of gloves, too, but the right one has holes in two of the fingers.

Ari climbs down from Lilja's back, and I slide after him. The ice coating the grass crackles beneath my feet. Ari and I both let our gifts flare through our fingers, lighting the landscape surrounding us. An ice forest stretches out to the south and west, every visible tree and branch and twig topped with snow. Directly to the north and east lies a gigantic glacier, a huge sheet of ice spreading almost as far as the eye can see. Only the distant mountain peaks on the horizon provide landmarks in the expanse of white.

"It's beautiful," Ari says quietly. He's right, but that's not what I'm thinking about.

What I'm thinking is that this is entirely the wrong season to be tracking icefoxes. The warmer summer temperatures mean that there's less snow sitting on top of the glacier. At this time of year, the top layer of ice will be thinner and slicker. Of course, there's no need to worry about the ice melting out from under us. The glacier is so massive that it would take *years* of warm temperatures to melt it. But a slicker surface means it will be slippery, without the help of snow to give our feet more traction, and there will be no icefox prints. The best time to find icefoxes is in the early spring, right after they first emerge from their dens but while there's still plenty of snow to show their tracks.

An owl hoots somewhere in the trees, and Lilja's head

swivels toward the sound. "No, Lil," I say quickly. "You need to stay here."

Together Ari and I set a quick boundary spell that will keep Lilja within a mile of this spot. Lilja snorts when she recognizes the feel of the spell, and Ari tosses her a berry. "Good dragon."

Lilja snorts again in response. Probably wondering why we're standing around in the cold and not giving her enough berries.

"So," Ari says, "which direction should we start off in?"

"Well, they hibernate in their dens in the caves during the winter, but during other seasons they will trek across the glacier from their dens to the forests, where they hunt. So the icefoxes have probably finished hunting in the forest for tonight and traveled back across the glacier to their dens. If we start walking in the direction of the nearest caves, we should come across signs of them that we can track. And if not, we should check the nearest caves anyway, to see if there might be icefoxes sleeping inside."

"But how do we know where the nearest caves are?"

I point to the horizon. "We should start to see rock formations that will create natural caves as we get closer to the northern mountain range. So we want to head that way, toward the mountains."

Ari gestures in that direction. "After you, then."

I whistle again as we take a few more steps away from Lilja, tossing her a berry when she turns my way. Her eyes look sad and confused as Ari and I head north, and she takes a single, tentative step in our direction.

"Stay there, Lil," I say. "We'll be back soon."

She lets out a low rumble of discontent, never taking her eyes off us. I force myself to turn away and focus on the horizon. She'll be fine. We won't be gone for long . . . probably. Unless we get hopelessly lost and die of frostbite or something.

I shiver and wrap my arms around myself as Ari and I set out across the glacier, surrounded by nothing but a dark expanse of ice. The howl of a sea wolf somewhere in the distance is the only sound aside from our footsteps.

"I haven't seen any tracks, have you?" I ask after a minute, just to break the silence.

Ari smiles. "Not on bare ice, no."

I roll my eyes even though he probably can't see it in the near dark. "I'm not just talking about prints," I say. "Obviously, there aren't any, but the foxes leave other traces behind."

"Like what?"

I point to the rock formation on our left. "Look at the patterns there. The edges of those rocks are jagged, and they aren't piled very high. Generations of icefoxes may use the same dens for decades or even longer, since they can remember every location they've been to. So many years of icefoxes traveling in and out tend to wear down the rock, making it smoother near the entrances of their caves. Like they carve out a little doorway for themselves. And they always prefer formations that are high off the ground and require lots of climbing. They're nimbler than most predators and want to use their climbing skills to their advantage."

"Which means . . . ?" Ari says.

"Which means that formation on the left would be a less likely place to find a fox den. Unlike, say, this formation over here, which is taller and looks like it has smoother surfaces up top."

"Oh," Ari says, nodding. "That makes sense."

I grin. "There's also the fact that there are icefox crystals piled along the rocks."

"What?" Ari's head swivels toward the rocks on our right, straining to see. "How can you tell?"

"Look at how much the moonlight sparkles over the rocks there, even in places that should be more shadowed. The light is reflecting in the crystals."

Ari frowns. "If you say so."

"You wanted me to share my knowledge," I say with a smirk. "I can't help it if it's too advanced for you."

Ari glares for a second, but then a slow smile edges onto his face. "Just for that, you'll pay," he says. Before I get the chance to respond, he cries, "First one there gets all the crystals!" and takes off.

I race after him, slipping and sliding on the ice, as we approach the den. He has a good head start and longer legs, so there's no way I'm going to catch him. But there's also no way he can collect *all* of the crystals before I get to them. So I veer to the right, heading for a different part of the rock than he is, where the light is especially bright. Ari reaches the rocks first and whoops in triumph, but then scrambles to find crystals when he sees me scoop one up beside him. The crystal is cold even through my gloves, a gleaming shard of ice barely bigger than my thumbnail. An entire rainbow of colors glimmers inside of it, more beautiful than any diamond. I stuff it into my pocket and reach for the next one.

After a few minutes of searching the rocks, we've found half a dozen crystals each, just on the lower levels. "Why are there so many?" Ari asks.

"The foxes shed a lot during the summer," I say. "Some of the crystals melt off during the warmer months. There's probably a whole lot of these things scattered out on the glacier too; it was just difficult to see them. Easier to spot when they're all piled together like this, and when you know where to look."

"Do you want to grab a few more?"

"This should be plenty," I say. "I didn't come all this way to see icefox crystals but not icefoxes. Let's climb a little higher, see if we can get a peek into their dens."

"Is it safe?"

I shrug. "They're generally friendly as long as they're not threatened."

Ari nods. "All right. I think I see a good handhold over here."

Ari and I carefully climb up the side of the rocks, scrambling over ledges and darting from one handhold to another. We're relatively quiet the whole way up, so it doesn't occur to me that we might be in trouble.

But once we reach the top of the formation and spy the entrance to the icefox den, I realize I made two mistakes.

One: I forgot that icefox mothers are extra defensive of their dens when their babies are inside.

Two: icefoxes are nocturnal, which means they're already awake.

As we cling to the side of the rocks, looking up into the den, a mother icefox bares her teeth from above, her hackles raised, her babies' eyes peering out from behind her. And every single one of her sharp, icy spikes is pointed directly at us.

NINE

The mother icefox glares down at us, her yellow eyes fierce.

"Um, Bryn?" Ari whispers. "She's really, really angry."

I think fast. "Don't make any sudden movements. Keep your hands visible. And tilt your head down! Icefoxes show deference to one another by bowing their heads."

"If I look down, I won't be able to see if she's lunging for my face or not!" Ari protests.

The icefox makes a hissing sound, her pointy teeth bared in his direction.

"Just do it!" I yell.

I don't wait to see if he listens. I lower my own head, fixing my gaze on the rocks below. We're too high to jump down. We could climb, but that would require moving our hands, and the icefox wouldn't like that at all. They seem to associate hands with claws, so she'll be watching ours closely.

The fox makes a low growling sound in warning, which means Ari probably isn't listening to me. "Use your gift to calm her down!" I say. I'm already casting mine out, but while I can feel the cold core of the fox's life source just fine, I can't do much to make her calmer. I can't sense her emotions the way Ari can. All I can attempt is to touch her life force with mine, so that she can feel it and sense that I mean her and her babies no harm. But she's too angry for me to attempt that right now. She'd see my encroaching magic as a threat and lash out.

"I'm trying," Ari says from somewhere to my left. "She's pulling away from me."

The sound of claws scraping against rock echoes above my head. "Try harder!"

I don't dare look up to see if he's doing anything, or if his magic is working. I try to remember anything Papa's ever told me about icefoxes that might be useful right now, and suddenly it hits me.

Clearing my throat, I start to hum a simple melody. It's an old lullaby, one Mama used to sing to me and Elisa before we went to sleep. But I'm no good at singing and can't remember all the words, so I just hum the notes as best I can. It's a soft, soothing song, the kind that lulls you into relaxation, and I hope it's enough. Papa always told me that when he befriended icefoxes to use as guides around the Realm, he'd hum or whistle melodies. "They like music," he'd say. "But don't tell the other Seekers. They haven't figured it out yet!"

He winked at me then, like it was a secret just for us.

I have to hope he was right, or I might be about to face the attack of an angry icefox.

"It's working, Bryn!" Ari yells. I'm not sure if he means my song or his magic, but I hum louder, trying not to imagine which sharp pointy thing will kill me first—the fox's teeth or its claws or its long icy spikes.

My fingers are losing their grip on the ledge, and I'm forced to tilt my head up quickly as I scramble to find a better purchase. I get a quick glimpse of the fox, who is still pointing spikes at us but no longer baring her teeth. She's watching me.

I reach out with my magic, just a little, and sense the presence of Ari's gift, already entangled with the fox's energy. I can't detect her emotions, so I have no idea if he's actually doing anything, but her energy *does* seem less bright than before, like maybe she's calmer.

"Keep going," Ari says as I reach the end of my song. "She definitely liked it."

I start the song over from the beginning, humming as loudly as I can. I want to ask him if his magic is working, but I don't dare stop humming.

"Almost there," Ari says, answering my question. "You can look up, Bryn. I've got her nice and calm now."

Cautiously, not quite ready to believe him, I tilt my head up. The fox's spikes are receding, her fur now covered only in small, harmless crystals. Her jaws are closed, and while her ears are pointed toward us in curiosity, she isn't growling or looking defensive anymore. I nudge her life source gently with my gift, letting her sense me. Her tail swishes.

"I think we can approach her now," I say. "She's not giving off any threatening signs."

Ari nods. "You're right. Her energy is curious but more relaxed."

Slowly, I climb to my knees on the ledge, while Ari does the same beside me. We scuffle forward on our knees, remaining at the fox's height, while she sniffs in our direction. Four pairs of eyes—her curious cubs—watch us from the dark entrance of the den.

"Hello, Mama Fox," I say quietly. "Sorry to have scared you." I place my hands flat on the ground in front of her, letting her sniff them carefully to verify that I have no threatening claws. Ari copies me, and she sniffs him too before sitting back on her haunches.

I raise my hand slowly, letting her see it, and when her body language doesn't change, I carefully touch her shoulder.

"She wants to be petted," Ari says, his hands still glowing yellow with his gift. "She likes the attention. I think maybe she's had an interaction with a Seeker before. She doesn't seem confused by what you're doing."

I hum a little bit more, softly, and begin to pet her, stroking all the way down her back with my gloved hand. Her fur is thick, and ice crystals break off under my touch, dropping to the ground.

As I give Mama Fox another pet, one of the babies emerges from the den, followed by another. Ari laughs. "They want the attention too!" he says, grinning.

"Make sure the mama is okay with it before you touch them," I say, and Ari follows my advice, keeping a wary eye on Mama Fox as he introduces his hand to the nearest baby and gives it a pet. The baby icefoxes are adorable: tiny bundles of white fluff, small enough that I could lift each of them with one hand. Their little paws patter against the rock, their tiny tails swishing. They're too small to form many crystals of their own yet, but I detect a few glimmers here and there. Give them a few more months in the Realm, and the magic will suffuse them so completely that they'll be brimming with crystals, just like their mama.

The one nearest to me lets out a tiny whine, asking for attention, and I use my free hand to pet it even as I continue stroking Mama Fox's fur. Within minutes, Ari has one fox cub curled in his lap and one nipping at the fabric of his gloves while he gives the third a scratch behind the ears with his other hand. The fourth cub nudges me insistently with her nose whenever I stop petting her for even a moment.

"That's the cutest thing I've ever seen," I say to Ari, laughing as the second cub tries to run off with his glove.

"These little fluffballs are attacking me!" he says jokingly, grabbing his glove from the runaway fox even as the one in his lap starts to nibble at his coat.

"They really like you," I say, grinning.

"A little too much," he grumbles, tugging his coat's button out of the baby fox's mouth. But he's smiling, and yellow light shines around his hands as he intertwines his magic with their life forces. I do the same with mine, strengthening the little foxes' sparks to make sure they'll stay healthy.

I wish we could play with baby icefoxes forever, but we have to move fast if we're going to get Mama Fox to lead us to some potential potion ingredients. The sooner we start looking, the more time we'll have.

Ari must be thinking the same. He looks over at me and says, "So how do we get her to lead us to anything?"

I bite my lip in concentration. Papa has told me before that icefoxes can act as guides, but he's never told me *how*. "Let's try visualizing," I say. "We should both picture what we want to find, and try to share that with her."

"Um, how do we share it?"

"We picture what we want to happen when using our gifts, right? Let's do the same thing, but share our gifts with her life force at the same time. Maybe she'll understand."

Ari looks doubtful, but he doesn't argue. "So what should we try to find first? I was thinking about meadowsweet."

"Really? Why?"

"It's got healing properties, right? The herbalist says it's always in demand, because he uses it for lots of things. Asked me to bring him some if I could ever find it."

I shrug. "Okay. Worth a shot." I know what meadowsweet looks like, since I've seen it in Papa's sketchbook. It has clustered, creamy-white flowers that shouldn't be too hard to identify.

Together, Ari and I close our eyes and start to visualize. I picture the meadowsweet flowers in my mind. As I imagine them, my gift flows through my fingers, and I reach out blindly for Mama Icefox's life spark. As our gifts mingle, I imagine the meadowsweet flowing toward her, mixing with her energy the way it fills mine.

I open my eyes. Mama Icefox tilts her head sideways, looking at me.

"Do you think you can lead us to more of these?" I ask. Which is dumb. It's not like she understands what I'm saying. But her ears perk up, and she leaps to her feet.

"Is it working?" I ask Ari.

"Her emotions changed," he says, closing his eyes in concentration, "but I'm not sure—"

Mama Fox is now nudging each of the four babies back into the den, out of sight. She makes a sort of yipping sound at them, communicating something, before turning back to us. Then she sniffs, makes a low whining noise, and begins picking her way down the rocks. She glances back at Ari and me, as if to ask us if we're coming.

"I guess that's a yes," Ari says. I follow Mama Fox back down the rocks, with Ari clambering after me.

Mama Fox makes it to the bottom much more easily than we do, jumping nimbly from one rock to another while Ari and I climb, but she waits for us at the bottom. I think my first instinct was right: she's had interaction with Seekers before. She knows how to guide us.

Still, she seems a bit impatient, swishing her tail back and forth as Ari and I drop to our feet at the bottom of the rocks. She takes off running across the glacier as soon as we reach the bottom, and we have to scramble across the ice to keep up.

Mama Fox scurries across the glacier and into the nearest forest, where the trees' limbs are choked with ice and a heavy layer of snow crunches underfoot. Ari and I travel in silence, just trying to keep up with the icefox, until suddenly I spot something clinging to a snow-covered tree.

"Hold on," I say to Ari, skidding to a stop. "Those are snowpetals!"

Ahead of us, Mama Fox senses that we're no longer following and turns around. She swishes her tail impatiently, but she waits as I approach the trees.

"Are you sure?" Ari asks. "All of these plants look so similar when they're covered in snow."

"I'm sure," I say. "I can feel it with my gift." Snowpetals are one of the few flowering plants that can flourish in frigid temperatures, drawing upon the magic of the Realm to actually feed off snow and turn it into fuel. I draw my knife from my pocket and cut two of the flowers from their stems, being careful to leave the roots so that they can regrow. The flowers are beautiful, with tiny white blossoms. I haven't seen one since the first round of the Seeker competition, when we were tasked with collecting them.

With a flourish, I hand one of the flowers to Ari. He examines it closely before tucking it into his pocket. "Thanks," he says.

I nod toward Mama Fox. "I think our guide is getting impatient. We'd better keep moving."

We continue through the forest for several more minutes before Mama Fox veers south, and the landscape begins to change. The layer of snow beneath our feet thins and then disappears altogether, even as it vanishes from the plants around us and the trees overhead. This far south, the trees are coated in moss rather than ice.

I'm beginning to suspect that this icefox is leading us in hopeless circles when Ari cries, "Look!"

Nothing is visible in the darkness of the trees, but Ari isn't looking with his eyes. He's using his gift. I do the same, letting my magic stretch out before me. Something sparks in the distance, something huge and flowing and full of life. No, more than one something. A bunch of tiny plants, all growing side by side.

I gasp and run forward, Ari on my heels. We follow Mama Fox, bursting through the trees and into a little hollow beside the stream. Strewn all along the ground are tall-stemmed plants covered in creamy-white flowers.

Meadowsweet.

There are so *many*.

Mama Fox sits back on her hind legs, panting from exertion but looking quite proud of herself. I channel a bit of my gift into her life source as a reward, giving her more energy.

Then I study the plants. It's important to make sure I can recognize them again; if this *does* end up being the right ingredient for Runa's potion, we might need lots more. I close my eyes and let my gift flow around me, taking stock of the surroundings to make sure that I can always find this place again. We're deep within the western forests, beside a stream, just northwest of the line of lava fields. . . .

Once I'm certain I've got it down, I dig up four plants and slip them carefully into my pockets. Ari joins me, grabbing a few flowers of his own.

We work in companionable silence for a minute. It's almost peaceful, somehow. "Thanks for helping me find these," I say finally. "I really think we can find a cure."

Ari glances sideways at me. "You're pretty set on this, aren't you?"

"Of course. What could be more important than saving the Realm?"

Ari smiles gently. "But we don't have to do it single-handedly. We're not on our own anymore. The other Seekers can help us. I think we should listen to what they have to say."

"I *am* listening," I insist. "But just because the other Seekers have a lot of experience doesn't mean they can't be wrong. And *they* don't listen to *me*. So I'll just have to prove to them that I can do this. That *we* can do this."

"You're already a Seeker," Ari says softly. "The time for proving yourself is over."

"Is it?" I look him straight in the eye. "Because no one seems to act like it. The other Seekers treat us like we're students, giving us training and not letting us go anywhere alone. They don't listen to us, and they don't let us make decisions. They should trust us, but they don't."

Ari frowns, but I can tell he's considering it. "You're pretty good at this, you know. Being a Seeker."

I smile. "You're not so bad yourself."

Ari tugs the flower free and tucks it carefully into his pocket. "Guess we'd better head back," he says. "It's getting late. Or early, really."

"Guess so," I say, slipping one last flower into my own pocket.

Mama Fox leads us back through the forests and out to the glacier at a more leisurely pace this time. After we ascend the rock formation, we find her cubs waiting in their den, and they rush out to greet us. We give all of them a few more pets, but then Mama Fox nudges them back inside. She turns to us one final time at the entrance of the den, and I give her a goodbye scratch behind the ears, sending a shimmer of crystals falling to the ground. "Thanks for everything," I say. "I'll come back to see you soon."

"Yeah, thanks for not eating us," Ari adds.

As we scramble back down the rocks, my heart is filled with the same kind of warm, fuzzy feeling I always get after spending time with Lilja or looking at Papa's sketchbook. The feeling that I get only when thinking about magical creatures. About how much I love being a Seeker. Nothing else in the world is like this. Nothing else makes me so light, so energized, so warm.

I knew it even before I won the competition: I was born to be a Seeker. My dream has come true—the Realm is all around, its magic filling my every breath.

Now I have to make sure I do a good job. I have to keep the Realm safe.

But as Ari and I trudge back across the glacier toward the edge of the ice forest, the warmth in my chest is replaced with a heaviness that sinks into my stomach. Maybe Ari's right. The other Seekers certainly have more wisdom and experience than us. What if there's nothing that can be done to make a cure? What if we lose all the gyrpuffs? What if the plague continues to spread?

After all this time, after working so hard to become a Seeker . . .

What if I can't save the Realm?

TEN

The next morning, the other Seekers give us absolutely nothing to do.

Seeker Larus arrives at the Point in a hurry and hardly glances at us as he calls his dragon. "We're focusing on boundary spells around the cliffs today," he says as his dragon appears in the sky, "so your assistance won't be needed. Enjoy the day off!"

As he flies away, Ari and I glance at each other. "Well," he says finally, "what now?"

"I'm going to go see Runa and find out if she's made any progress with the healing potion."

Ari nods. "I was thinking I might go visit Elder Oskar. He's one of my neighbors, and I've seen him around a lot since he retired from being a Seeker. I thought maybe I'd ask him some questions about the plague, see what he remembers from the last time this happened."

My eyes widen. "Ari, that's brilliant! Okay, you do that, and I'll talk to Runa, and then we can share what we've learned tomorrow."

Ari looks a bit relieved at my reaction, though I'm not sure why. Is he just glad we're on the same page? Or glad I'm not talking about going into the Realm on our own? Probably both.

We walk back down to the village and part ways. I head straight to Runa's.

She meets me in the sheep pasture, where her sheepdog, Hundur, runs straight toward me, wagging his tail. I give him a quick rub behind the ears, letting my gift flow with his.

"Should've known you'd be back so soon," Runa grumbles, straightening the sleeve of her tunic. "I haven't had time to do much yet, Bryn."

"I brought you a surprise," I say, drawing the meadowsweet from my pocket.

Runa's eyes widen. She reaches wordlessly for the plant, and I hand it over. "These are really useful in healing," she says. "They—"

"I figured you could try them in a batch of the potion," I say. "Maybe they'll work?"

Runa shrugs. "As good a try as anything, I guess. I still need to get some mountain avens, though."

"Have you spoken with Elder Ingvar yet? About the apprenticeship."

Runa looks away. "He's probably busy."

I frown. I know she'd be absolutely brilliant as an apprentice. And even if I didn't need her help, I'd still want her to get the job. I want to see her reach her dream of becoming a doctor, the same way I became a Seeker. She just needs someone to give her a little push.

And after all the help she's given me, I need to do something for her.

"Let's go," I say, turning on my heel and marching out of the field.

"What? Where are we going?"

"Come on, keep up!"

Runa races after me, hiking her skirt up to her knees, the meadowsweet still in her hand. "What are you doing?"

"We're going to get you an apprenticeship right now."

"Right now? But—"

"No time like the present!" I say cheerfully.

Runa stops in the middle of the path. "I don't know, Bryn."

I stop too and face her. "You do want to become an apprentice, don't you?"

"Well, yes," she says. "But they probably won't hire me, so there's no point."

"But if I could help you get the job, would you want that?"

"I . . . Yes."

"Okay, then. You're always doing all of these favors for me. Let me do this for you."

"But how are you going to do it?" She gives me a very suspicious look, which is completely unfair. My ideas are always good ones—well, okay, most of the time.

"You'll see. Let's go."

By the time we reach the village and stand outside the herbalist's shop, Runa is fidgeting with the end of her braid. She adjusts the collar of her shirt and brushes a tiny fleck of dust off her sleeve. I roll my eyes. "You look fine," I say. "Just follow my lead." I wrap my Seeker cloak more firmly around my shoulders so that it's clearly visible from the front, straighten my spine, and stride into the shop.

"Good morning, Seeker Bryn," Elder Ingvar says, glancing up from his desk at the back of the small, dimly lit shop. "What can I do for you today? Oh, and hello, Runa."

"Hello," she says back, her voice a little squeaky. I can't believe that Runa, my supremely confident friend, is suddenly so nervous. She must really want this job.

I decide that the direct approach is best—that, and making as many references to my new Seeker status as possible. "Elder Ingvar," I say, "I heard from Seeker Larus that you might be looking to hire an apprentice."

"Er, well, I suppose it's been a while since I took one on, yes, though I wasn't actively looking . . ."

"Well, that's good, because I have the perfect candidate for you."

"You do?" His brow furrows in confusion.

"The rest of the Council and I want to make sure that you

have all the help you need to keep this shop running smoothly," I say. "We've discovered several new magical plant populations in the Realm, so we expect that we'll have a lot of new plants to trade very soon. We want to make sure you'll be able to handle the influx of business, so we've taken an interest in identifying the brightest young healer in the village for the job."

Elder Ingvar still looks confused, so I'm not entirely sure that he's following along, but I plow ahead. The best way to appear confident and official is just to keep going like everything I'm saying makes perfect sense.

"Who did you have in mind?" Elder Ingvar asks.

I try to subtly gesture Runa forward. She takes a step closer.

"Runa could do it," I say. "One of the brightest healers in the village, and already very knowledgeable about herbs and magical plants. She'd be a perfect fit for the job."

"Is that so?" Elder Ingvar says, and I can't decipher his expression. "And do you want this apprenticeship, Runa?" he asks.

"Er, um, yes, I am interested in the position, yes," she stammers.

Elder Ingvar nods. "Well, you've always been one of my more knowledgeable customers, so I don't see why we couldn't try something out. It's not a paid position, you understand?"

"Yes, I know."

He smiles. "All right, then. Would you like to start tomorrow?"

We leave the shop a few minutes later, and as soon as the

door swings shut behind us, Runa jumps up and down with excitement. "Yes, yes, yes!"

I grin. "See, what did I tell you? He must already think you're brilliant, or he wouldn't have given you the job so easily, you know."

"True," she says, grinning back at me. "I don't think he bought any of your Seeker nonsense for a second."

"Well, I think he bought it a *little*, maybe."

She rolls her eyes. "Nope. It was entirely due to my brilliance."

"Okay, whatever. The point is, you have an apprenticeship! That's amazing!"

"I guess," Runa says with a shrug, like she wasn't just excitedly jumping around a second ago. "I'd rather be a doctor than an herbalist. But this seems like a good place to start, and I like Elder Ingvar."

"Maybe he'll let you experiment with some of the herbs in the shop, for the potion," I say.

"That's an awful lot to ask before I've really even started the job, but we'll see."

"You'll be whipping up cures in no time, I'm sure. And once everyone sees how brilliant you are, there's no way you won't be able to be a doctor."

Runa doesn't reply, but she smiles as we make our way out of the village and down the path toward her home. "So what's happening in the Realm?" she asks finally. "Has the plague spread?"

"I don't know." I cross my arms. "The Seekers still aren't letting me and Ari into the Realm much, so I don't know what's happening there. I don't know how the gyrpuffs are doing. Haven't seen anything except the icefoxes and the missing phoenixes." Quickly I explain to Runa what Ari and I observed the day before. Runa listens, nodding intently.

"I'll get to work right away, I promise," she says. "Oh, and there's one other thing. I could really use some peppermint; I think it will balance out the meadowsweet. But it doesn't grow on the island. I'll have to get it from the Laekens—it's Trading Day. Can you come with me and bring something to trade?"

"Of course," I say. "We always go together! Besides, the other Seekers haven't given me anything else to do."

"Great," she says, brightening a little. "But I don't have anything to trade, and peppermint is expensive, so you'll have to bring something from the Realm."

"No problem. You're looking at the best Seeker in the Realm, after all."

Runa would usually tell a joke in response, but now her eyes are serious. She brushes a finger over the petals of the meadowsweet and says, "Let's just hope the potion works."

I nod. "Good luck."

After a break for lunch, Runa and I head down to the docks, where the three mainland trading ships—from the Ermandi, the Laekens, and the Midjans—have already arrived, and the villagers are flocking to greet them. I'm always eager to visit the Ermandi ship, but Runa loves to see the herbs and medicines that the Laekens bring to trade.

We approach the tent that's been assembled on the dock beside the Laeken ship, where an elderly woman in a colorful shawl greets us.

"Hello, Elder Margret," Runa says. "We were hoping to find some peppermint today."

Elder Margret smiles. "Well, you're in luck. I have the highest quality you'll find anywhere." She leans forward and says, in a conspiratorial whisper, "The Ermandi have been trying to grow it themselves, but don't let them fool you. *Our* peppermint is the only way to go."

Elder Margret drives a hard bargain; she takes two silver dragon scales and the snowpetal flower in exchange for the peppermint, which Runa accepts eagerly.

"Do you want to see the Ermandi next?" she asks as we exit the Laeken tent and stroll along the docks.

I shake my head. "I'd rather just get to work on the potion. Is there anything I can do to help you with it?"

She shrugs. "I just have to finish putting everything in. Shouldn't take too much longer. I can have it ready for you tonight."

"Okay," I say. "I'll meet you in the pasture again after dinner."

Runa looks down at her feet. "Assuming nothing goes wrong with the potion. I might mess it up."

"Oh, please. The best healer in the village would never."
Runa looks uncertain.

I give her hand a squeeze. "You'll do great. I know it."

I say goodbye to her as we reach my family's hut, and she continues toward her home. I haven't made any other plans for this day off, and I'm not sure how best to spend it. Surely there's something else I can do to help the Realm. . . .

"Brynja," Mama says in surprise as I walk through the door. "Back so soon?"

"Yeah," I say glumly, sliding into a kitchen chair beside Elisa.

Mama frowns. "You and Runa used to love spending all day down at the docks when the ships come in. Is something wrong?"

"No," I say, too quickly.

Mama looks up. "Elisa," she says, "why don't you take your dolls outside for a moment?"

Elisa makes a face. "I want to hear the secrets!"

"Out," Mama says firmly, pointing to the door. Elisa slumps her shoulders and slowly makes her way to the door, pouting.

"All right," Mama says, turning to me. "What's been going on?"

"I'm not supposed to tell you. It's Seeker business."

Mama's eyebrows fly upward. "You told your papa, didn't you?"

"Well, yeah, but . . ."

Mama waits. I sigh.

"Okay, fine. There's an illness spreading in the Realm. A few creatures have gotten sick. The older Seekers have seen this illness before, and they say it's very deadly and very contagious to all of the Realm's creatures."

Mama's gaze softens. She sits in the chair beside me. "And what have the other Seekers proposed to do about this?"

"Basically nothing," I say with a huff. "They quarantined the area where we found a sick gyrpuff, but they're not doing anything to cure him."

"Let me guess," Mama says. "You've taken it upon yourself to come up with a cure?"

"Of course. I'm a Seeker now. It's my job."

Mama fixes me with her lecturing stare. "Being a Seeker isn't a solo job, Bryn. All of the Seekers are meant to work together to share experience and find solutions."

Share experience. Meaning, I don't have any, and the other Seekers do, so I should listen to them. I cross my arms over my chest. "I don't know why I told you this," I say. "You think I can't do it."

Mama leans back. "I never said that."

"I can tell. You don't think I can really do anything as a Seeker. You think I should just leave all the hard work to the others."

"I certainly don't think that." Mama stands, wiping her hands on her apron. "What gave you that impression?"

"Everyone thinks it," I say. "I thought once I won the

competition and became a Seeker officially, everyone would take me seriously. But they don't. Because I'm young, and because I'm a girl, nobody treats me the way they treat the other Seekers. Even the *other Seekers* don't take me seriously or listen to me. I have to do things alone, because I don't have any other choice."

Mama rests one hand on my shoulder. "You knew this would be difficult when you entered the competition," she reminds me. "And you'll prove yourself as a Seeker the same way you proved yourself in the competition. But do you remember how you accomplished that?"

I frown. "You mean stopping a Vondur attack and saving the whole village? I can't exactly do that again."

"No," she says, "before that. You teamed up with Ari in order to learn the skills you needed, remember? It was your teamwork—you and Ari together—that allowed you both to become Seekers."

"We can't be a team if the other Seekers don't want to be one," I say, shrugging her hand off my shoulder. "Even Ari doesn't listen to me, not when the other Seekers say something different."

Mama starts to speak again, but I stand up. "I'm going to go play with Elisa."

Elisa and I are still playing dolls when Papa strides up the path and enters the garden, returning from an errand. "Well, there are my two favorite girls!" he booms. Elisa flings down her doll and rushes into his arms, telling him all about our game (which currently features a flying unicorn, for some reason).

Papa sits down on the garden bench, pulling Elisa into his lap. "And how is my eldest daughter doing today?" he asks me, patting the bench beside him.

I sit down with a heavy sigh. "Well, I—"

"Papa," Elisa interrupts. "Tell us a story."

"A story?" His eyes twinkle. "What story do you want to hear?"

Elisa thinks for a moment, cupping her chin with her hand. "Tell the one about Finn and the fairies!"

Papa pretends to frown. "Oh, that old legend? Surely you don't want to hear *that* one."

"Fairies!" Elisa chants. "Fairies, fairies, fairies!"

"Once upon a time," Papa says, and Elisa quiets immediately. "There was a brave young Seeker named Finnur who set out to discover all the secrets of the Wild Realm." Papa winks at me, and I can't help but smile. Even though I've heard this legend a thousand times, Papa always makes it fun.

"One day, Finn was walking deep within the forest when he encountered an injured unicorn. Finn was an expert healer, so he quickly healed the unicorn and sent it on its way with an offering of figroses. To his surprise, a bright, golden light then appeared in the forest, and a soft voice spoke to him."

"What did the voice say?" Elisa asks eagerly.

"The voice said, 'Thank you, young Seeker, for healing the creatures of this forest. We would like to reward you for your selflessness.' As Finn studied the light, he was able to make out a small shape within it—the shape of a fairy, with wings like a butterfly. He couldn't believe his eyes. Fairies, in the forest! He thought he must be dreaming."

"But he wasn't," Elisa says.

"He wasn't," Papa says with a nod. "He followed the fairy still deeper into the forest, and she led him to a golden, flowering plant he had never seen before. Its petals were coated in golden dust, and Finn knew instantly that it was real gold. 'With this,' he said, 'I'll be rich!'" Papa's voice turns grave. "But it was here that Finn made his big mistake."

Elisa's eyes widen. "What was the mistake?"

"Finn got too greedy," Papa says. "Instead of taking only a few pinches of gold, as the fairy asked him to, he dug up the entire plant, roots and all, and carried it from the Realm. He took flakes of gold from its petals, and that evening, he went into the village and spent the gold wildly, telling everyone who would listen that he was now a wealthy man."

"Did the flower die?" Elisa asks, clutching her doll to her chest.

"No," Papa says. "Because, you see, the fairies are smarter than that. They knew that humans could not be trusted with such a precious gift. So they had enchanted the flower. Under the spell, all of the gold the flower created disappeared into thin air at dawn. So greedy Finn, who had tried to spend all of the gold, was now left with nothing but angry villagers when the gold he'd given them vanished. Worse, the flower no longer produced any gold. Desperate to repay his debts, he returned the flower to the Realm and replanted it exactly where he'd found it. Within a day, the flower produced gold again. This time, Finn took only the gold dust, as the fairy had instructed, and returned to the village. But the damage was done. The fairies no longer trusted him, and they didn't lift their spell. All of the gold vanished at dawn once more. When Finn returned to the Realm, he could never find the flower again."

"Never?" Elisa whispers.

"Never," Papa replies. "The Fairy's Gold had vanished. Some say that the magical golden flower still lives within the Realm, but it's revealed only to those who are worthy of it. And even those who find it must never be greedy with the Realm's gift, for the flower's gold will always disappear at dawn."

"What about the fairies? Did Finn ever see them again?"

Papa shakes his head. "No Seeker has ever seen a fairy in the Realm, before or since."

Elisa frowns. "Then how do we know what happened to the fairies? Are they okay?"

Papa smiles. "Don't worry. The fairies lived happily ever after."

Elisa wriggles down from his lap, holding her doll up. "I'm going to play a new game about the fairies! Bryn, come with me!"

"Okay," I say with a sigh as she skips toward the hut. I look accusingly at Papa. "You've created a monster."

He laughs. "But my storytelling skills have improved, eh?"

"The last time you told that story, it was a sea wolf that Finn heals, not a unicorn," I say accusingly.

"Was it?" Papa scratches his beard. "Well, I'm sure the unicorn is how it *really* happened."

I roll my eyes. "Sure, Papa." Everyone knows there's no such thing as fairies, and no Seeker has ever really seen one. Some do say that Fairy's Gold is real, but no Seeker has found it in decades. It's all probably just legend.

"Bryn!" Elisa calls. "Come on, I need you to be a fairy!"

I sigh. "A Seeker's work never ends," I say, and Papa chuckles.

I manage to survive playtime with Elisa and dinner that evening. Mama glares at me the entire time, apparently still upset from our conversation earlier, but she doesn't protest when I ask to see Runa after dinner. Runa is true to her word and meets me in the sheep pasture again.

Before I can even speak, she reaches into the pocket of her cloak and withdraws a small, gleaming vial. The liquid inside is pale yellow.

"One plague cure potion," she says triumphantly, holding it out to me.

I take the vial, which is so small it fits in the palm of my hand. "Are you serious? You really did it?"

"Obviously I don't know if it *works*," she says. "But I combined the ingredients, just like we talked about. I had enough for one vial, for now. But that should be plenty to test it out. If it works, I can make more, especially if I can get Elder Ingvar's help at the herbalist shop."

I tilt the vial in my hand, watching the pale liquid shimmer inside. It isn't much, but it's a start. "Have I mentioned recently that you're the best?"

"Not recently enough," Runa says with a grin.

I watch the liquid inside the vial shimmer. This could be it—the cure that will save the gyrpuffs.

"So," I say, "what's the best way to test it out?" I don't really want to give a mysterious potion to the sick gyrpuffs when we don't know exactly what it will do. We might have to risk it if it's the only way to save their lives, but . . .

"I have an idea," Runa says. "Follow me."

ELEVEN

Runa leads me into her family's barn, where she steps expertly around an assortment of farm tools. I stumble over everything in the dark, and Runa shushes me. "Don't let my parents hear you!"

At the back of the barn, she lights a lantern and reveals a worktable covered with a line of potted plants, all in a row. But not just any plants, I realize—magical ones. The meadowsweet, the mountain avens—all the remains of the plants I've been giving her for the potion.

"So what's your idea?" I whisper.

"Well, I was thinking . . . You said the plague feeds on magical energy, right? So we want the cure to do the opposite—to give the magical creatures more energy."

"I'm not sure, though," I say. "Because won't giving them more energy just give the plague more to feed off?"

"True. I don't think it's enough on its own just to boost

energy. We need something that will eradicate the plague itself. But it's impossible to know what will do that without testing it. Anyway, I thought that, at the very least, there should be some sort of test of this potion before you give it to the gyrpuff, to make sure that it won't harm them. Why not test it on these plants? We can't know if it will actually cure the plague with this test, of course, because the plants aren't sick. But at least you can see what happens to their energy. If the potion seems to give them a boost and keep them healthy, then we'll know it's probably safe for the gyr-puffs, or at least not likely to harm them. It's a safety check, you know?"

"Yeah, I see what you mean," I say. "But how do I give the potion to plants?"

Runa rolls her eyes. "Hand it over."

I pass her the vial, and she pours the tiniest of drops into the soil of the nearest plant. We wait a moment and then tentatively reach out with our gifts. The flower's energy is bright and strong and . . . growing. Yes, it's definitely getting stronger.

"It worked!" I say, and Runa nods. "Let's try the rest."

One by one, we pour a few small drops of the potion into each pot and study their energy afterward. All of the plants respond positively to the potion.

"Okay," Runa says. "Obviously, a gyrpuff is not a plant, so I can't say for sure how it will affect them, or how the plague will react to it. But at the very least, I think it's safe to say I haven't created some sort of horrible poison. It's certainly giving their magical energy a boost."

"Right," I say. "I'll still only give it to the sickest gyrpuff for now, just to be safe. If he reacts well, then we can make more of the potion and give it to other sick creatures in the Realm. I bet more have been infected by now."

Runa nods. "Let me know how it goes. Are you going to test it tonight?"

"Of course," I say. "The sick gyrpuff doesn't have any time to waste."

Now there's just one thing left for me to do. The one thing that all of the other Seekers, including Ari, have asked me not to do: enter the Realm alone.

Lilja is very confused.

She's used to me and Ari meeting her at Dragon's Point together, and it's been a while since I've flown with her alone. When she appears, her silhouette dark against the glow of the moon, she lands clumsily, stares at me in confusion, and yawns.

"Sorry to wake you up, Lil," I whisper. "But we have a secret errand to run, okay? You remember how we used to train at night?"

She blinks sleepily.

If only Ari were here—he could use his empathy gift to make her feel more energetic and awake right now. But Ari doesn't approve of what I'm about to do, so this is one task I'll have to undertake on my own.

I climb onto Lilja's back, letting my gift swirl around her energy in a feeble attempt to perk it up a bit. Lilja makes a grumbling noise but raises her wings and takes off shortly afterward.

I steer her straight for the southern cliffs.

I feel the energy of the boundary spells before the cliff even comes into view. The other Seekers did a very thorough job. There's so much magic in the air that it ripples ahead of us, and Lilja slows down, not liking the feel of the barrier.

"It's okay," I tell her, giving her scales a pat. "Let's find a place for you to land farther away." I need to keep her out of the quarantine zone, so there's no risk that she'll be exposed. Since humans can't get the sickness, there's no risk of *me* breaking quarantine, but I have to make sure that no magical creatures cross the boundary. I find a safe spot to land about a mile from the base of the cliffs, well outside the quarantine line. I give Lilja a few berries and set a spell to keep her in place, and then I head out.

I have to do a *lot* of hiking.

I'm not sure how long it takes me to get all the way to the right cliff, but it feels like ten years. By the time I finally cross the boundary spell, I'm already tired, but I still have work ahead of me.

My original plan was just to open up a gap in the boundary spell around the quarantine. But, as it turns out, I can't do that. I've never broken a boundary spell this strong before, and I don't know how. I'm not a defender, and my gift isn't much of a match for Seeker Ludvik's skill. I broke a Realm boundary once before, the day the Vondur came to the island in the middle of the Seeker competition. But I was feeling urgency and desperation then, and I'm not feeling it now. I don't know how to break the spell open.

But after a couple of minutes of examining it, I realize that the spell *doesn't* restrict humans from going in and out. It's more than enough magic to deter Lilja or another magical creature, but I don't think it will stop me if I try to walk through it.

I feel a swell of victory as I finally enter the quarantine zone, but it quickly dies as I realize I'm not nearly done yet. I still have to climb down the cliff to the gyrpuff nests, administer the cure, and then climb back up.

This is going to be a long night.

Another issue I didn't anticipate is how different the cliffs look in the dark. It takes me several minutes to orient myself, and I can't see handholds or footholds in the rock in this blackness. I use my gift to illuminate the cliff and seek out the presence of gyrpuffs, which helps a little, but it still takes ages to climb down.

At long last, I reach the first nest, the one Ari and I found with eggs inside. The egg we found before is still there—the baby gyrpuff hasn't hatched yet.

I slip into the crevasse behind the nest, to the place where we found the first gyrpuffs, still marked with Ari's blue ribbon. Seeker Ludvik's magic is even stronger here.

I can practically feel it in my bones as I walk through the darkness, the green light of my gift casting eerie shadows against the rocky walls.

I almost miss the sick gyrpuff. His life spark is so feeble, so tiny, that I don't notice it at first. He's just as still as before, lying tucked against the wall, but clearly one of the other Seekers tried to make him more comfortable—he's surrounded by grass and feathers to make a cozy nest, and there's a small pile of fresh fish for him to eat. I crouch down beside him, and he barely lifts his head in my direction. His eyes are still an eerie, pupil-less black.

"Hey, little buddy," I say. "It's time to take your medicine."

I pull the little glass vial from my pocket. My hand curls over the stopper, and I hesitate. What if our tests on the plants weren't enough? What if it's some kind of poison? What if it makes things worse?

The gyrpuff blinks slowly at me, barely able to move, and I uncork the vial. If I don't do something, he will definitely die. If I give him the potion, there's a chance he'll live. It's risky, but it's the only option.

"Here you go," I say. I coax the gyrpuff with my gift, urging him to open his beak. He resists at first, but he's so weak that eventually he gives in, cracking his beak open a tiny bit. Carefully, I tilt the vial and pour the potion into his mouth. After a moment, the gyrpuff swallows.

I sit back and wait.

Nothing happens. The gyrpuff seems to have fallen asleep, his eyes closed. His chest is still moving up and down with shallow, labored breaths. He doesn't seem better, but he doesn't seem worse. His life spark hasn't changed.

Should it have worked by now? How long do I have to wait?

I walk to the opening of the crevasse, checking the moon's position in the sky, and then return to my vigil. Maybe the potion needs more time to work.

I've been waiting for what feels like forever when a sudden noise startles me. It's a thudding sound, like something big moving around outside the cave—or someone.

As quietly as I can, I creep forward to the cave entrance, straining my eyes to see in the dark. I don't dare use my gift, in case it's one of the other Seekers—

"Caught you," says a familiar voice.

"Ari," I say, exhaling in relief. "You nearly gave me a heart attack. I thought you were one of the Seekers!"

"I am one of the Seekers," he says.

"You know what I mean."

"You mean, you thought I was someone who was going to get you into trouble for sneaking into the Realm against the rules?" He raises his hands, and the yellow glow of his gift illuminates his face. His gaze is unreadable. "What makes you think I'm not?"

"Oh, come on," I say. "You're not supposed to be here either. You can't tell on me without getting in trouble yourself."

"Sure I can," he says, and he can't quite hide his grin. "I could claim to have seen you sneaking up to the Point and just spied on you while you called Lilja and went into the Realm. They'll never know I was here too."

I tilt my head. "How *did* you figure out I was here?"

Ari rolls his eyes and holds up his glowing hands. "Empath, remember? I know everything."

"I'd hardly call it *everything*. Seriously, how'd you know?"

Ari scoffs. "Please. Your emotions have been clear as day. Ever since the last Seekers meeting, you've been feeling determined and stubborn and reckless. Even more so than usual, I mean, which is really saying something. And you've been talking nonstop about how we need to take action and do something to save the gyrpuffs ourselves, and I knew you were working with Runa to make a potion. It wasn't hard to guess you'd come here alone."

"I—okay, you make a good point. But if you really intended to get me in trouble, you would've done it already instead of coming out here to meet me. So it's not hard for *me* to guess that you're here to help."

"I can't let you have all the fun without me," he says. "Besides, someone has to stop you from doing something reckless."

"When have I ever done something reckless?" I say with a grin. "But how'd you get here? I put a boundary around Lilja, so she couldn't have met you at the Point."

"I copied Seeker Ludvik's whistle and rode Snorri."

My eyes widen. Ari's only ridden a fully grown dragon once, when we fought the Vondur. "How'd you manage that?"

"Wasn't that hard. Snorri's a pretty easygoing dragon. I left her with Lilja, and they were already becoming friends."

"Well, we should probably get back to them," I say. "I already gave Runa's potion to the gyrpuff, but I don't think it worked. Nothing happened. I'll come back and check again tomorrow, but I doubt anything will change. The potion must still be missing something."

Ari starts to respond, but we both jump as a loud thud echoes from somewhere overhead.

"What was that? The dragons?" I ask.

"No. They're too far away," Ari whispers. "I think someone else is up here."

"Quick, stop using your gift so the other Seeker doesn't—"

But Ari's gift flares more brightly around his hands as he gazes toward the top of the cliff. "I don't think it's a Seeker," he whispers.

"What?" I ask. But somehow I know what he's going to say before he says it. Dread coils in my stomach.

"Vondur," he whispers.

For a moment neither of us speaks. Another thud sounds from above, but it's fainter this time.

"Are you sure?" I whisper.

"Yes. I can feel their magic."

I remember the feeling of Vondur magic and shudder. Ari

wouldn't mistake that for anything else. "What are we wait-ing for, then? Let's get up there and stop them!"

Ari and I race up the cliffside as fast as we can, but it's hard to climb in the dark, especially while trying to make as little noise as possible. By the time we finally scramble to the top of the cliff, no one is in sight. We both cast our gifts out wide, searching for a life spark—

"There," I say, detecting something in the distance. "Moving away from us."

Ari nods, and we break into a run.

We're much less concerned about making noise as we race to catch up, plunging through the thick trees surround-ing the cliffs. Branches snap and leaves crunch as we run, the green and yellow lights of our gifts bouncing wildly off the trees.

"I don't know if we're going to catch up," Ari says, pant-ing. "Their energy feels fainter than before."

"Wait," I say, skidding to a stop and holding up my hands. "Do you see that?"

Ari follows my gaze. There, imprinted in the dirt ahead of us, is a trail of paw prints.

Ari's eyes widen. "Sea wolves," he says.

I nod. "Looks like it."

Ari raises his hands, illuminating the tracks with his gift. "They're fresh."

"Looks like they abandoned their usual dens. They must have come this way."

"Headed north," he agrees, studying the tracks. "But why? Did they sense the plague in the cliffs?"

I let my gift fly wide, searching the surrounding area. To the south, I can sense it.

"Water," I say. "There's a stream south of here. And it feels like there's something wrong."

Wordlessly, Ari and I rush through the trees, following the sea-wolf prints south to their origin point. Eventually, the ground gets firmer and the tracks disappear, but we keep moving toward the sound of running water straight ahead.

We break into a low clearing near the coastline. The same jagged cliffs we just climbed down rise before us, and descending from one of them is a bubbling stream, rushing rapidly over the rocks and disappearing into the forest.

"Do you think—" Ari says, but he stops. I follow his gaze and gasp.

The banks of the stream are covered in fairy clovers, which isn't uncommon—they often grow near water. But most of the flowers are wilted and drooping. As we walk closer to the cliffs, following the stream to its source, more and more flowers are drooping and even dying. Ahead, the banks of the stream are charred and blackened, all of the flowers and even the grass reduced to nothing but ash.

I don't need to use my gift to confirm the truth, but I do it anyway. I can't find a single life force in this part of the stream or the area surrounding it. No fish, no moss, no flowers. Everything close to this stream has died.

"The sea wolves," Ari says quietly. "They ran in the opposite direction. They were fleeing from this."

"And this stream goes into the cliffside," I say, pointing. "I'll bet you anything that its source is where the gyrpuff colony gets its water too."

"Either this stream is the original source of the plague," Ari says, "or it's been contaminated by the source of the plague. And the animals are getting infected by drinking the poisoned water."

"The sea wolves were smart enough to recognize that the water was contaminated," I add, "but gyrpuffs aren't as intelligent. They didn't know any better."

"And they may not have had another water source. They can't migrate as easily as the wolves, not when they're nesting."

"We need to follow it," I say, walking closer to the stream. The dead plants crunch under my feet. "We need to find where it starts and—"

"Careful!" Ari calls. "The Vondur is around here somewhere!"

"But we found the source! If we can get there, we can—"

"I think we need to go for help." Ari steps forward and places a hand on my shoulder. "Please, Bryn. We need to tell the other Seekers about this. They'll know what to do."

"Ari, that Vondur could be doing something terrible right this second! We have to stop this fast. We don't have time to go for help."

"Whoever that was, they're long gone by now. I can't sense them anymore. But if we get the other Seekers, we can all spread out and find them."

At that moment, a terrible cry rises over the trees. Ari and I stare at each other with wide eyes.

It's Lilja, and she sounds like she's in trouble.

TWELVE

Lilja!" I call, running toward her as fast as I can, with
Ari right on my heels. We both whistle for her, but it's
no use. My boundary spell is trapping her in the place
where I last left her, so she can't come to us.

"It must be the Vondur," I gasp, ducking under a low tree
limb. "They must have found her!"

"We don't know that for sure," Ari says, but he runs faster.

"We have to find her." I leap over a rock and burst through
another clump of trees, hardly caring that the branches are tear-
ing at my clothes. "Lilja! Lilja!"

I fling my gift out as wide as I can, seeking Lilja's familiar
life source. As we move farther from the path of the stream, the
dying plants gradually disappear, but I still can't believe how far
into the forest the damage has traveled. The plague is spreading
fast.

Finally, we reach the clearing where I left Lilja, and I catch sight of her silvery scales. "Lil!" I yell, hardly caring if there are a hundred Vondur who can hear me. "Lil, are you all right?"

She bounds toward me, breaking the limbs off nearby trees as she goes. Her ears perk up at the sight of us, and her tail thuds the ground.

"What's wrong?" I ask her.

She yawns, revealing a tongue stained blue with bilberry juice.

"Look," Ari says, pointing behind Lilja. Through the trees, I can just make out several clumps of bilberry bushes. And lurking just behind them is a massive brown dragon—Snorri. He's lying with his head on his front feet, staring longingly at the bilberry bushes.

"Um," Ari says, "do you think maybe . . . they were just arguing over the food?"

I look around for anything else that might have been distressing, but there's nothing. No danger. No signs of the plague. No Vondur.

"Lilja!" I say. "Did you cry like that just because Snorri tried to eat some of your berries?"

Lilja happily thuds her tail against the ground again, looking delighted with herself.

I sigh. "You're *ridiculous.*"

Ari shakes his head. "Honestly, Lil, we need to work on your training. And you need to get along better with the other dragons!"

She huffs a breath at him, rustling his hair.

"Let's get out of here," Ari says. "We need to tell the other Seekers what we found."

"Um, Ari," I say, looking at the ground. "You know they're going to be *really* mad that we came out here alone again."

"Yeah." He tilts his head, and I suspect he's reading my emotions with his gift.

"I think . . ." I take a deep breath. "I think I should take the blame for this one. I'll say I came out here alone and describe what I saw. They don't need to know you were here."

"No," Ari says. "I *am* here, and if you're getting in trouble, then I should too."

"But I don't think *either* of us should get in trouble," I say. "Why let them punish us both? What happens if they decide to kick us off the Council for breaking the rules again? We don't want that to happen to both of us. And besides, you wouldn't even be out here if you hadn't come looking for me. It was my idea, and my fault. I'll take the blame for it this time, if they're mad about it."

"I'm pretty sure it's more of a 'when' than an 'if,'" Ari says. "It isn't fair, though. I'll take the blame too."

"No." I look up and give him my firmest glare. "I'm taking this one. It just makes sense. You can owe me one for next time, okay?" Before he can protest further, I hop onto Lilja's back. "Come on, we don't have any time to waste. We have to tell the Seekers."

Ari decides to fly Snorri, just to make sure that the dragon isn't going to stay out here close to the poisoned stream. The dragons drop us off back at the Point and then head straight for the Valley of Ash, probably wanting to catch up on some sleep after this long night.

Unfortunately, Ari and I don't have that option. We run to the chapel and ring the emergency bell. Within fifteen minutes, the other three Seekers have joined us in Seeker Larus's hut.

Seeker Freyr is last to arrive. "What's happened?" he asks as he takes off his cloak.

Seeker Larus nods at me. "Seeker Bryn was just about to tell us."

Ari glances at me, and I can tell what he's asking: *Are you sure you want to take the blame for this?*

I ignore him and gaze at the other Seekers, clearing my throat. "The plague is spreading beyond the quarantine, and I sensed Vondur magic in the Realm."

Silence rings in my ears. Finally, Seeker Larus says, "What do you mean?"

"I went into the Realm alone tonight," I say. "I wanted to check on the sick gyrpuff. While I was there, I sensed the presence of another person and what felt like Vondur magic. I tried to follow them, and as I did, I found signs of the plague, outside of the quarantine barrier." Quickly I describe the sight of the stream and the dead plants that surrounded it.

Seeker Larus is already rising from his chair before I finish. "Ludvik," he says, "we must extend the boundary at once. This stream, and any other water source it connects with, must be quarantined."

"Right," I say, "and we also need to search the Realm for the Vondur."

"How many creatures reside in the area?" Seeker Freyr asks Seeker Larus, as if I haven't spoken.

"Sea wolves, unicorns," Seeker Larus says, ticking them off on his fingers, "possibly some vatnaveras—"

"We need to find the mouth of this stream," Seeker Ludvik adds. "If it empties into a larger river, we could be looking at many more infections. One of the central rivers could spread the plague to every corner of the Realm!"

"Yes," I say, "but what about the Vondur—"

"This must be what the phoenixes sensed," Seeker Freyr says, again talking over me. "Their water source may have already been infected. That's why they fled north."

"If so, the dragons and firecats aren't safe either," Seeker Ludvik says. "They all rely on the same water."

"But the dragons would likely have sensed it as well, and we haven't seen them relocate yet," Seeker Larus says. "There may still be time."

"Excuse me," I say, raising my voice. Finally, the three Seekers turn in my direction. "But what are we going to do about the Vondur? They're back in the Realm!"

To my surprise, Seeker Freyr makes a scoffing noise. Seeker Larus at least seems to consider me for a moment, but then he says, almost gently, "Bryn, did you actually see a Vondur in the Realm?"

"Well, no, I didn't *see* him, but I followed him. I could sense his magic!"

Seeker Freyr makes the scoffing sound again. "With a nature gift? You could detect a subtlety in a human life force while they were still so far away as to be out of sight? And detected it clearly enough to follow it for miles the way you described? Ridiculous."

I bite my lip. He's kind of got me there—Ari sensed the Vondur, not me, because his gift is more sensitive to that than mine. But I have to make them understand that the threat was real. "I know what I sensed," I say firmly.

"Bryn," Seeker Ludvik says softly, and at first I think he's going to be on my side. "Is it possible that you sensed something else? I know the events of last month have left us all feeling a bit . . . concerned about the Vondur. It was late at night, and you were in the Realm alone. Isn't it possible that you just . . . thought you sensed what you were afraid of?"

I blink at him incredulously. "You think I'm making it up? You think I was *afraid* in the Realm?"

Seeker Freyr stands abruptly, waving one hand dismissively through the air. "That's enough of this," he says. "There's no point in arguing over a child's imaginings. We must see to the matter at hand and correct the boundary spell."

"I didn't imagine it!" I say, leaping to my feet to face him.

He towers over me, and I have to crane my neck to look into his eyes, but I stand my ground.

He gazes down at me. "Then perhaps you invented it deliberately. Did you think that hallucinating Vondur would be enough to escape censure for rule-breaking this time? Don't think we've overlooked *that* little omission in your story."

"What? That's ridiculous!"

"Is it?" He furrows his brow. "Because it sounds to me like you broke the rules to go into the Realm, then realized that the plague had spread and you needed help. Then you added a few details about this so-called Vondur in the hope that we'd all go rushing off to handle this emergency and conveniently forget to address your punishment."

"That's not what this is," I say, but no one seems to hear me.

"Now, Freyr," Seeker Ludvik says, "I don't know that we can accuse her of deliberate falsity. Perhaps she simply imagined—"

"I didn't imagine it!" I yell again. I glance helplessly at Ari, who's staring at the floor. He looks up and catches my eye, and I know what we have to do. Ari has to confess that *he's* the one who detected the Vondur. I bet they'll believe him. They think I'm a silly little girl making up stories. But Ari? He's a boy and an empath. They'll believe him.

"Tell them, Ari," I say, and the room falls silent.

All of the Seekers are staring at us now. Ari seems to

fold in on himself under their gazes, shrinking back into the chair.

"It wasn't me who sensed the Vondur tonight," I say. "It was Ari."

"Is this true, Seeker Ari?" Seeker Larus asks.

Ari opens his mouth to speak . . . and nothing comes out.

In the silence, my racing heartbeat drums in my ears.

Freyr makes a disgusted sound. "Trying to cast the blame on others won't help your cause. Stop wasting our time with this foolishness."

He takes a deep breath like he's gearing up for a rant, but Seeker Larus cuts in. "All right," he says. "We will discuss the rest of this at a later date. For now, we must go to the stream and determine how far the damage has spread, and then—"

I tune out the rest of the meeting. Ari glances at me a couple of times, but I stare pointedly away from him, my jaw clenched.

After everything we went through in the Seeker competition, I thought I could trust him, but I guess I was wrong.

I don't have a single true friend on the Council of Seekers.

So I'll just have to do things my way. And I'll have to do them alone.

Thirteen

After the Council meeting, the older Seekers rush to check out the stream, leaving me and Ari alone. I can barely look at him.

"How could you do that to me?" I ask after the silence stretches unbearably. "Why didn't you tell them the truth?"

"I—I don't know. I panicked. Not telling them the truth was your idea!"

"But I didn't know that they wouldn't *believe* me. I needed you to back me up!"

"What makes you think they would've believed me if I'd said it?"

I raise my eyebrows. "Do you really not know the answer to that? Don't you see how differently they act toward me? Sure, they still treat both of us like we're babies, but it's mostly *me* they baby. When I say I sensed a Vondur, they think I'm just some scared little girl who imagined things, or worse, that I'm a liar. But if *you'd* said it—"

"You don't know how they would've reacted," Ari says, rising from his seat. "You're the one who told me you wanted to take the blame for everything, and now you're mad at me for letting you? I don't get it."

"I think it should've been obvious that the plan had changed when *nobody believed me* and I specifically *asked you for help.*"

"Well, I'm sorry I didn't read your mind and figure out exactly what you wanted. You know, because we always go along with what *you* want. I told you not to go into the Realm alone, and I told you not to take the blame for it, and now you're mad at *me* because it didn't work out how you wanted?"

"Really, the *empath* is complaining about not being able to read minds? I think it was pretty clear when the rest of the Seekers were accusing me of making things up that I needed some support! You don't have to be a mind reader, or even an empath, to see that."

"Well, maybe *you* should be an empath," Ari says quietly, "and learn to listen to other people for a change."

Before I can respond, he walks out of the hut and slams the door behind him.

As I exit Seeker Larus's hut, the first rays of dawn are creeping into the sky. I sneak back through the village, down the lane, and inside my hut, falling into bed beside Elisa. I haven't slept all night, and I forgot just how exhausting it would be. I can't wait to fall asleep. . . .

Unfortunately, it seems like mere minutes later when Mama wakes me to help with breakfast. I feel a little like I'm going to die.

But I will do it all over again tonight, and the next night, and the next—as many times as it takes to get a cure that works and save the Realm. The other Seekers might not listen to anything I say, but that doesn't matter. I'll prove them all wrong and cure the plague myself, even if it means I don't sleep another night.

The day passes by in a blur as I help Mama with chores around the hut. I tell her simply that I have the day off from Seeker duties, and she doesn't ask any questions. I even manage to work in a nap in the afternoon, when she catches me nodding off while scrubbing out the soup bowls. As soon as the rest of my family goes to bed for the night, I grab my cloak and satchel, lace up my boots, and head for the door.

With the stars glittering in the sky overhead, I walk to Dragon's Point alone.

I fly Lilja to the same place where I left her the night before, safely outside the boundary spells surrounding the quarantined area. I cross the border just like before and make my way to the gyrpuff cliffs. I still need to find the source of the stream, but first I want to check on the gyrpuff who drank some of Runa's potion to see if he's cured.

The gyrpuff caves are eerily deserted, which isn't a good

sign. Either the other gyrpuffs have fled somewhere, or they've all gotten sick and are hiding deep in the caves.

My heart sinks when I finally catch sight of the little gyrpuff. He's still huddled in his cave, with no signs of improvement. His breathing is shallow and weak.

Runa's potion didn't work, and I don't know how much longer he can survive.

Luckily, I thought to bring some supplies with me this time. If it's his water making him sick, maybe giving him clean water will help him get better. I withdraw a bowl I stole from the kitchen (which Mama can never know about) and place it right next to the little gyrpuff's head. I fill it with cool water from my jug, which was drawn from our well at home rather than in the Realm. But I'm not sure the gyrpuff is strong enough to lift his head on his own, so I also coax him with my gift, getting him to open his beak and take a drink. He does manage to swallow a trickle, which seems like a good sign.

I lay out some more fresh herring to make sure he has plenty to eat too. Unfortunately, there's not much else I can do. I'm tempted just to sit with him and make him drink clean water all night, but finding the cure is more important, especially if he's not the only animal who's sick.

"Get better, little guy," I say to him. "I'll bring you the real cure soon. I promise."

I crawl back out of the cave and onto the rocky ledge along the cliff. I reach for a handhold, preparing to climb back up—

Something rustles in the nest beside me. I freeze, one hand on the rock.

Another rustle, and a tiny black head pokes up out of the nest.

A baby gyrpuff.

I glance around and realize my mistake. In my hurry to get to the sick gyrpuff, I didn't even notice before that there are discarded eggshells scattered around.

The egg hatched.

And the little gyrpuff's parents are nowhere to be seen.

A baby this little should never be on its own. The mother might be going to get food, but there's no sign of that. No food stockpiled in the nest for this baby, and it looks to be at least a day old already. Its eyes are open, and it's hopping around the nest on its own, tottering awkwardly. If its mama were taking care of it, there'd be a pile of fish here by now. Either its mama is sick, or she fled the nest to get away from the plague and left the egg behind.

This little baby's been abandoned.

I don't even have to think about what to do next.

"Hey, little guy," I say, extending a hand.

Gyrpuffs are notoriously shy. An adult gyrpuff is more likely to disappear at the first sign of trouble, or shriek at a predator to defend their nest. But babies are different—they haven't learned to disappear yet, and they're not as defensive as adults. This baby just looks up at me, cocking his head to the side.

"It's okay," I whisper softly. I keep my hand still and steady, not moving any closer to him. "Come say hello," I murmur.

I keep myself frozen in place, letting him come to me. He takes a little hop forward, stumbling on his new legs. When I don't move, he takes another, hesitant hop, his bright eyes examining my hand. I can tell exactly what he's thinking: *Is this food?*

I release a tiny wisp of my gift, letting him sense my presence. His life spark brushes happily against mine. He likes the feeling of my magic.

"That's it," I murmur. "Just one more little hop . . ."

He rustles his feathers and hops again, practically tumbling into my hand. I let him stay there for a moment before I slowly raise him up, closer to my face. He chirps, but he doesn't seem to be afraid. He studies me with wide, curious eyes.

"Hello," I say. "I bet you're hungry." With my free hand, I dig some bilberries from my pocket and offer one to the baby gyrpuff. He eats it eagerly right out of my hand. He looks thin, and I have to wonder if he's been able to eat anything at all since he hatched.

"Okay, baby gyrpuff," I say. "I can't just leave you here all alone with no food. So you've got to come with me, all right?"

He ignores me, tapping his beak against my palm as if to summon more food.

I hadn't exactly planned to carry a baby gyrpuff around, so I don't know how to transport him. Will he be afraid if I tuck him into my pocket? He's definitely small enough to fit in there.

I bend down, careful not to jostle the baby from my hand, and pluck some grass from the nest. I stuff it into my pocket, creating a familiar lining for him, and then drop a few more berries inside as well. The baby gyrpuff follows the food with his head, and he doesn't resist at all when I slip him into the pocket as well. He keeps his head buried inside, seeking out all the tasty food.

Now I have to figure out what to do next. I had planned to follow the stream to its source, to see if I can identify the cause of the plague. But I don't want to do that with this baby gyrpuff. If he hasn't been exposed to the plague yet, taking him closer to its source is risky. Still, if the plague really does originate in the water, then he should be fine as long as he doesn't drink any of it. If I keep him in my pocket, I don't think there's any chance of exposure. Unless I'm wrong about the water . . .

It's a risk I'm going to have to take. The gyrpuff who's been infected doesn't have much more time, and neither do any other magical creatures who have been exposed. I need to find the cause of the plague as quickly as possible, so I can also find the cure.

"Stay in there, Little Puff," I say to my wriggling pocket. "We're going on an adventure."

By the time I climb all the way back up the cliff, the gyr-puff has settled in, occasionally popping his head out to look around before hiding himself again. He's mostly still as I trek back toward the stream Ari and I found earlier. It's harder to locate in the dark, but the trail of dead plants surrounding it is a clear sign I'm in the right place.

Little Puff lets out a chirp, and I give him a reassuring nudge with my gift. "Stay in there, okay? Don't come out."

He chirps again, and his head slips back into the pocket.

I trudge through the dead grass along the stream's bank, climbing over the increasingly large rocks as I follow it up into the cliffs. The climb is steep, and I scrape my hands trying to get a steady purchase on the rocks. Another chirp issues from my pocket, but Little Puff doesn't stick his head out again. I wonder if he can sense the dead plants around him, or the plague itself.

The stream twists and turns through the rocks, seemingly without end. After about an hour, we're deep within the cliffside, surrounded by rocks. The stream flows faster here, making me think we must be getting close to its source. Little Puff blinks sleepily up at me, clearly wanting to stop exploring and take a nap.

"Almost there," I reassure him, following the stream around a bend, but I'm not sure if that's true or not. "Surely we must be almost . . ."

My voice trails off as I round the corner and stare at the sight in front of me. Here, the rocks fall away, and looming out of the darkness is a solid, frozen mass. A glacier, rising as high as a mountain, standing sentinel against the dark.

This is the source of the stream. Chunks of ice float in the current here, melting into the rest.

I cast my gift wide, running it along the stream's current, trying to get a sense for any magic that might be here. The stream is completely devoid of life, as it has been for miles. Anything that lived here before has been killed by the plague, I suspect. But I do feel something, something magical.

As my gift inches closer and closer to the glacier, my heart pounds in recognition.

There's something dark and strange and pulsing inside the heart of the glacier—something that doesn't feel at all like the magic of the Realm.

But I know what it *does* feel like.

Vondur magic.

Little Puff peeks out of my coat, his eyes wide, and I gaze back at him in shock.

"Ari was right," I say to him.

He gives me a tiny, concerned chirp.

"We *did* sense someone in the Realm last night. The plague . . . it came from the Vondur."

FOURTEEN

I don't know how it's possible, but I know I'm right.

It all makes a horrible kind of sense.

The Vondur have poisoned the Realm.

I rush back down the rocks as fast as I can, the urgency of this discovery giving me the strength to run. By the time I emerge from the cliffside, the baby gyrpuff has fallen asleep in my pocket, and dawn is only an hour away.

I expect that I might have to break the quarantine boundary spell to get Little Puff out, but I quickly discover the flaw in Seeker Ludvik's spell—since it doesn't affect humans, as long as Little Puff is in my pocket, the spell doesn't stop him, either.

I find Lilja where I left her, sleeping peacefully beside a cluster of now-bare bilberry bushes. She wakes reluctantly and gives a snort of indignation when Little Puff pops his head out of my pocket. Little Puff trembles at the sight of the dragon, then looks up at me with a questioning chirp.

"It's okay," I say to both of them. "We're all friends here."

Lilja snaps her jaw closed and huffs.

"Don't be so dramatic," I say, rolling my eyes at her. "He's just a baby bird. He's not going to hurt you."

Lilja makes a great show of turning away from me when I try to climb onto her back, but the promise of more bilberries and a little coaxing from my gift eventually calm her down, and she's steady for the entire flight back to Dragon's Point. She gives Little Puff one last, distrustful examination before nudging me with her snout in farewell and flying back into the Realm.

I look down at Little Puff. "Well," I say. "Looks like it's just you and me again."

Now, of course, I have a new problem. Magical creatures aren't supposed to leave the Realm—I certainly learned my lesson about that during the Seeker competition. But I don't know where to take Little Puff within the Realm where he'd be safe. He's too vulnerable to be on his own, and most creatures in the Realm would view a tiny, defenseless bird as a nice snack. Ordinarily, I'd take him straight to Seeker Larus and ask him what to do. But given how much trouble I'm already in for sneaking into the Realm, that seems like a bad plan. I could lie and say I found him elsewhere, but something tells me Seeker Larus won't fall for it.

So it looks like I'm just going to have to break the rules. Again. Not to mention breaking a few more boundary spells on the way out of the Realm.

"Come on, Little Puff," I say, giving my pocket a gentle pat. "I know where you'll be safe."

The sun is just peeking over the horizon by the time I reach Runa's farm. Luckily, she and her family rise early, and she's already walking into the field with Hundur the sheepdog by the time I crest the top of the hill.

"What happened?" she asks as soon as I reach her. "Did the cure work?"

"No," I say. "The gyrpuff is still sick."

Runa's face falls. "I'm sorry. I hoped I'd gotten it right."

"It's not your fault," I say. "I think I've figured out why we can't cure it."

Quickly I explain about the stream, the glacier at its source, and the pulse of Vondur magic I felt inside.

Runa's eyes go wide. "That's why our healing magic doesn't work on this plague!" she exclaims. "The Vondur are dark magicians. Their spells feed off natural sources of magic like ours. That's what my papa said, anyway, after they came onto the island. That's why the plague seems to feed off healing gifts instead of being cured."

"I don't know how the Vondur did this," I say, "but maybe we can figure out how to cure it, now that we know what it is."

Runa nods. "There must be some kind of ingredient that we could . . ." She trails off, deep in thought.

I close my eyes, picturing the Realm. What's the most powerful plant there? Something so magical, so legendary, that it could—

"Oh!" My eyes fly open.

"What? What is it?" Runa asks.

"This is going to sound ridiculous. In fact, it might be impossible."

"What is it? What are you talking about?"

"Fairy's Gold," I say, and Runa's mouth drops open. "I know it's impossible," I add quickly. "Probably just one of those legends everybody repeats. But . . . it's supposed to be the most magical plant ever to exist in the Realm, right? What if that's the missing ingredient? And that's why the Seekers never figured out the cure the first time—they never had any Fairy's Gold to try. Papa's told me so many stories about it. What if there's a reason those stories exist?"

To my surprise, Runa seems to be considering this idea seriously. "But even if that's true, how will you find any? How will you even know where to look?"

"I don't know," I admit, "but I'll figure it out! At least now we know what to look for. If I *can* find it, I bet it will be the perfect missing ingredient for your potion, and then we can cure the plague for good!"

"I don't know for sure that it will work," she says doubtfully, tugging at one end of her braid.

"It has to. The more I think about it, the more perfect it seems. Fairy's Gold is supposed to cure everything, and to be one of the strongest magical plants Seekers have ever found. Exactly what we need. If I can find it, can you work with it?"

"I suppose so," she says. "I can whip up another batch

of the potion and have it ready for you. But *how* will you find it?"

"Leave that to me," I say. "I have a plan."

Runa looks skeptical, but I grin at her. "Did I mention you're a genius?"

She waves a hand. "We knew that already."

Little Puff chooses that moment to make a tiny chirp in my pocket, and Runa freezes.

"Bryn," she says slowly, "why is your pocket moving?"

"Oh," I say, giving Little Puff a nudge, "there's one more thing I need to tell you."

Little Puff pops his head out of my pocket, blinking up at Runa, and her eyes widen. "That's a gyrpuff!"

"Yes."

"In your pocket!"

"Yes."

Runa blinks, steadies herself, and fixes a stern look at me. "Bryn. Why is there a miniature gyrpuff in your pocket?"

"He's a baby," I say. "His egg only just hatched. But the rest of the gyrpuffs abandoned their nests because of the plague, so he was left behind. He doesn't have anyone to take care of him, and he's too vulnerable to leave in the Realm alone. Not until he grows up."

Runa knows me too well and figures out exactly where I'm going with this.

"No," she says immediately. "No, no, no."

"Please?" I say, giving her my cutest pleading expression.

"Don't even think about it. I am *not* hiding a baby gyrpuff for you."

"You literally can't get into any trouble for this," I say. "I'm an official Seeker now! Taking care of the Realm's creatures is my job. So if I ask you to look after him, you're just helping a Seeker."

Runa wrinkles her nose. "Something tells me the rest of the Council won't see it that way. And my parents *definitely* won't."

I huff. "The rest of the Council doesn't matter. I get just as much say as they do—or I *should*. And your parents don't have to know. He's tiny. Just hide him in a safe place."

"How would I even take care of him? I don't know anything about gyrpuffs."

I grin, knowing that she's already agreeing to help. Quickly, I give her a few instructions about feeding times and nesting materials.

"I don't know . . . ," she says, but I can tell she's caving in.

"Here." I reach into my pocket and withdraw the baby gyrpuff, holding him up for her to see. "I've been calling him Little Puff for now."

The gyrpuff shakes out his feathers and blinks up at Runa, his big eyes fixed on her.

"He's so cute," she whispers. "And so *tiny*."

I smile. "Do you want to hold him?"

Five minutes later, Little Puff is snuggling in the palm of Runa's hand, and the two of them are already becoming fast friends. "I'll be back to check on him," I say. "And to let you know how the Fairy's Gold search is coming. Have a potion ready to go for when we find it."

"Okay," Runa says, not taking her eyes off Little Puff. I give the baby gyrpuff a goodbye pat and head for home, knowing I couldn't have left him in better hands.

By the time I reach my own hut, it's well past dawn, and Mama is standing in the doorway, watching me walk up the garden path.

Oops. I gulp.

"Brynja," Mama says loudly. "Do you want to tell me where exactly you've been at this hour? Are you sneaking out of this hut again?"

I consider my words carefully. There's a chance Mama knows how long I've been gone, and getting caught lying will only put me in more trouble. But there's also a chance she *doesn't* know I've been out all night, in which case I don't want her to find out. "I went to see Runa," I say slowly. "I needed to ask her a question about healing magic before heading into the Realm today, so I had to leave the hut early. Sorry if I woke you."

Mama gazes at me for a beat too long. "Just because you're a Seeker now," she says finally, "doesn't mean you don't have to follow the rules of this house. There will be no sneaking out without telling anyone where you're going. Understood?"

"Yes, Mama."

She thrusts the well bucket in my direction. "Fetch the water for breakfast."

I sigh. "Yes, Mama."

Apparently even Seekers have to do chores.

I rush quickly through breakfast, thinking about the plague and the possible cure. Papa picks up on my distraction instantly. "Something wrong, Bryn?" he asks, raising a spoonful of oatmeal.

"No," I say. On second thought, I add, "Papa, what do you know about Fairy's Gold? The real thing, not the stories."

Papa slurps his oatmeal for a moment, considering the question. "Some say it's a myth," he says finally. "No Seeker has seen any Fairy's Gold in a hundred years. But there are enough stories about it to suggest that it's real—or may have been real, once."

"If it's real, why can't anyone find it?" I ask. "If, say, you had an icefox to guide you to different plants in the Realm . . . Couldn't you find Fairy's Gold that way?"

Papa raises a brow. "I suppose you could try," he says. "If the plant is real, I suspect it's so rare that even the icefoxes may not have seen it. They can only guide you to things they've seen, remember. But it might be possible."

I perk up. That "might" is all I need. "Thanks, Papa."

"Don't spend too much time chasing myths, now," he says. "I'm sure there's plenty of work to be done in the Realm."

"Of course," I say. I decide not to share my theories about the cure—not yet. I'm afraid Papa might be too skeptical, and I don't want anything to kill the hope that's rising in my chest. I consider telling him about the Vondur magic too, but Elisa is still at the table, playing with one of her toy unicorns, and I don't want to scare her by mentioning the Vondur. She's had a couple of nightmares about them ever since they interrupted the third trial. I'll have to ask Papa about all of that later.

"Speaking of work," I say, quickly slurping down the last of my meal, "I'm going to be late to meet Ari. We wanted to get an early start this morning."

Mama nods at my empty bowl. "Dishes first."

I sigh. "Yes, Mama."

Luckily, the delay in leaving the hut is exactly what I need. The other Seekers should have left Dragon's Point by now; they have too many things to do in the Realm to worry about sticking around to discipline me. And they'll be focusing their efforts on the spread of the plague around the southern cliffs, which means that I can sneak up to the northern forests without being seen. Probably. And if they do see me, well, how much more trouble could I get into, really?

So I'm not expecting to encounter anyone as I stride up the plateau to Dragon's Point—which is why I'm shocked to see a silver dragon lying at the top, with a figure cloaked in green sitting at her side.

Lilja. And Ari.

I don't even know what to say to him after our fight. How could he betray me like that?

I don't want to tell him what I saw in the Realm last night either. Clearly he can't be trusted to back me up in front of the other Seekers, and what if he tattles? No, best not to tell him for now. He already knows about the Vondur, anyway, so he understands what we might be facing.

I glare at him and cross my arms over my chest. "What are *you* doing here with *my* dragon?"

I say this just to get a rise out of him, so I'm surprised when he says simply, "Hey." He brushes a stray curl behind his ear as he stands, one hand on Lilja's side to steady himself. A faint yellow light dances across his fingertips. He's probably using his gift to read my emotions again, which is irritating. "I figured you'd be here, once the other Seekers had left."

"Oh, so *now* you can read my emotions. It's just when I need your support that you can't seem to figure out what I'm thinking."

"I'm sorry, okay? I didn't mean for that to happen. I was caught off guard, and . . . And the other Seekers intimidate me sometimes. I'm not as good at speaking up to them as you are. I just froze."

"Yeah, well . . ." I actually wasn't expecting an apology, and now I don't know how to respond. "Well, I'm still mad at you."

"I know."

"I thought you were on my side."

"I don't want to be on anybody's side. I think we all need to work together."

"But I already told you before that none of the other Seekers ever listen to me or take me seriously. You were the only one who might stick up for me, and you didn't."

"I'm sorry. Really. But *I* also need *you* to listen, Bryn. Sometimes you're so busy moving forward with your own ideas that you don't listen to anybody who disagrees. I tried to tell you that we should've just been honest with the other Seekers from the beginning, and I don't think it's fair that you're blaming me for a problem that *your* lie caused."

"I'm not trying to blame you. But the reason I have to be focused on my own ideas is because nobody else listens to them. I've been saying from the beginning that we need to find a cure for this plague rather than just focusing on establishing the quarantines, but no one is listening. If I don't do it myself, nobody else will."

"But do you even know *how* to cure it?"

"As a matter of fact, I might."

That gets his attention. He shoves his hands into his pockets and rocks back on his heels, studying me. "What do you mean?"

"I think I figured out what the missing potion ingredient is. Fairy's Gold."

Ari frowns. "Be serious, Bryn. I thought you really had something."

"I *am* serious."

His frown deepens. "Fairy's Gold is a myth, just like . . . well, just like fairies. No one's ever seen it."

"That's not true. It's just been a while since anyone's seen it, but that doesn't mean the stories aren't true. Besides, I have an idea."

Ari sighs loudly. "Nothing ever goes well after you say that."

"It's a brilliant idea, thank you very much."

"Sure it is," he says skeptically, brows raised.

"Well, fine, if you don't want to hear it . . ."

"Okay, okay. Tell me your idea."

"Icefoxes. What if that mama fox we met before could lead us to Fairy's Gold? If she's ever seen it, she could take us there!"

Ari still looks skeptical, but he tilts his head, considering this. "Icefoxes only travel in the northern and central forests, so the Fairy's Gold would have to be located somewhere in those regions. If it exists anywhere else, the icefox wouldn't know about it."

"But those forests are some of the largest territories in the Realm. So there's a good chance it exists in one of them, at least."

"Seems unlikely, though. I mean, no one's been able to find Fairy's Gold for ages, if it even exists. What are the odds we'd be able to find it?"

"Odds have nothing to do with it. We're the only ones determined enough to actually *look* for Fairy's Gold. I bet the other Seekers never bothered because they thought it would be too hard to find, or they thought it was just a myth. *We* could be the ones to find it, if we try. Besides, do you have any better ideas?"

Ari sighs again. "I suppose it's worth a shot. But this time, let's agree that if we're caught, we're *both* going to take the blame for it, and we're going to stick up for each other. Agreed?"

I grin. "Agreed."

We might still be a little angry at each other, but at least we both care about the same thing: saving the Realm.

FIFTEEN

L ilja is very upset about our destination, and she makes
sure to let us know.

She hates the cold of the northern forests, and she
knows from our previous trip that she'll be left behind while
Ari and I walk across the glacier to the icefox dens. So as soon
as Ari and I try to steer Lilja farther north, soaring high above,
she begins her temper tantrum.

Huffing loudly, she ignores the nudge of my gift and starts
to turn away from the forest. Her spikes rise in indignation, as
does a rumble in her throat.

"Lilja!" I say. "Where do you think you're going?"

She leans harder into the turn, forcing me to grip her scales
for dear life instead of steering her with my gift. Behind me, Ari
nearly loses his purchase on her back, and he lets out a curse.
"Stubborn, *disobedient* dragon!" he shouts into the wind.

I can sense his gift in the air as he tries to calm her emotions and get her to respond to us. I add my gift to the mix, pushing even more firmly against her.

"Lilja," I say, "only cooperative dragons get bilberries!"

Lilja grunts in annoyance, but she straightens up reluctantly.

"Come on!" I shout to her, giving directions again with my gift.

Finally, we persuade Lilja to land just outside the barrier that prevents her from getting closer to the icefox dens. She grumbles loudly at us as we set boundary spells to prevent her from wandering too far, and grumbles even louder when we walk away.

"Who let that dragon become so spoiled?" Ari mutters.

"Certainly wasn't me," I say with a grin.

"Wasn't *me*, either," he says, and for a moment it feels like nothing has changed between us. But then I remember the meeting, and the grin slides off my face. Ari picks up on the change in my emotions immediately and falls silent, stuffing his hands into his pockets.

The walk to the icefox den is long and cold, and by the time we reach the spot where we last saw Mama Icefox and her cubs, I'm wrapping my scarf more firmly around my neck and fastening the highest buttons on my coat.

"Well," Ari says, finally breaking the tense silence as he stares up at the rock formation housing the foxes, "guess we should start climbing."

I nod, and we move forward together, finding handholds

and footholds in the rock until we reach the top.

"Better be quiet so she doesn't snap at us like last time," Ari whispers as we scramble to our feet.

"I don't think she will. She'll remember us. Besides, they're nocturnal. They'll all be asleep at this time of day."

Ari and I peer at the entrance to the den. No foxes emerge.

"Must be why they're not coming out," Ari says. "Bet they're asleep."

I cast my gift cautiously into the cave. Several bright life sparks are definitely in there, but they're not moving around. "Yep. Cubs are asleep," I report.

Ari's gift joins mine in the air, and he stiffens suddenly. "Bryn," he says. "Do you feel that?"

"Feel what?" I focus on my gift again, but I'm not sure what I'm supposed to be feeling. Sometimes the perceptiveness of Ari's gift is *really* annoying. "Feel what?" I ask again.

"It seems like . . ." His eyes are wide. "The plague. It's here."

I gape at him. "What are you talking about?"

"One of them has the plague, Bryn."

"How do you know?"

"The energy. It's all wrong. It feels the same way the sick gyrpuff did. It *must* be the plague. Can't you feel it?"

I close my eyes and focus on my gift again. One ordinary life spark, two, three, four . . . Wait.

There.

One of the sparks inside the cave doesn't feel like it should. It's weak and trembling.

Just like the sick gyrpuff.

I don't think. I move forward on instinct, crouching down and crawling into the den to see for myself.

A baby icefox blinks sleepily at me as I shine my gift around the dark space, and another tumbles forward to sniff my shoes, but they don't seem sick or threatened by me. I glance around. Maybe one of the other cubs—

No.

Oh *no.*

It's Mama Icefox who has the plague.

She's curled up in the corner of the den, panting weakly. Her fur looks dingy and flat, and her ears are pressed tightly against her head. As she turns slowly toward me and blinks in the light of my gift, her pupils shine a solid, horrible black.

I do a quick count of her babies and check their eyes. No black pupils anywhere, and they all seem healthy enough.

But how long can that last? They can't be taken away from their mama at this age—they're too little. But if they stay with her, surely they'll all get the plague.

Mama Icefox can't lead us to the Fairy's Gold. She's too sick to stand. She needs a cure, and she needs it now—or every one of these babies is going to get sick too.

"Bryn," Ari says quietly. He's crouched at the entrance to the den, peering inside. "Bryn, come on. There's nothing we can do to help her in here."

As much as I hate to admit it, he's right. Using my gift won't cure this, and there's nothing else I can do right now.

Leaving the baby icefoxes to their sleep, I crawl back out of the den and stumble into the harsh sunlight outside.

"We need to get food and water," I say to Ari. "Mama Icefox can't feed herself right now, and the babies won't leave the den without her. We have to bring them something."

"All right. But then we have to tell the Seekers about this, Bryn. The plague's spread much farther than any of us thought. If we don't do something to contain—"

"Let's focus on one thing at a time," I interrupt, and Ari nods.

We spend the next few hours catching fish and gathering raspberries and bilberries. Icefoxes will eat just about anything, but salmon are their favorite snack, and the berries will last a few days. I use my gift to braid some long grasses tightly together, creating a makeshift bowl, and, after climbing back up to the icefox den, I pour water from my jug into it. I crawl back inside the den and leave both the water bowl and the food where Mama Icefox can reach it without moving far. The babies immediately run to the water bowl and slurp some of it up. It must have been ages since they've had anything to drink. They can lick the ice off their fur, of course, but they tend not to do that, since they like to have their ice crystals for protection, and the babies are still forming theirs for the first time.

"That water won't last them long," I say to Ari as we climb once more down the rocks. "We'll have to come back and refill it."

We walk across the glacier in silence for several minutes before Ari, looking down at his feet, says, "How are we going to find the Fairy's Gold now?"

I don't have an answer.

We can't find the Fairy's Gold, we don't know any other way to cure the plague, and if we don't figure it out soon, Mama Fox and her babies will die, along with the gyrpuffs and any other Realm creatures who have been exposed.

We're running out of time.

SIXTEEN

Ari insists on telling the other Seekers about the ice-foxes right away, and I don't argue this time, even though I know what will happen. Sure enough, the minute we inform the others, Seeker Freyr starts ranting at us about "disobedience" and "rule-breaking." But Seeker Larus reminds him of the urgency of the situation and promises to discuss our punishments while Seeker Freyr and Seeker Ludvik scurry off to set boundary spells around the icefox dens and search the surrounding area for more sick creatures. Ari offers to lead the way to the den. I remain mostly quiet during this conversation and stay behind as they leave.

I must be a little *too* quiet, because Seeker Larus casts me a knowing look as soon as the others are gone. "Something on your mind, Seeker Bryn? Contemplating more ways to sneak into the Realm alone, perhaps?"

I bite my lip. I decided not to argue with them about the

rules, because I know it's useless at this point. I'll just check on the icefoxes myself, like I've been doing for the gyrpuffs. It doesn't matter if the other Seekers want to punish me for entering the Realm or not—I'm still going to visit the sick creatures and make them as comfortable as possible, and I'm still going to try to find the cure.

But I guess my sudden silence has made Seeker Larus suspicious.

"I was just thinking, Seeker," I say finally. "About how we might cure the plague. Ari and I went to visit the icefoxes today because we were hoping that maybe they could lead us to some rare plants that could be used for the cure." I don't specify Fairy's Gold, because he'd probably laugh.

Instead, he nods, looking thoughtful. "A great idea," he says. "Few creatures know the Realm better than the foxes."

"Except now the mama is sick," I say, "and others may be as well. I don't know if we can find another icefox who can help us."

Seeker Larus leans back in his chair and considers me for a moment. "If I may make a suggestion, Seeker Bryn?"

This is the first time any one of the other Seekers has *asked* before telling me what to do, so I nod. "I would appreciate your advice, Seeker."

"The icefoxes are helpful guides, it's true," he says, "but a good enough Seeker can find anything they need in the Realm even without a guide. You simply have to trust yourself, use your gift, and follow your instincts."

I shift in my seat. "That doesn't sound very 'simple,' Seeker Larus. No offense."

He laughs. "Easier said than done, I agree. But anything can be found in the Realm by a Seeker who's determined to look for it."

I bite my lip before blurting it out quickly. "What about . . . Fairy's Gold?"

Seeker Larus is momentarily taken aback. His eyes widen, and he remains silent for a long time. "No one has ever seen anything resembling a golden plant in the Realm. It is legend, not reality."

"Are we sure about that? What if that legend is based in reality?"

He studies me for a moment. "What makes you think so?"

"Well, the story had to originate somewhere, right? And aren't there still secrets to the Realm that we haven't discovered? Places we haven't explored?"

He pauses for another minute. "An interesting theory," he says finally. "You think it might exist *and* be the cure to the plague?"

"I think it's something we haven't tried yet."

He nods, and I realize he's taking me more seriously than I expected. "Well. That is a challenge, I will admit. I have never seen Fairy's Gold in all my years in the Realm, and I do not expect that we ever will. But if I have learned anything in my time as a Seeker, it is that nothing is impossible in those lands. The wilds of the Realm contain many mysteries, and Fairy's Gold could, in theory, be one of them."

"So you don't think it's a waste of time?"

Again, he takes the question seriously, considering his answer for a moment before speaking. "I don't know how or if we could locate Fairy's Gold quickly enough to stop the plague," he says finally. "But if you think you can locate it, then by all means, give it a try. At this point, I'm afraid there's little else we *can* do to find a cure. We've exhausted every other possibility."

His answer surprises me, and it takes a second to form a response. "How should I begin? Where should I look first?"

"That I cannot tell you," he says, "though I may offer a theory. Many Seekers have speculated about a potential location for Fairy's Gold, and I believe it was your papa who suggested that, if such a powerful magical item did exist, surely it would be located in the very heart of the Realm, where magic is strongest."

"The heart of the Realm," I repeat. "But what does that mean?"

"You've sensed, I'm sure, how much magic flows within the Realm? Well, your papa and I observed that the Realm's magic was strongest in its center—where the forests grow the densest, where unicorns tend to dwell, where we could feel the magic like a pulse surrounding us. But the terrain there is difficult to navigate, and the farther you walk toward the center, the thicker the forest becomes. We always wondered what secrets might lie hidden there. . . . But in our attempts to reach the center, we were always forced to turn around once the forest became impassable."

I slump back in my chair. "So you don't think I could go there."

He leans forward, and a small smile creeps across his face. "You were chosen as a Seeker for a reason, Bryn. I haven't forgotten, and neither should you."

A tiny flutter of hope stirs inside my chest. He's right. I *am* a Seeker for a reason. I earned it. And I didn't let anything stand in my way—not Seeker Agnar, not the other competitors, not even a Vondur invasion. I'm not going to let *anything* stop me from protecting the Realm. I'll prove to everyone that I can do this.

If I have to comb over every inch of wilderness to find the Fairy's Gold and cure the plague, then I will.

"Thanks, Seeker," I say. "I won't forget."

He smiles and raises his teacup. "What are you waiting for, Seeker Bryn? You have work to do."

I'm distracted during dinner that evening, and Mama asks me three times if everything's okay. But I don't want to talk about the plague in front of Elisa, who might get scared for the animals and who *definitely* won't keep it quiet, so I say nothing. After I pick at my stew for the hundredth time, Mama excuses me from the table in exasperation, and I flee to the front garden.

Papa finds me a few minutes later. He leans heavily on his walking stick as he makes his way down the garden path and settles on the bench beside me. "What's happened?" he asks immediately.

I sigh. "The plague is spreading, the Seekers don't know how to cure it, and my idea for finding a cure didn't work. I've got to figure out the solution, but I don't know how I'm going to do it."

Papa nods thoughtfully. "Have you spoken with the other Seekers?"

"Seeker Larus encouraged me to find the cure, but . . . he didn't seem to know how either."

Papa's bushy eyebrows rise. "And you didn't ask your own papa for advice? I'm offended," he says, smiling to let me know he's teasing.

But he's right, actually. Why *didn't* I ask him for his advice? I want to prove to him—to everyone—that I can do this, but that doesn't mean I can't ask Papa for help, and he knows the Realm better than anyone.

"Papa," I say, "you remember when I asked you about the Fairy's Gold? We were going to ask the icefoxes to guide us to it, but—the icefoxes are sick now, and I don't know how else to find it. What would you do?"

A familiar gleam shimmers in Papa's eyes. "I always assumed that such a powerful magical item would exist in the heart of the Realm."

"Yeah, that's what Seeker Larus said." I sigh. That doesn't

do me any good if the heart of the Realm is as impenetrable as Seeker Larus claimed.

"Well, did Seeker Larus tell you I nearly made it through that forest once?"

I perk up, straightening my shoulders. "Really?"

"I didn't tell you this before because I didn't want you to waste time on what could very well have been a fever dream. But if it's your only remaining option . . ."

"What happened?"

"I was tracking an injured unicorn, hoping she'd let me close enough to heal her. As I pursued her, she led me deeper into the forest than I'd ever been before. The trees were so high they blotted out the sky, and I could almost taste the magic in the air. The forest was quiet, but I sensed the presence of magical creatures there, watching me. I reached out with my gift, trying to find a path forward through the trees."

"And?" I prod when he pauses, a distant look in his eyes.

"And I thought I found one. For a moment there was a light—a sort of golden glow, shining between the trees. But I was exhausted by this point; I'd been tracking the unicorn for several hours, and my gift was weakening. By the time I stumbled toward the light, it had vanished, and the trees seemed even thicker than before. I was forced to leave the forest, but I resolved to return the next day, when my gift was replenished."

"And did you?" I ask, leaning forward in excitement.

"I did. In fact, I tried to return many times. But I never

found that place—or that golden light—again."

"Papa!" I exclaim, leaping up from the bench. "That could've been it! That golden light—it could've been the Fairy's Gold!"

Papa smiles. "Yes, that thought had occurred to me. But it's also possible that, in my exhaustion, I was seeing things that weren't there. Perhaps the golden light was nothing more than sunlight reflecting off the trees."

I study him for a moment, and the gleam in his eye gives away the truth. "But you don't believe that. You don't think you imagined it."

"I don't know what to believe, Bryn. I never found the Fairy's Gold, no matter how hard I tried. So either I imagined it . . . or the forest didn't want me to find it."

I return to the bench beside him, gripping the edge in anticipation. "Papa, where was this place? What do you remember about where you saw the light?"

"It was the trees I remember most," he says, his expression distant again. "There were three rowan trees, all with intersecting branches. And the tree in the middle—there was a circular pattern in the center of its trunk that reminded me of a dragon's eye."

"A dragon's eye?" I repeat.

"I'm sorry I can't be more helpful than that," he says, looking sheepish. "But that's all I can remember of the place. That, and the light, and . . . the birdsong."

"Birdsong?"

"There are more birds in the heart of the Realm than anywhere else on the island," Papa says. "I remember hearing the larks singing in the trees."

I nod. It isn't much to go on, but it's *something*. "Thanks, Papa. That really does help."

Papa wraps one arm around me. "Whatever happens, Bryn, remember that your mama and I are very proud of you."

"Thanks."

His expression deepens. "But do be careful, all right? The center of the Realm is full of magic that no human on this island has ever fully understood. Trust your instincts, and get out if you need to. And don't go alone. Take Ari or one of the other Seekers with you. Promise?"

"I promise," I say, rolling my eyes. "Honestly, Papa, I'll be fine."

He gives my shoulder a squeeze. "I know you will. Now, what do you say we go back inside for dessert? I think I spied your mama baking a bilberry pie."

I leap up from the bench again. "Why didn't you mention that sooner?"

Papa chuckles. "Between you and that dragon of yours, this island's going to run out of bilberries!"

After I eat two slices of pie and Mama refuses to serve me any more, I leave the hut again and head down the hillside to Runa's. I have a *lot* to fill her in on.

But first I check in on Little Puff, who's been given a warm and cozy nest inside the stable near Runa's horse, Starlight.

"He seems fine here," Runa says, "and my parents hardly ever come in now that mucking out the stables is *my* chore." She wrinkles her nose.

"Hi, Little Puff," I say, nudging him with my gift. He chirps and hops closer to me. I lower my hand, and he rubs his beak against my finger. "Is he hungry?" I ask Runa. "Have you been feeding him?"

"Of course," she says indignantly. "I wouldn't let him starve."

I cup my hands, and Little Puff nestles happily onto my palms. "I have so much to tell you," I say to Runa as Little Puff chirps contentedly.

Runa listens with wide eyes as I explain about the Vondur magic I sensed in the Realm, the sick icefoxes, the Fairy's Gold, and the hints Papa gave me.

"Wow," Runa says when I'm finished. "Do you really think you can find it?"

"I have to try. The plague is spreading fast, and I don't know if the attempted quarantine is working. If there's even one creature who didn't get behind the boundary spell, or if it's still spreading through the water . . . the whole Realm could be infected unless we make the cure."

"I've been refining my potion technique," Runa says, beaming. "The meadowsweet and peppermint balance each other out well. Elder Ingvar helped me find a more effective way to chop the figrose roots, and I whipped up a much stronger batch. All it needs is one more ingredient. If Fairy's Gold really does exist, it could be the missing piece."

"It's settled, then," I say. "I just have to find the Fairy's Gold, and the cure will be ready."

Runa's eyes widen. "Are you going to search for it tonight?"

I sigh. "I don't think so. For one thing, the forests will be really dark, so I won't be able to see where I'm going. And for another, I promised my papa that I wouldn't search alone. He thinks the magic in that part of the Realm might be dangerous."

"Sounds smart," Runa says. Little Puff chirps from my hands as if to agree.

I roll my eyes. "He's just being overly cautious. But I *did* promise. And anyway, I need to check on some of the creatures in the quarantine tonight. I've been bringing the sick gyrpuffs food and water, and now I need to do that for the icefoxes too. By the time I finish all that, I won't have time to search for Fairy's Gold. So I'll have to wait until morning. I'll convince Ari to go with me first thing."

"That's a good plan," Runa says. "Is there anything you need me to do?"

"Keep a fresh batch of the potion ready," I say. "As soon as I find the Fairy's Gold, we'll need it."

"I can do that. Elder Ingvar has been helping me with it."

I frown. "You haven't told him what it's for, have you?"

"Of course not. I haven't told anyone about the plague. I just said that you asked me to make a potion with these ingredients and that I didn't know why."

"And he accepted that?" I ask, raising my eyebrows.

Runa laughs. "Bryn, you're a Seeker now. Everyone in the village respects the Seekers, and none of us have any idea what you actually *do* in the Realm on a daily basis. So most people just do what the Seekers want without asking any questions."

"Really? They're not curious to learn more about what the Seekers are doing?"

Runa rolls her eyes. "Just because *you've* always been endlessly curious about being a Seeker doesn't mean anyone else is. Most people don't ask a thousand questions about magic on a regular basis, you know."

"Well, they're missing out," I say. "If I didn't ask a thousand questions, how would I ever learn anything?" I give Little Puff a gentle pat, and he ruffles his feathers. "Isn't that right, little guy?"

Runa smiles. "I guess that's why you're a Seeker now. That, and the fact that you have a very talented healer friend helping you out all the time."

"You're right. I'll have to thank my very talented healer friend the next time I see them. I'd be lost without them."

She shoves my shoulder lightly. "Yes, you *would* be lost without me, and you're welcome."

"Thanks, Runa. Seriously. I know you're working hard on the potion."

She grins. "Go find me some Fairy's Gold, then, Seeker Bryn."

Little Puff chirps in agreement.

SEVENTEEN

C ome *on*, you silly dragon!"

Lilja snorts indignantly, shaking out her wings and refusing to budge. She's tired of going near the ice forests and knows perfectly well that I'll leave her behind once we hit the boundary. But I don't have a choice. I have to check up on the icefoxes, and Lilja can't come with me into their territory. Not to mention that I have to go through the new quarantine spells to get anywhere close to the icefox caves, and I don't want Lilja on the other side.

Try explaining all of that to a stubborn baby dragon.

"It's only for a minute, I promise! The little icefoxes need food!" I wish Ari were here to help soothe her emotions, but he was exhausted after Seeker Ludvik and Seeker Freyr asked him for help in the Realm today, so I told him to go home and sleep, and he was too tired to argue. But now that I've got a defiant dragon on my hands, I'm regretting that decision.

Lilja's ears pull back, and she raises her chin haughtily.

"I know you don't want to go closer, but it's too far for me to walk by myself." I cross my arms over my chest and give her a stronger push with my gift. "Just take me a *little* farther, Lil!"

For a moment she doesn't move, and I think I've convinced her. But then she huffs, and gray smoke shoots from her nostrils. With a rumble of protest, she folds her legs and lies down on the ground.

"Lilja! I'll give you a whole bilberry pie or something, okay?"

She doesn't move.

"Lilja! Come on!" I say in my most enticing voice, pretending I'm not frustrated. "This way! Let's go! It'll be fun."

She blinks once before closing her eyes.

"You've got to be kidding me. Are you taking a *nap*?"

I reach for my gift, prepared to surround Lilja's life force with an even bigger push—

Something flickers in the trees, and my gift is drawn to it. Another life force, a big one. Cautiously I send my gift closer, trying to figure out what's moving through the trees. Lots of things live in this forest. It could be a sea wolf or a unicorn or—

It's human.

I freeze.

Lilja senses either my tension or the new arrival or both. Her eyes snap open, and she's on her feet in seconds, opening her jaws wide, her spikes rising.

There are only two possibilities I can think of, and

neither one is good. The first is that another Seeker is in the Realm, and I'm about to get in trouble again.

But the other possibility is even worse.

The Vondur that Ari and I sensed before might be back.

An image of the plague-infected glacier full of Vondur magic flashes in my mind, and I shudder.

As quietly as I can, I slip down from Lilja's back. A low growl fills her throat, but I hush her, giving her scales a pat, and she quiets down, though her body is still tense and her spikes are standing on end.

I try to use as little of my gift as possible so that the light won't give me away. Carefully, I creep forward toward the mysterious life force, stepping gingerly around fallen branches and twigs so as not to make any sound. Even Lilja is moving more quietly than usual, her feet sliding almost soundlessly across the forest floor.

The figure appears to be walking rapidly, their life force moving through the trees at a brisk pace. I nearly have to run to keep up, dodging tree limbs and darting around bushes blocking the path. It's too dark to see well, and I can't make out any sign of them ahead.

Following the flicker of their life force, Lilja and I race south through the trees until we break into a small clearing. I halt Lilja at the tree line and study the darkness before us. At the end of the clearing, a massive shape is moving, and I identify the second life force that has joined the first.

Another dragon.

The mysterious figure is just barely visible as a shadow against the trees, climbing onto the dragon's back. I let out a sigh of relief. It's got to be a Seeker. I don't know what they'd be doing here so late, but maybe Seeker Ludvik was checking the boundary spells of the quarantine or—

No, that can't be right. I know all of the Seekers' dragons, and this one's life force is completely unfamiliar to me. From what I can see of the shadows, it's a small dragon too—smaller even than Lilja, which means it's got to be a baby. Could someone be riding Vin?

I send a little bit of my gift closer, trying to hide it in the trees so that the light won't be visible at the other end of the clearing. The mysterious person's life force doesn't feel right—there's something off about it, something . . .

Fear jolts through my spine, and Lilja stiffens beside me.

Vondur magic.

I couldn't sense it earlier, but we're close enough now that it's unmistakable. That's a Vondur in front of me. Riding a dragon. *In the Realm.*

I leap forward, but I'm too late—the dragon is rising into the air, taking its rider with it.

"Hurry, Lilja!" I cry, spinning toward her, no longer caring about being quiet. I have to catch up to the Vondur and stop them. Whatever they're doing, it can't be good.

Lilja immediately lowers herself to the ground so that I can scramble onto her back, and she whips her wings out without a second of protest. She bursts into the clearing and takes a running start, and we're in the air in seconds. Unfortunately, the other dragon is fast too, their shadow rapidly disappearing in the distance.

"Hurry, Lilja!" I cry. "Follow them!"

She doesn't need to be told twice.

With a burst of speed I've never seen from her before, she lunges forward, nearly throwing me into the back of her neck. I cling to her scales for dear life as she whips through the dark sky, rapidly gaining on the other dragon.

I don't know what we're going to do when we catch up to them, but I can't just let them disappear. I have to know who this Vondur is, where they came from, and what they're doing here. This might be the person who used magic to infect the glacier with the plague.

Lilja is flying so fast that her breathing is short and rapid. She wheezes suddenly, and her whole body rattles beneath me.

"It's okay, Lil, we're almost there," I say, but something is wrong. She wheezes again, and her wingbeats rapidly slow.

"Lilja?"

I reach for her energy with my gift. Her life force is weaker than usual—*much* weaker. Maybe she flew too fast and overexerted herself?

"Take it easy," I say, trying to soothe her with my gift. "It's okay, you can go slow—"

She wheezes again, and suddenly we're falling.

"Lil!" I scream, but her wings don't beat again to catch us, and we keep falling.

The other dragon is nothing but a smudge in the distance as we drop right out of the sky.

"Lilja!"

As we near the trees, some of her strength seems to return to her. Her wings give a few halfhearted flutters, slowing our momentum, and she rolls sideways, narrowly avoiding a collision with some trees and aiming instead for a clear patch of land ahead. With a start, I realize that it's Dragon's Point. We've gone much farther south than I thought.

For a second I think we're going to crash right into the plateau, but somehow Lilja saves the landing, skidding across the rock and stumbling to a halt. I lie against her back, panting, my hands clenched so hard around her spike that for a moment they're too stiff to move.

When I recover, I immediately slide down from Lilja's back, filling the air with my gift. Her life source is still weak and trembling, but I don't see any injuries. "Are you okay, Lil? What happened up there?"

I circle around to her front. She gazes at me, and I gasp.

Her eyes, usually a bright and clear yellow, are now dotted with spots of black.

I reach frantically for her snout, running my hands over her scales, willing it not to be true. Maybe I'm imagining things in the darkness, maybe—

The glow of my gift illuminates her face, and I can't deny the truth.

Lilja has caught the plague.

EIGHTEEN

I bang on the door of Ari's hut so loudly that the chickens in the yard's coop squawk indignantly, and a light flickers on in the neighboring hut. My fist aches, but I keep pounding.

Finally, the door opens, and Ari's mother stares back at me, eyes wide, the blue light of her gift dancing around her hands. She wraps a shawl around her shoulders. "Bryn—I mean, Seeker Brynja? What's wrong?"

"Sorry to wake you, Elder Eydis," I say. "But it's urgent. I need Ari, now."

"What's wrong?" Ari calls, padding to the door and rubbing the sleep from his eyes. His curls are even more disheveled than usual, sticking up in all directions.

"It's Lilja," I say, and his eyes widen instantly.

"What happened?"

I glance at his mother. I don't know whether he's told her about the plague. "Come with me," I say.

"Not so fast," Ari's mother interrupts, and for a second I think she's going to forbid him. "Grab your cloak, Ari. It's freezing out here."

Ari shuffles from view for a moment and returns, wrapping his Seeker cloak around his shoulders. His mother thrusts a pair of boots into his hands, and he stumbles into them.

Finally, I manage to herd him outside. His mother watches from the doorway as we run into the street, and I head straight for Dragon's Point.

"Where are we going, Bryn? What's wrong with Lilja?"

"The plague!" I say, forgetting to keep my voice down in my panic. "I think she's got it!"

"WHAT?"

As rapidly as I can between breaths, I tell him about the Vondur in the Realm, our rushed pursuit, Lilja's fall, and the black I saw in her eyes.

"It's dark," Ari cuts in finally. "Maybe you didn't see her properly. Maybe she just tried to fly too fast. Maybe—"

"See for yourself," I say. "She's at the Point."

We race to the top of the plateau without another word, panting in the darkness.

Lilja lets out a happy cry when she sees Ari, but she doesn't rise from where she's lying, a clear sign that something's wrong.

"Lilja?" Ari whispers, his gift filling the air as he rushes toward her. He stares into her eyes, and for a long moment he doesn't speak.

"Her life force feels all wrong," he says finally, nearly choking on the words. "I can tell she's sick. She knows something's wrong."

"And her eyes?" I ask, knowing what he'll say yet hoping I'm wrong.

"I see it. The black. I think you're right."

He spins toward me suddenly. "What happened, Bryn? Where did you go?"

I swallow hard. "Just the usual, like I've been doing every night. I bring food and water to the gyrpuffs, and I was going to visit the icefoxes—"

"How close did you bring her to the sick animals?"

Maybe it's the darkness, but there's an expression on Ari's face that I can't read, that I've never seen before. I take a step back without thinking, and my next words come out in a jumble. "I—I've been making sure that she stays outside the quarantine zones. I don't know how she was exposed."

"But we already knew there was a chance that the plague had spread outside of that. How close was she to the boundaries?"

"I don't . . . I don't know. But she didn't come in contact with any other creatures. She never saw the icefoxes or gyrpuffs directly. Well, except for . . ."

"Except for what?" He stares me down, waiting for my response.

"Except for Little Puff," I say quietly. "I . . . I found a

baby gyrpuff abandoned in a nest, and I took it out of the quarantine zone."

"And Lilja came near this gyrpuff? The one that had been in the center of the plague zone?"

"Yes. But I don't think—"

"Right, obviously you weren't thinking. How could you take a risk like that?"

"We don't know that Lilja got sick from Little Puff. Like you said, the plague's been spreading outside the boundaries, and who knows where she travels when we're not around, or if it's reached the Valley of Ash. She could've gotten it anywhere."

"But she *could* have gotten it from this baby gyrpuff. One that you exposed her to. I can't believe you'd do something that reckless!" He spins away from me, and I'm not sure if he's trying to hide his anger or his fear.

If only I were an empath too, so that I'd know what to say.

"I kept trying to tell you," he says finally. "I kept telling you not to keep going into the Realm, that you didn't have to cure this thing by yourself. But you thought you didn't have to listen to anyone else. Even when the other Seekers warned us about not breaking the quarantine and allowing the gyrpuffs to expose other creatures. You're so convinced you can cure it when no one else can that you put Lilja at risk, and look what happened."

"That's not fair," I protest. "I took precautions, and I never let Lilja cross any boundaries, and she barely interacted with

Little Puff at all. We don't know how she caught it, or . . ." But my voice drifts off, because I don't know how to defend myself. Is he . . . right? Did I do this to Lilja? Did she get the plague because of me?

Without another word, Ari climbs onto Lilja's back, moving carefully so as not to hurt her. "I'm going to try to get her back to the valley. She'll be safer in her den, instead of exposed out here."

"I'll come with you and—"

"No," he says, not looking at me. "Just get out of here."

"But we need to heal her," I say. "Together, maybe we can—"

"Bryn," he says. "Just listen to me for once. Please."

He's never sounded like this before, so sad and angry all at once, and something twists inside my stomach.

Without another word, I turn and run back to the village, leaving Ari and Lilja in the darkness behind me.

The sky is lighter by the time I reach Runa's farm, and the tears on my cheeks have nearly dried.

Her mama opens the door to their hut when I knock and is only slightly less surprised to see me than Ari's mama was. "Runa!" she calls without asking any questions.

Runa shrugs on her coat and follows me into the yard, yawning.

"You have to help me," I croak. "It's Lilja. She's got the plague now."

Runa's eyes fly open. "I've kept the potion ready like you asked," she says. "Did you get the—"

"I haven't found the Fairy's Gold yet. That's what I need your help with."

She frowns, studying me. "What do you mean? I can't go into the Realm."

"That doesn't matter right now. Someone has to go with me, and Ari—he's not speaking to me at the moment. You have to help. We need the Fairy's Gold *now*, before Lilja gets any sicker."

"But, Bryn, I'm not a Seeker! I'm not allowed!"

I laugh, the sound hollow. "I've already broken every other rule, so what does it matter? Just don't use your magic in the Realm unless I tell you it's okay, and we should be fine."

"But if the other Seekers find out—"

"Runa! This isn't the time to play by the rules! Are you going to help me or not?"

She hesitates, biting her lip, but something in my expression—the desperation, probably—convinces her. "Okay, okay. But if Lilja is sick, how are we getting into the Realm? Can she fly?"

"I don't think so, but it doesn't matter. I've got a backup plan."

Breathlessly, we run to Dragon's Point. Ari and Lilja are gone by the time we get there—as I suspected, he's found a way to get her back into the Realm, though I don't know how far she could've made it. I try to force the thought of her crash-landing again out of my mind and focus.

Runa is looking around in awe. She's never been to the top of the plateau before. "You can see the whole village from here!" she whispers, gazing at the landscape surrounding us.

I grin. "If you think that's something, watch *this*."

I step to the edge of the plateau and let out a whistle. Three high, clear notes echo back to us.

For a moment I think it isn't going to work. I don't know how often the other Seekers used that whistle, and we haven't had much practice, so maybe he didn't—

"Look!" Runa cries as a big red shape fills the horizon, flying toward us.

Vin soars into view, and his head bobs back and forth in excitement when he spots me below. Runa and I take a few steps back as he lands, a little less gracefully than Lilja usually does, and rushes toward us.

Runa lets out a very undignified squeal as he charges, but I use my gift to steady him, and he halts right in front of her, tail lashing back and forth eagerly.

"Runa, this is Vin," I say. "Vin, meet Runa."

Runa has seen dragons before, of course—she's met Lilja, and she saw Gulldrik in the arena during the Seeker competition. But she still gazes in awe at Vin, and I can't blame her. Dragons are incredible every time I see them.

"Hi, Vin," she says, giving him a little wave. Vin does a happy snort in response, tilting his snout toward her.

"Come on," I say to Runa. "He's our ride."

"Um, how are we going to get *up* there?" she asks, gazing at his back.

"Like this." I scramble up first, demonstrating, and then reach down to help her up. Runa hesitates. "Come on," I say. "You love riding horses. Think of this as a *really* big horse."

Runa gulps and reaches for my hand.

I manage to get her settled on Vin's back behind me. "Okay," I say, "remember what I said about using your gift? I'm going to guide him with mine, and I don't want him to get confused if he feels yours too. So try not to use it."

"Okay." Her voice shakes, and a new thought occurs to me.

"Runa, are you scared of heights?"

"Um," she says, "I don't normally try going anywhere high, so I'm not sure?"

Well, this should be interesting. "Okay, no problem. See that spike in front of you? Grab on to that, and hold *very tight*."

She does so, and I give Vin a tiny nudge with my gift. He's so excited to have passengers that he jerks up immediately, and I nearly slam my forehead on his back as we lurch forward. Runa knocks into me and lets out a squeal.

"Hold on!" I shout over the sound of Vin's wingbeats. Within seconds, we're airborne.

The wind rushes in our ears as we climb higher and higher, bursting through the clouds. The Realm spreads out below us, and Runa gasps sharply in my ear.

"Are you okay?" I call over the wind.

"It's incredible!" she shouts back, and I grin. I know exactly what she means.

She hasn't seen *anything* yet.

I direct Vin to the central forests and find a safe space to land. He stumbles a bit, jostling us as his claws scrabble the earth, and Runa lets out a muffled shriek.

"You okay?" I ask again as Vin slows to a stop and gives his leathery wings a shake.

"Um. I think so?" Runa says, taking a deep breath. "That was amazing. And terrifying. And amazing!"

I laugh. "Welcome to the Realm, Runa."

We climb down from Vin's back, and she looks around with wide eyes. We're in a small clearing full of wildflowers and long grass that glimmers in the pale moonlight. The edges of the forest encroach on all sides, the trees dark with shadows.

"It looks a little more impressive during the day," I admit, using my gift to bring light to my fingertips.

"So how will we find the Fairy's Gold?" Runa asks, gazing into the trees. "How big is this forest?"

"Big," I admit. "But Papa gave me some clues. We need to go deep into the center of the forest and find three rowan trees with intersecting branches. One of them has a pattern in the trunk like a dragon's eye."

"Well, that narrows it down," Runa says grimly. "There's only a thousand trees in there."

"Probably more like a million," I say, putting false cheer into my voice. "So we'd better get started."

Runa groans. "How did I let you talk me into this?"

I set a couple of quick boundary spells around Vin, who seems perfectly content wandering the clearing and sniffing clumps of wildflowers. Then Runa and I cross the tree line, our gifts illuminating the path.

I send my magic out wider, trying to get a feel for the flow of energy through the forest. The stronger the magic, the closer we are. "This way," I say, leading Runa deeper into the trees.

The forest is mostly quiet as we walk. The underbrush is dense and snags at us, so I use my gift to move the branches out of the way, forming a small dirt path. But we still stumble over tree roots and stones and uneven ground as we make our way forward in the near darkness.

An owl hoots above us, and Runa jumps. "Bryn?" she says quietly. "What kinds of creatures live in this forest?"

"Unicorns!" I say immediately, and she relaxes slightly. It's technically not a lie, although I didn't mention the fact that there are plenty of other things living in these trees too.

We walk for what feels like hours. The landscape doesn't change much—just tree after tree after tree—but I sense the magic around us getting stronger. The forest is brimming with it, and my gift feels stronger here, more powerful. Runa feels it too, casting the blue light of her magic out wider.

"I don't see any rowan trees," she says, watching the blue light flit ahead of us.

"We'll just have to keep looking," I say, trying to sound optimistic, but my heart is sinking. We could comb this forest forever and never find it. And we don't even know if what Papa saw was real, or if it will lead us to the Fairy's Gold.

And Lilja doesn't have much time.

"Do you feel that?" Runa asks suddenly, her eyes widening.

"What?"

"It's like . . . I can feel a pulse. In the magic. It feels like . . . a heartbeat."

I close my eyes. There's so much magic in the air around us that, at first, I'm not sure what she means, but then I feel it. The magic ebbs and flows, and there's a rhythm to it—like a pulse. And the farther into the trees we walk, the stronger the pulse is.

"We're getting closer," I say.

Runa nods. "Closer to *something*," she says darkly.

The trees around us are the tallest I've ever seen, towering so high that the sky is barely visible between their branches. Even our gifts, which are so much stronger here, are barely bright enough to illuminate the darkness surrounding us.

"Papa said it looks like this!" I whisper, taking a few steps forward. "We just need to find the right tree."

"I don't like this, Bryn," Runa says quietly. "It feels like . . . like we're not supposed to be here."

A high sound breaks through the trees, and I spin toward it. "Do you hear that?"

"It's a bird," Runa says. "It sounds like a lark singing." She pauses. "Bryn, do larks usually sing at night?"

"I don't think so," I say. "We must be close! Papa said he heard birdsong. We need to follow it!"

Runa sighs but doesn't argue. We continue stumbling through the darkened forest, following the high, clear singing. The farther we walk, the more birds join in the song, until it's a whole chorus.

We're so close. I can feel it—the pulse of magic filling the air and thrumming in my veins. I've been in the Realm plenty of times now, but I've never felt magic as strong as this. If the Fairy's Gold exists, it's got to be here.

"Bryn!" Runa says. "Look!"

I follow her gaze. To our left, three rowan trees are clustered together, their branches intertwined. I race forward, and Runa stumbles after me. I cast my gift all along the trunk of the center tree, searching, searching—

There.

In the middle of the trunk is a circular pattern in the wood, shaped almost exactly like a dragon's eye.

"This is it!" I yell. "This is it!"

"Shh," Runa whispers. "I think we're making it angry."

"Making *what* angry?" I ask, turning to her.

"The forest." Runa's eyes are wide as she gazes around. "Bryn, I don't think we're supposed to be here," she says again.

"What are you—" I stop.

All around us, the trees are moving.

Magic swells in the air, and the branches of the trees rise, creaking and groaning, as if manipulated by naturalist magic. But no naturalist could control so many massive trees at once. The branches grow and twist, spreading out, almost as if they're—

"They're reaching for us!" Runa yells, and this time I don't argue.

I'm not a defender; I can't make a shield to protect us. But my Seeker instincts kick in. I reach for the trees with my gift, funneling it into the branches, trying to turn them away from us. The branches writhe and quiver as my magic reaches them, but they don't stop growing. They grow *faster.*

"It's getting worse!" Runa says, and she pulls her own gift in, the blue light vanishing. "They don't like our magic!"

"That doesn't make sense," I say. "The Realm always likes natural magic . . ." I pause as a memory floats back to me. At the first Seeker trial, the arena had been filled with trees, and I tried to use my gift to manipulate them, only to see them rise up against me, much like this. And I remember how I got through it.

I can't force the trees to move with my magic. I have to coexist with them.

The wind has picked up, and twigs blow into our faces as the nearest branches get closer and closer, reaching for us like skeletal limbs. I stop trying to move them with my gift, but I funnel more of it out, letting it fill the air with a green glow. This time, I just let it mingle with the energy of the trees, weaving in and out, making my magic a part of the forest. The branches slow their thrashing, and after a moment, they stop moving altogether, frozen at unnatural angles. A second passes, then two, then three. Nothing moves.

Runa exhales. "You did it," she whispers. "You—"

The ground buckles beneath us.

"Runa!" I yell, reaching for her hand, but the ground rolls again, and I fall backward, away from her. Everything trembles beneath me as the earth rises, and hills and dips suddenly form all around. I scramble to my feet only to be knocked down again as the shaking increases.

"Bryn!" Runa yells, but I can't see her around the massive hill rising between us.

I try to repeat the same trick with my gift, sending it into the ground and letting it flow alongside the magic, but it isn't enough. I don't have enough magic to combat this. Runa was right—the Realm doesn't want us here.

But why?

I cover my head with my hands as a tree above me cracks, its branches tumbling down, the earth still rocking beneath me. Papa was right. Humans aren't supposed to enter the heart of the Realm. It senses our presence, and it's fighting back.

I close my eyes. I think about Runa, struggling against this magic where I can't help her. I picture Lilja, her eyes gradually turning black. I picture Little Puff and the other gyrpuffs, lying still and silent; I picture Mama Icefox and her cubs, their eyes all turned to shadows; I picture the rivers and lakes of the Realm running black with the plague.

Then I imagine the Fairy's Gold. I don't know what it looks like, but I picture a golden light, a warm magic that chases away the darkness of the plague and fills the Realm with healing.

We're so close. Please. Please.

The shaking stops.

I open my eyes and lift my head. Nothing moves. The trees and the earth are still.

"Runa?" I call.

"I'm here!" A moment later, her head pops up from behind the hill that now rises between us. "Are you okay, Bryn?"

I stumble to my feet and check myself for injuries. "Yeah, I'm okay . . . I think. You?"

"Fine," she says. "What *happened*?"

I open my mouth to reply, but suddenly a golden ball of light rises from the trees ahead. My eyes widen, and Runa spins around to look.

"This is it," I say, and Runa nods wordlessly.

The golden glow fills the forest, and we step forward.

NINETEEN

The light is like an illusion. Every time I think we've almost caught up to it, suddenly it seems farther away than ever. Runa and I stumble through the thick foliage as fast as we can, the glowing light constantly illuminating the way forward.

"How much farther?" Runa pants, swiping a strand of hair from her forehead.

"I'm not sure," I say, dodging a tree root. "Feels like we've been in here for hours."

We press forward, the trees getting thicker as we walk, like they're closing in around us. The light beams steadily, always right ahead of us, just out of reach.

My gift presses against the edges of my fingertips, but I'm barely using it. There's so much magic everywhere that sensing it is overwhelming. I don't know how we'll ever be able to find the Fairy's Gold, if it exists, when I can't even tell apart the life sources—

But *that* seems odd. "Do you feel that?" I ask Runa, tentatively releasing my gift.

"Feel what?" she asks, slowing to a stop beside me.

I follow the prickle of magic with my gift, trying to determine the source. There's something strong here. Not *big*—not like a dragon or anything. But strong.

"What is it?" Runa whispers. "I don't sense anything."

"I think we found it," I whisper.

Wordlessly, I step forward, leading the way between two massive trees. On the other side, the golden light glows overhead, illuminating the forest floor.

Directly beneath the golden light is a single flower.

In shape, it looks a bit like a daffodil, one with particularly wide, full petals. But no daffodil could ever be this golden. It glitters even in the dim light, like someone dipped it in shimmery paint. I reach out carefully, just brushing the edge of one of its petals, and specks of gold coat my fingertip.

"Fairy's Gold," Runa whispers, and I nod.

"This is it," I say. "It has to be. This is the cure we need."

"But . . ." Runa hesitates, studying the flower. "There's only one. How am I supposed to make a big batch of the potion, for all the creatures, with only one flower?"

"Wait . . ." I spin around, searching the area, but there aren't any more flowers. Just one. "You can't take it," I say.

"What? We came all this way—"

"Not the whole flower," I explain, gesturing to it. "It's

the only one. It has to be preserved. If we pluck it, who knows if another one will grow back?"

Runa frowns, biting her lip. "So what do we do?"

I glance down, studying the flower again. The speck of gold dust on my finger sparkles in the light. My eyes widen.

"What if we don't need the whole flower?" I say. "What if we just need some of the gold dust? Couldn't you sprinkle some of this into a potion?"

Runa leans closer to the flower, examining it. "I guess so. But I thought the legends said you aren't supposed to take gold from these flowers? Isn't that bad?"

"The legends say there's a catch," I explain, remembering Papa's story. "Once you remove the gold from the flower, it disappears the following dawn. Some of the stories say that fairies enchanted the gold to disappear so greedy humans wouldn't destroy the flowers. Or maybe fairies don't exist and it's just the flowers' way of preserving themselves. Anyway, the reason you're not supposed to take the gold is because it's worthless—by dawn. But what if we put it in the potion and give it to Lilja before then? As long as she drinks it by sunrise . . ."

Runa tilts her head, considering. "I don't know how much of the gold we need to make the potion work. What if one flower isn't enough?"

"We have to try. For Lilja, and for the rest of the Realm."

Runa nods. "All right. Here, help me with this." She draws two glass vials out of her pockets. The herbalist's symbol is etched into each of them. "We can collect the dust into these."

We quickly set to work. As gently as possible, I brush the gold dust from the petals off the flower and into the vial. It's messy, and more of the gold dust ends up on my fingers and on the ground than in the vial, but it works. There's a ton of gold on each petal, and my vial is filled after only three.

"Ready?" Runa asks, holding up her own vial, now filled to the brim with glittering gold.

"Ready," I say, rising. I glance up at the golden light that led us here, still glimmering in the sky. It's so bright that it's hard to look at, like a miniature sun. "What do you think that is?"

"Magic," Runa says with a shrug.

"I know, but what kind? I've never seen anything like it before."

The heart of the Realm, says Seeker Larus's voice in my head.

"Bryn," Runa says, "come on. I don't know how long it will take us to get out of here. Dawn might not be far off."

I tear my gaze from the golden light and focus. Runa's right. I can't tell if we've been in here for five minutes or five years, and the trees overhead block any glimpse of the sky. We need to hurry.

Unfortunately, finding our way *out* of the trees is even more difficult than finding our way in, now that the light isn't guiding us.

"Do you think we're going the right way?" I ask, scanning a row of identical trees.

"We must be," Runa says. She points to the shadows ahead of us. "There's that hill that rose up when the forest attacked us. See it?"

I squint at the shape in the distance. "That's brilliant, Runa," I say. "I knew you should've been a Seeker!"

She rolls her eyes. "It's not brilliant to point out the obvious."

We make our way past the place where the ground is uneven, the only remaining sign of the forest's attack, and continue into the trees. From there, the journey gradually gets easier as the forest thins out. A few minutes later, we burst into the clearing, where Vin is waiting for us.

But something else flares against my gift—another life spark—and I realize too late that there's someone else waiting for us in the clearing.

A tall figure wearing a black cloak steps toward us. I sense the Vondur magic immediately, and my heart hammers in my chest—but Vondur magic isn't the only thing I can sense. As the realization sinks in, bright-red light dances around his hands and illuminates his face at last.

"I knew you'd find it," he says, his voice all too familiar.

It's the one person I never thought I'd see again. The former Seeker, turned traitor. The reason the Vondur came to our island last time.

It's Agnar.

TWENTY

Stay back!" I call, and my gift flares to life, glowing green around my hands. "Get away from our dragon!"

"*Your* dragon?" He laughs, and the sound is harsh and bitter. "I trained this dragon myself!"

"You let the Vondur keep him in chains," I say. "*I* trained him. He belongs to the Realm, not to you."

"I'm not here for the dragon," Agnar says. His gaze is fixed on the glowing vial in my hands.

"What could you possibly want with this?" I say, genuinely surprised. "The gold vanishes at dawn."

"Don't recite the legends to me, girl," he says with a sneer. "I was a Seeker for years, and I explored every inch of the Realm. I always knew there might be some truth in those old legends. But I could never quite find it." His gaze flickers between the vial I'm holding and the one in Runa's hands. "The heart of the Realm requires an equally pure heart, as the legend says.

It never accepted me, but you, a *child* . . . I knew you'd get there eventually. I've been following you every night, waiting . . ."

I think back to the times I sensed Vondur magic, and the figure Ari and I tried to follow, and then the one I saw tonight with Lilja. "So it was you," I say. "You poisoned the Realm. The dark magic was yours. But why? You always claimed to love the Realm. Was that a lie?"

"I didn't poison it!" he snaps. "The other Vondur did. It was what they wanted to do from the beginning, you know. The original plague, all those years ago, it was caused by their magic, when they tried and failed to take control of the Realm. They wanted to try that again, but I convinced them otherwise. I traded the items they would need, helped them plan the attack during the competition . . . But then it went wrong, no thanks to *you*, and so they ignored my advice and went for their original plan. They don't actually care if the Realm's creatures are alive or dead, you see. They need magical items for their spells, and it matters not at all how they get them. But I don't particularly want to see the Realm killed. I've been trying to stop them."

"Stop them? If that's true, why didn't you come to the Seekers and tell them—"

"The Seekers cast me out! They never would have listened to me. I have to prove to them that I have always had the Realm's best interests at heart. I will cure the Realm myself, using those golden vials you have there."

I frown. Something about this story doesn't quite add up. "So you really think they'll reinstate you as a Seeker or something if you cure the plague?"

"No," he says, and his mouth twists into a horrible smile. "I think I'll offer them the cure for the plague in exchange for what I want."

"Ah. Now it makes sense. You're going to try to blackmail them. Well, good luck with that."

I glance at Runa, who's still frozen behind me, clutching one of the vials tightly. "Get ready," I whisper to her.

"Now, now," Agnar says loudly, taking a step forward. "There will be no whispered plotting between you two. Stay *exactly* where you are."

"Um, I don't think so," I say. "I'm a Seeker now, so I don't have to take orders from you. We're leaving, and we're taking these vials, and you can't stop us."

"Can't I?" he says, and his gift flares brighter, the red light filling the clearing. His strong warrior gift.

Runa and I have strong gifts too, but they're not suited for fighting. The only way I can see us getting out of here is if I distract Agnar so that Runa can get to Vin—

"Did I mention," Agnar says casually, "that more of the Vondur are about to arrive?"

Overhead, the beat of a dragon's wings fills the air. I don't have to look to know that it isn't one of the Seekers coming to help us. It's more of the Vondur.

Agnar gives me another horrible smile. "Surely you didn't

think I'd spend all this time *chatting* for no reason, did you? We've simply been waiting for my associates to arrive."

"Yeah, well, give them my regards," I say. "Because we've *really* got to go."

This time I don't risk warning Runa. I whistle a sharp, clear melody.

Vin leaps up, responding eagerly to the signal I taught him. Before Agnar has time to react, Vin charges toward me, plowing right past Agnar. I race to meet him and scramble onto his back as quickly as I can, clutching the vial tightly in one hand. As soon as I'm steady, I glance back for Runa, who's scrambling up Vin's back with slightly more difficulty. I grab her hand and pull her up as Vin races excitedly through the clearing.

Agnar shouts something behind us, but I don't look back. I summon more of my gift and channel it toward Vin, directing him into the air.

"Hang on tight!" I shout to Runa. "We're going to go *fast!*"

"Don't you know any *calmer* dragons?" she shouts back, but she's composed enough to wrap her arms around one of Vin's spikes as the baby dragon lurches into the sky.

The clouds are heavy, making it difficult to see, so I can barely make out the silhouette of the other dragon as it lands in the clearing below us. By the time they get it into the air again, we'll be too far ahead of them—I hope. But we'll have to be fast.

"Vin," I say, "time to fly as quick as you can!" I release more of my gift, which feels strong and full after so much time spent in the heart of the Realm, and direct it to mix with Vin's energy, letting him sense what I want him to do. This time, I don't give him any gentle nudges. I give him a *push*.

Vin responds with a wild cry of joy and surges forward, pumping his wings at full speed. Runa lets out a gasp as we fly low and fast toward Dragon's Point.

"What's the plan now?" Runa shouts. "How do we stop Agnar?"

"Same plan," I shout back. "Create the cure and save Lilja first, before the Fairy's Gold disappears. Then we get the other Seekers and go after Agnar."

I cling to Vin's back for dear life as the wind rushes past us, the ground nothing but a blur below. Runa closes her eyes, her fingers clenched around one of Vin's spikes. "I don't like this ride anymore!" she yells.

"Almost there!" I call back, watching Dragon's Point loom closer on the horizon. I nudge Vin into a much calmer descent, and he handles it even better than I expect, easing up in plenty of time to make a smooth landing.

I stumble from Vin's back, brushing my windswept hair from my eyes. Runa clings to his spike for a moment longer before opening her eyes, straightening her shoulders, and climbing down. "Next time, I'm steering him," she says. "You can't be trusted."

"You got it," I say as Vin spreads his wings and takes off again, heading back into the Realm. "Next time we're flying a dragon out of the Realm in order to cure a plague and save all of the magical creatures while at the same time being chased by the Vondur, I'll be sure to let you take things slow."

"Why do I even help you?" Runa huffs. "I've been up all night, I nearly died falling off a dragon, and there is *dirt* in my *hair*. Honestly, the things I do for you."

"I'll shower you with gratitude later. I promise," I say. "Right now we have a potion to make. Let's go."

We run through the dark, empty streets of the village, and Runa leads the way to the herbalist shop. "The potion is all ready to go in the back," she says as we reach it. The shop's door is closed, and the lights are off.

"Please tell me you have a key," I say.

"Um."

"Runa!"

"I didn't think about it," she says, tugging on the door handle. Sure enough, it's locked. "Elder Ingvar is usually here."

"Where does he live?" I ask, pacing in front of the door. Surely we didn't brave the wilds of the Realm just to be thwarted by a locked door. Lilja does *not* have time for this.

"We can't just wake him up!" Runa protests.

"I'm a Seeker. I'll tell him it's a Seeker emergency. Which it is."

"I've got a better idea," Runa says, walking away. "I think I can get us in through the back."

We circle the squat stone building, and Runa leads me into a tight alleyway. "Um, Runa? There's no door back here," I say, gazing in dismay at the impenetrable stone wall in front of us.

"No," she says, "but there is a window. Up *there*."

She points, and I crane my neck to follow her gaze. Way, *way* above us is a tiny square opening, barely visible in the dark.

"You've got to be kidding."

"On the other side is a big storage cabinet," Runa says. "It's nearly as tall as the window, so it should be easy to climb onto it once you get through."

"But *how* do I get through? I'm not a dragon, Runa. I can't fly!"

She sighs impatiently. "You're a Seeker, aren't you? Don't you, like, climb trees and cliffs and things all the time? Or don't you have some kind of Seeker magic you can use?"

"Being a Seeker doesn't mean having a magic spell for everything!" I protest. But I study the wall more closely. Her first point . . . well, she's not entirely wrong. This is old stone, the jagged kind used on some of the earliest structures in the village, and it's not very smooth. There are dips and ledges in the wall here and there that might—*might*—be big enough to serve as handholds and footholds. For someone who's scaled Realm cliffs before, how hard can it be to scale a wall?

"Okay," I say finally. "We'll have to try climbing it. But please have your healing gift ready if we fall and break any bones."

"We?" Runa says. "Oh no. *I'm* not climbing it."

"But you have to! I don't know how to find the potion and add the gold dust by myself."

"But once you're inside, you can just open the front door for me," Runa says, grinning. "I'll leave the rock climbing to the experienced Seeker."

I glare at her. "You're lucky you're the best healer in the village," I grumble, "or I'd find someone else."

"Good luck," Runa says sweetly, gesturing to the wall.

Okay. I can do this. How hard can it be?

I use my gift to illuminate the wall, seeking the best place to start climbing. Finally, I identify the largest ledge and use it as a handhold, hauling myself up. My feet dangle uselessly for a moment as I scramble to find purchase. Finally, the end of my boot manages to wedge itself in place, and I search for the next handhold.

In theory, this is way less dangerous than any of the climbing I've done in the Realm. The wall isn't nearly as high as the cliffs we scaled to reach the gyrpuff nests. But at least the cliff had plenty of crevices that made it easy to scale. I've never had to climb something as smooth as this wall before, and it's slow going. The window feels impossibly far away, the footholds too few and far between to make it.

"There's one!" Runa says, her gift swirling around a ledge, and I jump sideways to reach it, my palm scraping against the rough stone. "You got this! Keep going!" Runa cheers.

Finally, after what feels like a century, I reach the open window ledge. It's such a short window that I have to crawl through headfirst and hope Runa's right about what waits on the other side. I let my gift brighten the dark room, but it's still hard to make anything out in the shadows as I dangle halfway in, gripping the window ledge, my feet hanging behind me.

"It should be right below you!" Runa calls, her voice muffled. I look down. There's definitely a large object of some kind beneath the window. I stretch as far as I can to reach it—

My other hand loses its grip on the window, and gravity does the rest. With a tremendous crash, I tumble headfirst from the window and land in a heap on top of the wooden chest below.

"Bryn! Are you okay?"

I lie still, taking quick stock of my injuries. Limbs: still attached. Bones: unbroken. Heart: absolutely pounding.

"All good," I croak, sitting up slowly. "Go to the front and I'll let you in."

Runa's response is too muffled to hear as I scramble off the furniture, my feet hitting the floor with a thud. I make out a doorway in the darkness and head for it carefully. Something clinks to my left as I bump into a table covered in glass bottles. I duck into the front room, climb over the counter, and finally reach the front door. With a twist of the lock, it swings open, revealing Runa on the other side.

"Took you long enough," she says with a grin.

"Next time, you're the one climbing through the window," I grumble.

Despite her teasing, Runa's all business once she's in the shop. She lights a lantern and leads the way into the back, ducking around cluttered tables and cabinets to reach a tiny workbench, where a single iron pot rests, covered with a large lid.

"This is it?" I ask skeptically as Runa takes the lid off and peers at the concoction inside.

"It's a test batch," she says. "Obviously I'm not going to make a giant vat of this stuff until I'm sure that it works."

"Fair enough," I say. "So what now?"

Runa reaches for a long, slender spoon and gives the potion a few quick stirs, the blue light of her gift flowing around her. "Consistency is good," she murmurs, more to herself than to me. "Smell is fresh. Should be ready to add the gold." She draws one of the vials from her pocket, the gold dust glimmering in the dim light.

"How much do you need to use?" I ask.

"Not sure exactly. But since it's going to vanish at dawn, might as well use it all, right? We can't save it for anything."

"Good point."

Runa dumps both vials of gold dust into the potion and starts stirring. Within moments, it transforms from a brownish-yellow color to a bright, shimmering gold. Pure magical energy radiates from the pot, and I can't help but grin.

"This has to be it," I say. "How could this much magic *not* be the cure?"

"We'll see," Runa says, biting her lip nervously. "I wish I had more time to batch-test. . . ."

"You've done great," I assure her. "This will work. I can feel it. Now we just have to find Lilja."

"There's that 'we' word again," Runa mutters.

"I need you in case it doesn't work. You can see what it does and modify the potion from there, if you need to."

"That means flying on a dragon again, doesn't it?"

I grin. "Want to see if we can go even faster this time?"

Runa closes her eyes. "We're doomed."

TWENTY-ONE

Vin is *very* confused when we whistle for him at Dragon's Point again, but he thumps his tail happily, waiting for us to climb aboard. Overhead, the moon is dipping low in the west, threatening the horizon. Will the potion still work after dawn? Or will the gold dust within it disappear? We hardly have any time left.

"Do you actually know where Lilja is?" Runa asks as we climb onto Vin's back. "I thought Ari took her."

"He did," I say. "But I'm pretty sure he would've just taken her to her den, where she'll be the most comfortable. I know right where it is."

Runa wraps her arms around Vin's front spike and squeezes her eyes shut. "I'm ready," she says.

I give Vin another big push with my gift, and within moments, we ascend.

At this speed, it takes us only a few minutes to reach the

stretch of volcanoes that the dragons call home. I direct Vin toward Lilja's den, and he swoops down eagerly, happy to be in familiar, comfortable territory. After a bumpy landing that causes Runa to shriek more than once, we clamber down from Vin's back and proceed the rest of the way to Lilja's cave on foot. Vin happily flies to the entrance of his own den and disappears inside.

"I changed my mind," Runa says with a shudder, taking in the landscape around us. "The Realm isn't incredible. It's just terrifying."

Admittedly, the volcanic terrain surrounding us does seem pretty intimidating. The landscape is nothing but rocks and ash, and the volcanoes rise on all sides like they're closing us in. Still, I feel the need to defend the Realm.

"You've only seen the scary parts," I tell her. "Just wait until you see a unicorn, or look at the view off the western cliffs, or—"

"I don't think so," Runa says, breathing heavily as the ground grows steeper. "You can stick to Seeker-ing or whatever it is you do, and I'll stick to the village."

But there's wonder in her eyes as she gazes around, taking in the sights, and I know she doesn't really mean it. If only I really could take Runa with me into the Realm. There are so many things she'd love to see. We could explore the forests, hike the cliffs, fly around the mountain peaks on Lilja's back, find sea wolves and saellons and unicorns. . . .

"You know what I just realized?" I say as we draw closer

to the Valley of Ash. "You're, like, the only person aside from the Seekers who's been here. Ever."

Runa slows, taking in the view. "Okay, it *is* pretty incredible," she concedes, brushing a flake of ash from her cheek. "But also terrifying. First we get attacked by a forest, and now we're going to get eaten by dragons."

"We're not going to get *eaten*," I protest. "Dragons don't eat humans."

"That's a relief."

"I mean, they *would*, but we're a bit difficult for them to digest—"

Runa throws her hands over her ears. "Don't tell me! I do not want to think about it." She glances around again. "How many of them are in these lairs anyway?"

"They're not *lairs*, they're *dens*," I protest. "The Realm's dragon population is small—probably about fifty or sixty altogether."

"Sixty!" Runa's eyes widen. "And they're all here? Right now? Watching us?"

"Well, no, some of them are probably out hunting," I say, and Runa sighs in relief. "But there are usually about ten or fifteen of them who stay behind to guard the dens, plus a lot of them are probably sleeping—"

Runa shudders again. "Just. Stop. Talking. The sooner we get this potion to Lilja and get out of here, the better."

"We're almost there," I say, and it's true. We ascend another slope, dodging the larger rocks that block the route, and make our way across the twisting path that leads to Lilja's den. Runa grumbles something about "paths crumbling under us" and "falling to our deaths" as we climb, but we make steady progress to the top.

"I never knew you were so afraid of everything," I tease her.

"Until this experience, I wasn't," she says grimly.

I expect Lilja's den to be filled with the yellow light of Ari's gift, but it's surprisingly dark. Using our gifts to guide us, Runa and I proceed into the depths of the cave, our footsteps echoing on the rocks. "Lilja?" I whisper.

A soft, sad whimper responds to my voice, and I break into a run. "Lilja! Are you okay?"

Her silver scales glimmer in the green light of my gift as I reach her. She's curled up in a ball, her head resting on her tail. She doesn't rise to greet me, which is how I know she's really sick. Her eyes fix on me, and her pupils are nearly black, with only a few remaining flecks of yellow.

"Hurry, Runa, hurry!" I yell. Runa rushes up behind me, blue gift swirling as she holds up the vial of potion.

"Um, how do I give it to her?" Runa asks, glancing back and forth between Lilja's massive jaws and the tiny vial of liquid.

"Hang on," I say, letting my gift mix with Lilja's. Her energy is weaker than I've ever seen before, barely responding to my magic. The heavy blackness of the plague is spreading through her life source, weighing it down. "It's okay, Lil," I murmur. "Runa's going to help you, all right? You just have to take this potion, and then you'll feel better."

I direct my gift at Lilja's jaws and gently give her a nudge, encouraging her to open her mouth. She protests at first, turning her head away from me, but she doesn't have the energy to keep it up. After only a moment, she opens her mouth wide.

She must *really* be sick if she's not even going to be stubborn about it.

"Just pour it on her tongue," I tell Runa, who's staring at Lilja's teeth with wide eyes. "She won't bite you, I promise."

"Likely story," Runa grumbles as she tears the cork from the potion vial and steps closer to Lilja. "'How did you lose your arm, Runa?' 'Oh, you know, I just stuck it in a dragon's mouth like a total fool. . . .'"

"Hurry," I say. I know Runa isn't really scared. She's healed Lilja before, after all. If anything, she's probably afraid that her potion isn't going to work.

I'm afraid it isn't going to work. But I can't think about that. It has to work. There's no alternative. No backup plan. Just this.

Runa takes a deep breath and steps toward Lilja. In one quick movement, she rushes forward and tilts the vial, letting the golden liquid splash onto Lilja's tongue. The dragon's eyes widen in surprise, and Runa quickly darts away as soon as the last drop falls from the vial. Lilja closes her mouth, considers the situation for a moment, and then swallows.

"How long will it take to work?" I ask, studying Lilja's eyes again. They're still black.

Runa sighs. "This is all experimental, remember? I don't know how long it will take." She hesitates, and I know what she's going to say: *It might not work at all.* But then she closes her mouth and doesn't say anything.

I lean back on my heels. "Well. I guess we wait, then."

Lilja closes her eyes, tucking her head closer to her body like she's taking a nap. I give her scales a soft stroke.

Runa glances around the cave. "Where's Ari, anyway? I thought he'd be here."

I look up. "Good question. I can't believe he'd just leave Lilja like this, not when she's so sick."

"Maybe he saw Agnar and the Vondur and went to get one of the other Seekers for help?"

"Maybe." Still, something about it doesn't feel right. He left Lilja without water? Food? A pile of bilberries, at least? Knowing that she's too weak to leave the den alone? Something doesn't seem right. "He must be getting help," I say, but I don't fully believe myself. "He's been weird lately, so who knows."

"Weird how?" Runa asks. She sits down next to me, no longer pretending to be afraid of Lilja.

"We had a fight," I admit. "I snuck Little Puff out of the quarantine when I wasn't supposed to, and Ari thinks that's probably how Lilja got sick."

Runa studies me for a moment. "Is he right?" she asks softly.

I look down at the floor of the cave, nudging a pebble with my foot. "I don't know," I say. "This plague has been spreading quickly—it's in the water—and I don't know if we managed to quarantine all the affected areas in time. Lilja could have picked it up somewhere else. And Lilja hardly interacted with Little Puff. But it's possible, I guess. And since Ari didn't want me entering the Realm alone at all, let alone sneaking magical creatures out of it, he got all mad about it."

"I can see why," Runa says, her tone gentle. "Lilja is his dragon too. You should've decided on these kinds of risks together."

"That's the problem. We *couldn't* decide together, because he didn't listen to anything I said. None of the Seekers do. Every time I pointed out that we needed to do more, they ignored me."

"But it's not your job to single-handedly save the Realm, Bryn. The Seekers are supposed to work as a team, aren't they?"

I sigh. "Yeah, but how am I supposed to work with people who don't want to work with me? Who don't think of me as a teammate?"

"You do it by proving that you're their teammate."

"That's what I was trying to do!"

Runa raises her eyebrows. "Were you? I think you were trying to prove *yourself*, sure. But as an individual, not as a team player. You've already proved that you're a good Seeker, Bryn. You've saved the whole Realm before! We all know that. But you have to prove you're good at being a member of the team, too. That means listening to what the others have to say, and compromising, and helping the whole group.

Doing your own thing without listening to the others doesn't prove to them that you can be a Seeker."

"Curing the plague does," I say, but my heart sinks. Is Runa right? Did I mess everything up by not listening to the Seekers? Maybe it *is* my fault that Lilja got sick. I never should've taken the risk of introducing her to Little Puff. Is she going to pay for my mistake?

Something echoes in the back of my mind, and it takes a moment to place the words:

They never would have listened to me. I have to prove to them that I have always had the Realm's best interests at heart.

It sounds like something I would've said about the Seekers' rules. But it wasn't me who said that tonight. It was Agnar.

Maybe I've been acting too much like him all along—thinking that the rules don't apply to me and that only I know what's best for the Realm. I should've known better.

"Excuse me, which one of us actually made the cure?" Runa jokes, interrupting my thoughts. "*I* cured the plague, thank you very much."

"Yeah, but I—"

Lilja snorts suddenly, and both Runa and I turn toward her. She shifts her weight, her eyes still closed, and snorts again, a gust of hot air bursting from her nose.

"Something's happening!" I say, leaping to my feet.

Runa and I watch, hardly daring to breathe, as Lilja slowly, slowly opens her eyes.

TWENTY-TWO

Runa gasps. I blink, making sure I'm not imagining it. Lilja's eyes are yellow again.

"It worked!" Runa whispers. "It worked!"

Lilja yawns and sits up, gazing around the den as if seeing it for the first time. She stretches her wings and shakes her head, her scales glistening. I move my gift closer to her life source, and a familiar warm energy rushes to greet me.

"You did it, Runa! This is the cure!"

She grins. "I can't believe it worked!"

"We have to get this to the rest of the creatures right away! How much is left?"

Runa gestures toward her bag. "Just the rest of that bottle," she says. "But it didn't take much to cure Lilja, and I'm sure the smaller creatures will need even less. We just have to get it to them before sunrise."

I gulp. In my worry for Lilja, I'd nearly forgotten—the gold dust in the potion might disappear by dawn. "Let's get moving," I say immediately, cutting our celebration short. "We need to get the other Seekers to help us find Agnar and the Vondur, and then we need to start giving the potion to the gyrpuffs and the icefoxes."

"Do you think Lilja's well enough to fly us already?" Runa asks, studying her. Lilja tilts her head to the side curiously, probably recognizing her name.

"I'm not sure," I say. "But she's better trained than Vin. Let's see if we can coax her out of here. If not, we'll call Vin instead."

It turns out that Lilja doesn't need much coaxing. Although her energy does feel more depleted than normal, she's still wide awake and eagerly follows me out of the cave. She happily snaps up the bilberries I offer her, and within moments we emerge from her den into the rocky landscape outside.

"What's that light?" Runa asks as we step out. "Is it sunrise already?"

I follow her gaze and spot it—a flickering yellow light in the distance, near some of the larger dragon dens. At first I think it's Ari, but it looks more like—

"Torches," I whisper, watching the way the light flickers. "Someone up there's using torches."

"The other Seekers?" Runa asks. "Maybe Ari brought—"

"No," I say, my voice sharp as fear slides down my spine. "Seekers don't use torches. We don't need to when we have our gifts. It's got to be Agnar and the Vondur."

Runa freezes, and Lilja stiffens as she picks up on our moods. "What would they be doing here?" she whispers. "They've already spread the plague. What more do they want?"

"I don't know. But we need help. We have to get out of here and find the other Seekers before—"

A shout echoes through the valley, and suddenly one of the flickering torches charges right at us.

It's too late. They know we're here.

"Quick, get on Lilja!" I shout to Runa, scrambling up the dragon's back. I pull Runa behind me as Lilja charges forward, snapping her wings open. I don't even have to give her directions. She picks up on my panic and acts instantly.

But we're too late. Another dragon blocks Lilja's path, and she doesn't have enough room to take off. A hooded figure sits on the dragon's back, a flickering torch held in one hand. More torchlights are visible in the distance, growing closer.

"You'd better leave now!" I shout. "All of the Seekers are here!"

The figure doesn't respond, but the other dragon snarls suddenly, baring his teeth. It's hard to make out his features in the dark, but I don't recognize him—his scales are a dull, mossy green. He's not very big—close to Vin's size. Lilja bristles, spikes rising along her back, and I wish Ari were here to keep control of her emotions—

"Bryn!" a familiar voice shouts, and I glance toward the torchlights in the distance. That was Ari!

"Bryn?" Runa whispers from behind me. "What's happening?"

"Hold on," I mutter, tightening my grip on Lilja's spike and summoning more of my magic. "I think this just became a rescue mission."

I give Lilja a nudge with my gift, and she lunges to the side, startling the other dragon, who rears back, creating just enough room for Lilja to slip past him. The sudden movement extinguishes the rider's torch, and I can't make out the figure anymore.

"Hurry!" I shout to Lilja, guiding her toward the other lights, where I heard Ari's voice.

Lilja whips her tail toward the green dragon, causing him to snarl again, but he doesn't stop us as Lilja rushes forward. The rider clearly doesn't have much control as the dragon snaps his jaws and lashes out so quickly, he almost sends his rider tumbling off his back. Luckily, Lilja is too fast and breaks away from the other dragon, running so hard that the earth trembles beneath her steps.

"Bryn!" Ari shouts again. "Lilja!"

Lilja's ears whip up as she recognizes the voice and charges straight toward him. As we draw closer to the flickering lights, I can make out more shadows, more torches. I don't see any more dragons, so maybe they're only in control of one. . . .

But there's something dark and thick in the air, a feeling I recognize instantly as Vondur magic. I don't know enough about how their magic works to know what kind of threat they might pose, and we're clearly outnumbered—there are at least four or five Vondur. And Agnar's probably lurking around somewhere. I have to get Ari out of here and get the other Seekers—

"Over here!" Ari shouts, and his gift flares up in the darkness. One of the Vondur charges toward him, but he backs off as Lilja emerges from the darkness, roaring at the top of her lungs. Ari is huddled on the ground, hidden behind a large cluster of rocks. As Lilja passes by, he leaps to his feet and scrambles toward us. Runa reaches down, grabs his hand, and hauls him up onto Lilja's back.

"What happened?" I shout to him as Lilja turns, snapping her jaws at the nearest torch-bearing Vondur. "What's going on?"

"I was headed for Gulldrik's den," Ari explains, gasping for breath, "to get him to fly me back to Dragon's Point. I was going to ask the other Seekers for help with Lilja once I got her settled in her den. But then I heard the Vondur coming, and I couldn't get to the den without them seeing me. I've been trapped back there, hoping they wouldn't notice me and trying to figure out what they're doing."

Another Vondur approaches Lilja, waving his torch. She takes one look at it and huffs. Her breath extinguishes the flame in a single gust.

"What *are* they doing?" Runa asks.

"Take out all the torches!" Ari shouts. "They're using magic to—"

His warning comes a second too late. One of the Vondur raises a torch into the air and shouts something that sounds like a spell or an incantation. Within seconds, flames explode from the lit torch, filling the air with fire. I duck behind Lilja's neck as heat surrounds us, and the flames quickly coalesce into a twisting, writhing shape.

A dragon soars through the air above us, sparks shooting from the tips of its wings, made entirely of fire.

For a moment, none of us can speak. Then Ari finishes his sentence. "They're using magic to set the dragon dens on fire."

TWENTY-THREE

The fire soars above us, filling the sky, sparks raining down. It looks just like a dragon, its wings beating, its jaws gaping wide. More flames pour from its mouth.

"I couldn't stop them alone," Ari says, almost apologetically. "I tried to use my empathy gift, but there were too many of them—"

"It's okay," I say quickly. "You were right to wait for help. Now, what are we going to do about *that*?" I point to the sky.

Lilja lets out a low rumble, somewhere between a warning and a whine, and watches the fire-dragon. The crests on her back shoot upward, signaling danger.

"But dragons breathe fire," Runa says. "Aren't they immune to it? Do their scales protect them?"

"Yes," I say. "That's why they live near the volcanoes. They *like* fire."

"Then why burn them out?" Runa asks, and she makes a

good point. Lilja snarls as another Vondur tries to approach us, and the fire-dragon overhead lets out another burst of flame. Luckily, the Vondur seem more focused on controlling their fiery creation than on us.

"I think they're trying to smoke the dragons out of the dens," Ari says. "I don't know why, but they've been trying to get the dragons to come out."

The fire-dragon lets out a sudden, booming roar. The sound fills the valley, and for a second I think it's just the echo—but no.

The dragons of the Realm are responding.

As smoke fills the air, I catch sight of one dragon emerging from the caves—then another, and another. Gleaming yellow eyes peer down from gaping holes in the rock walls surrounding us. Vin emerges, red scales gleaming, looking around with his spikes raised and letting out his own attempt at a threatening roar, which comes out more like a squeak. The valley is filled with heat and smoke. I wipe the sweat from my brow.

The Vondur have grouped together in the center of the valley, all except the one riding the green dragon, who is watching like a sentinel at the far end, blocking the only wide escape point. The Vondur are chanting something, and I can practically taste their magic on my tongue, as thick as the smoke in the air.

As the chanting continues, the Vondur form a rough circle, and suddenly I realize where they're standing and gasp.

"What is it?" Ari asks, following my gaze.

"The water. They poisoned the water. They're using the plague!"

Ari and Runa both follow my gaze, and Ari's eyes widen in understanding. "They're beside the water," he says.

Sure enough, the Vondur have grouped themselves around the large, warm pool that bubbles up from the fissure beneath the easternmost mountain. It's the primary source of water for the dragons when they're in their dens, and probably the main reason they haven't gotten sick from the plague yet. This pool doesn't connect to the stream I found before that was contaminated by the plague. This water is clean . . . or *was* clean, until now.

"They poisoned the water, and now they're forcing the dragons to drink it," I say, and Ari nods.

"Why would the dragons drink it?" Runa asks, looking from me to Ari and back again.

"They may be immune to fire," I say, "but even dragons get thirsty when exposed to a lot of smoke. The Vondur are trying to smoke them out of their dens and lure them to the water."

"What do we do?" Runa asks. Both she and Ari are looking at me.

I take a deep breath and regret it, nearly choking on the smoke. I cough to clear my throat.

"Okay," I say. "On the count of three, we need to steer Lilja toward Vin. Once we reach him, Runa, you can jump on Vin's back. Then Ari and I will charge the Vondur together on Lilja. If we distract them long enough, we can at least keep them from chanting and get them away from the water. Then we'll try to set a boundary spell around it to keep the dragons from drinking. In the meantime, Runa, you need to fly Vin out of here. Go to Dragon's Point, then run to the chapel and ring the bells. That will call the other Seekers to us."

"But I don't know how to fly a dragon!" Runa protests.

"You've seen me do it now," I say. "Did you see how I used my gift to direct Vin before?"

"Yeah . . . ," Runa says slowly.

"You can do it. I know you can."

"Don't overthink it," Ari adds. "It's all about instinct."

"Why can't you fly Vin?" Runa asks, looking at him.

"Because only the two of us know how to set boundary spells," I say, "and if something should happen to one of us while we fend off the Vondur . . . well, the other might need to set boundary spells alone," I say grimly. "You've got this, Runa!"

She doesn't look sure, but we don't have time for any more arguing. I tighten my grip on Lilja and summon more of my gift. Ari's magic joins me in circling Lilja's energy. "One," he says.

"Two," I say.

We move our gifts at the same time and speak in unison. "Three!"

Lilja charges forward, roaring. Her claws scrape against the blackened, rocky ground. As she moves, the fire-dragon suddenly dives toward us, heat filling the air. For a second I think the flame is going to rain down on us, but a burst of blue light suddenly fills the air, emanating from Runa. Her gift must startle the Vondur controlling the dragon, because it stops its attack for a moment—and a moment is all Lilja needs. She tears across the valley, heading straight for Vin, who rushes out to meet her.

"Get ready!" I shout to Runa. "Jump!"

Lilja pulls up beside Vin, and Runa leaps, flying through the air and landing on Vin's back. She nearly slides off, but at the last second she manages to grab hold of one of his spikes and hauls herself up. The blue light of her gift fills the air again, and within moments Vin darts away, spreading his wings and preparing for takeoff. I can only hope Vin has enough energy to get Runa all the way to the Point and that she understands how to steer him—

"Look out!" Ari yells, and I duck as Lilja spins around, dodging a blast of flame. The fire-dragon is overhead, pouring fire down on us.

"Why couldn't I have been a defender?" Ari mutters. "I could so use a shield right now!"

"Ari, that's brilliant!" I say. "Can you make a boundary around us to keep the flames out?"

"You're the naturalist!" he shouts back as Vin takes to the air at the far end of the valley, narrowly dodging the green dragon still waiting there and soaring into the sky. "Isn't fire supposed to be your thing?"

I sigh. "All right. You steer Lilja toward the water, and I'll work on it!"

I close my eyes, anchor my gift in the life sparks of the dragons around us, and picture what we need. I imagine the flames shooting toward us from all directions—and I imagine a burst of water dousing anything that comes close. I try to pull the water from the air, which is no easy task. The fire-dragon has nearly sucked the air dry. But it's the only thing I can think of. Any water in the ground might be poisoned with the plague, and I have no idea how that might affect it.

I can feel Lilja running and keep my hands wrapped tightly around her spike, but I don't open my eyes. One of the Vondur shouts, so we must be getting close, but I can't peek. I have to focus. I need more water from the air, more and more and more—

"Now, Lil!" Ari shouts. I picture the boundary spell one final time, and when it feels right, I open my eyes. Lilja is bearing down on a Vondur, swiping in his direction with her claws. He ducks, and she spins around, heading for the water. A burst of flame heads straight toward us from the fire-dragon overhead.

"Did you do it?" Ari shouts.

"I hope so!" I yell back, watching the flames descend.

Just before they reach us, my water shield works. It bursts over our heads, maintaining a steady stream that gradually douses the flame. Real fire wouldn't go out so quickly, but this is a test of magic, and the water is stronger.

Lilja leaps past one of the Vondur and reaches the edge of the bubbling pool, snapping her jaws at anyone who tries to get close.

"I'll do the spell this time," Ari volunteers, and I nod.

"I'll hold them off. Just keep the dragons away from the water—including Lilja!"

"Is she . . . ? Did you cure her?" he asks.

"Oh, yeah. Runa made a potion, and it worked. Tell you about it later!"

I turn my attention to the Vondur magicians closing in on us. Lilja does a pretty good job of fending them off on her own, but I help direct her attention, making sure she's aware of the ones who try to creep up from the side.

Their fire doesn't reach us anymore, but it doesn't stop them from trying—my water spell is constantly extinguishing the flames. They're testing the limits of the spell, trying to see if it'll give out eventually, and they might be right. There's only so much water, and my energy will be spent sooner or later—

"Got it!" Ari shouts. "Spell's done."

"Are you sure it will work?"

"No!"

"I trust you," I say. "Help me with Lil!"

For a moment we fend off the Vondur silently, directing Lilja's attention here and there as the Vondur try to approach. She swipes with her claws, bares her teeth, and shoots wave after wave of fire in their direction. They give up on directing flames toward us, and my water vanishes from above. But the fire-dragon is still shooting flames into the dens, and more and more dragons are emerging all around us. I reach for their energy to replenish my gift, which is fading from using the water shield.

"What are they doing now?" I ask Ari, ducking as Lilja spins around, knocking a torchbearer off their feet with a quick lash of her tail.

"Either they don't know my spell's protecting the water, or they've got a different plan to hurt the dragons," he says.

I glance up at the sky. No sign of Runa or the other Seekers.

"We don't have time to wait for help," I say finally, turning to face Ari. "We need to capture the Vondur ourselves before they hurt the dragons."

"Any ideas?" he asks, his gift swirling around his fingers as we direct Lilja toward the nearest Vondur, who narrowly manages to escape her claws.

"One," I say, "but it's ridiculous."

"When aren't your ideas ridiculous?" he says with a grin.

"I'm serious."

Ari meets my gaze. "I trust you, Bryn."

I swallow hard. "You shouldn't. You were right about everything. I shouldn't have exposed Lilja. I—"

"Doesn't matter now. You cured her. You were right about being able to do that. We've fought the Vondur together before, and we can do it again. What do you need me to do?"

I smile. "I need you to make all of the dragons feel really, *really* angry."

Ari grins back. "This does sound like a terrible plan," he says. "But I can do it."

"Okay. You make them angry, and I'll direct them. Got it?"

Ari nods. Above us, the fire-dragon lets out another roar as it blasts a cavern with flames. The earth trembles beneath us, and ash tumbles from the sky.

We close our eyes and cast our gifts out wide.

TWENTY-FOUR

The dragons' life sparks are easy to find, surrounding us on all sides. I can't read their emotions the way Ari can, but I can sense the effect of whatever he's doing with his gift—their energy is moving fiercely, roiling like waves on a stormy sea. I let my gift bleed into them all, letting them sense my intentions. Vondur magic is in the air too, but mine and Ari's is familiar to them. They accept us even as they push the Vondur away and resist their magic.

One by one, I bond my gift with the dragons of the Realm. One by one, I guide them forward.

And they respond.

Dragons swoop down from the caves, filling the air with wild roars and the frantic drumbeats of their wings. Plumes of fire rain down on the Vondur, and the fire-dragon above loses its form as the Vondur magicians shift their focus. Two of the magicians run toward the caves, seeking shelter, only to be stopped by a majestic blue dragon whose roar sends them to their knees.

Suddenly a shout rises up, and I follow their gaze to the sky. Four dragons are racing toward the valley, coming from the direction of Dragon's Point.

Runa brought reinforcements.

Seeker Larus, flying his golden dragon, lands first, directly beside Lilja. Seeker Ludvik and Seeker Freyr, both on their own dragons, land on the other side of the Vondur, strengthening the barricade. Lastly, Vin arrives, a smiling Runa on his back, and lands on Lilja's other side. Vin tosses his neck and snorts happily, like he's proud of himself.

The rest of the Vondur run toward the far end of the valley, where their moss-green dragon is still waiting. Ludvik and Freyr immediately begin casting boundary spells, preventing the Vondur from leaving the valley.

Suddenly the moss-green dragon leaps into the air, the rider on its back directing it. The dragon passes over the group of Vondur and lands directly in front of Gulldrik and Seeker Larus. Now that the green dragon has come closer, its rider is finally visible.

Agnar.

"It doesn't have to be this way, Larus," Agnar says, like he's negotiating.

"You're right," Larus says, and his voice sounds sad. "It didn't."

Without warning, the red light of Agnar's gift flares toward Seeker Larus.

"Look out!" I shout, and Seeker Larus ducks.

Ari glances at me, and I nod. We coordinate without needing to speak, reaching for the green dragon with our gifts. Agnar is distracted by attacking Seeker Larus and is not paying attention to his dragon. Vondur magic is all tangled into the dragon's life source, but he's watching the chaos with wide, confused eyes.

Ari and I flood the moss-green dragon with our gifts, drawing strength from the rest of the dragons, and Agnar's hold on him breaks. The dragon rears up, sending Agnar tumbling from his back. The dragon snarls and leaps into the air, out of Agnar's reach.

There's no escape now. Agnar and the Vondur will never make it far on foot, and they need a dragon to get out of the Realm.

"We've done it!" I shout to Ari, but he shakes his head.

"We can't let them leave the valley! What if they contaminate more of the water?"

I bite my lip. "We have a cure for the plague now . . . ," I start, but then I glance at the sky, noticing how quickly the moon is descending. "But I don't know for sure if it will work after dawn."

"What?" Ari shouts, but I don't have time to explain about the Fairy's Gold.

"You're right. We have to stop them before they infect any more creatures!"

"Are you thinking what I'm thinking?" he asks, looking up at the angry dragons around us.

"I think so," I say, wiping an ashy lock of hair from my face. "Let's do it."

Agnar is down but not out. He's still using his gift to attack Seeker Larus, who continues to fend him off. Seeker Ludvik and Seeker Freyr are at the far end of the valley, blocking the exit. But the Vondur outnumber them, and casting boundary spells is time-consuming. They need help.

Together, Ari and I use our gifts to guide the dragons into the air. The blue dragon and a plum-colored one go first, circling the valley and landing in a line in front of the Vondur, cutting off their escape. At the same time, Ari and I move Lilja to cut them off from behind, and Runa steers Vin beside us. Stretching my gift as much as I can, I reach for two more dragons to follow us, flanking Lilja and Vin on either side.

Without Ari, I don't know if I could handle this many dragons at once. Their life sources give me more strength than I would've thought possible, but spreading my gift across the whole valley leaves me feeling stretched thin, my attention drawn to a hundred places at once. But Ari helps fill in the gaps, nudging dragons forward when my control slips, and I do the same for him, noticing where his gift is weakest. We work together. As a team.

We guide the army of dragons across the valley, trapping the Vondur on all sides.

A few of them are trying spells, I think, though I don't understand the words of their enchantments. But most of them have stopped trying to fight. They're watching the dragons with wide eyes, searching for any possible escape. Even the moss-green dragon remains on our side, roaring at any Vondur who dares to get too close.

When Lilja gets within speaking range, I bring her to a halt and stand up on her back, showing the Vondur that I'm in complete control of her.

"We are Seekers of the Wild Realm," I yell, "and we will defend it."

One of the Vondur sends a spiral of flame toward us, but my boundary spell bursts into life again, dousing it. The Vondur murmur among themselves, but I don't think they're casting spells this time. They're trying to find a way out.

I glance behind us. Seeker Larus finally seems to have gotten the best of Agnar, who's now trapped behind a glowing boundary spell. Seeker Larus slides down from Gulldrik's back and approaches the remaining Vondur, drawing himself up to his full height. "What brings you to our lands?" he says. One of the Vondur responds, but his voice is so low I can't hear it. Seeker Larus says something else, his tone harsher, and several of the Vondur call out responses, seemingly defending themselves. After a moment, Seeker Larus declares, "You were exiled from this land a few months ago after attempting to take it from us. Then, we let you go freely. But now you have poisoned our lands and tried to kill our creatures. We cannot be so lenient."

Around us, the dragons are shifting restlessly. They're probably still worked up after Ari stoked their emotions. He seems to be thinking the same thing and leans toward me to whisper, "Should I start calming them down?"

"Seems like a good idea," I whisper back, not wanting to interrupt the grand speech Seeker Larus is now giving the Vondur. "Why don't you try to calm them, and I'll start leading them back to their dens? The boundary spell should contain the Vondur, and I'm sure Seeker Larus has them under control."

Then I turn to Runa, who's waiting patiently on Vin's back. "How was your flight?" I ask, grinning at her.

"Fast," she grumbles. "I'm never doing any favors for you ever again. You owe me times one million."

"I'm about to owe you one million more," I say. "We still have a job to do. It's almost dawn."

She nods. "I don't know if we have enough time for the potion to work."

"We have to try. Just let me lead these dragons back to their homes, and then we'll start giving out the potion as fast as we can."

Ari and I quickly start calming the dragons and leading them to their dens. Fortunately, the Vondur flames seem to have died down now that they're not actively using their magic, and the boundary spell around the contaminated water seems to be holding, for none of them approach it. Meanwhile, the older Seekers converse with each other and the Vondur, making some sort of arrangement.

Finally, I turn to Runa, who hasn't been idle—she's poured the potion into several smaller vials and passes one to Ari and one to me. "We'll be able to cover more ground if we split up," she says. "I just need someone to show me where to go."

"Okay," I say. "Ari, how about you head for the icefoxes on Lilja? I'll fly with Runa on Vin to the gyrpuff cliffs. Once we're there, Runa, you and I can tackle separate nests."

"All right," Ari says, gazing at the shimmering potion. "How much do I give them?"

"It's strong," I say. "One vial was enough to cure Lilja, so you should be able to split it among the icefoxes with no problem."

I hop down from Lilja's back, and Ari takes off immediately. Seeker Larus glances up in surprise, watching him go, and I quickly approach him to explain.

"We have a cure for the plague," I say, and all three Seekers stare at me in surprise. "It's a long story, and we don't have much of it, and we only have until dawn to administer it. If you've got everything under control here, Ari and Runa and I are going to find the sick creatures and give them all the cure."

"Of course," Seeker Larus says. "Go at once. We can

all meet at my hut when we're done with our tasks to discuss, yes?"

"All right," I say.

Seeker Larus nods toward Runa, who's still waiting for me on Vin's back. "Bring your friend to the meeting as well." He says it with no emotion, so I can't tell how much trouble we're in. Probably a lot.

I join Runa, and we quickly take to the air. A few minutes later, Vin lands at the edge of the quarantine zone, and I lead Runa down the cliffs. She has quite a few complaints for me when she sees how far down the cliffside we have to climb, but she handles it like a pro. I direct her to one of the larger gyrpuff nests before continuing to the very first sick gyrpuff myself.

I find him in the same place, too feeble to move but still breathing. "Here you go, little guy," I say gently, pulling the stopper from the vial. "I've got something that will make you feel better. I'm just sorry it took me so long."

He pinches my finger the first time I try to coax his beak open, but I finally manage it and pour a few drops of the potion into his mouth. For a moment nothing happens. Then he startles, his whole body trembling. A moment later the black fades from his eyes, and he hops up. He takes a few teetering steps toward the pile of herring I left beside his bed, then hops triumphantly toward it and begins to eat.

"Great job, buddy!" I say. "Glad to see you're feeling better!"

He lets out a happy little caw. I grin and leave him to his dinner.

I reunite with Runa at the top of the cliff, and together we find the remaining nest of infected gyrpuffs and distribute the last of the cure. As the little birds leap to their feet and regain their sight, the first rays of dawn emerge on the horizon.

"We did it," Runa says, throwing her arms up in triumph. "We did it!"

"Mostly it was you," I say. "You're the one who came up with the cure!"

She shrugs. "You gave me all the ingredients and told me what to put in. I just mixed it all together and added a little healing gift. *And* you're the one who led an army of dragons to attack the Vondur while I was off ringing some church bells and finding the other Seekers."

"We couldn't have done this without your potion and your healing gift," I argue. "*And* you flew a dragon by yourself without any help, *and* you brought reinforcements when we needed them. Are you sure you want to be a doctor instead of a Seeker? 'Cause I think you'd be pretty good at the job."

She laughs. "Last I heard, this was a job without any openings. Besides, if I've learned anything tonight, it's that you do *way* too much climbing on a daily basis. I'm not sure which is worse—scaling volcanic rock to find dragon dens or climbing down cliffs to gyrpuff nests." She shudders. "And I prefer riding horses over riding dragons, thank you."

Vin gives an indignant snort, and I laugh. "Well, if you

change your mind, there probably *will* be a vacancy after the meeting we're about to have. Pretty sure bringing a non-Seeker into the Realm is breaking the rules. Not to mention all the other rules I broke."

Runa's smile fades. "Do you think they'll fire you? *Can* you be fired from being a Seeker?"

"Well, they fired Seeker Agnar, so I guess it's possible." I try to make it sound like a joke, but I'm not entirely kidding.

Runa's eyes widen. "They *exiled* Seeker Agnar. Do you think they'll do that to you?"

"Of course not. I didn't lead Vondur into the Realm, at least! Surely it isn't an exile-able offense."

Runa looks unconvinced. "So what should we do?"

"Right now all we can do is meet the other Seekers and see how angry they are with me."

"We? I'm invited?"

"Seeker Larus requested your presence," I say gravely.

"Oh great, that means I'm in trouble too!"

"Probably," I say with a grin. "But at least we'll be in trouble together!"

Runa sighs. "I don't know why I let you talk me into these things."

I give her a nudge with my shoulder. "Because it's always an adventure!"

"That's one word for it."

"Hey, I owe you two million favors. I won't forget."

She laughs. "I'm pretty sure we're up to two *billion*."

TWENTY-FIVE

Dawn lights up the sky as Runa and I arrive at Seeker Larus's hut, where the rest of the Seekers, including Ari, have assembled. Now that the excitement is over, everyone looks exhausted—deep shadows line Seeker Freyr's eyes, Ari can barely keep his open, and Seeker Ludvik is cradling his mug of tea like a lifeline.

Seeker Larus greets us as Runa and I step through the door, and he doesn't seem angry with us—yet. He presses mugs of steaming tea into our hands and ushers us to the seating area, where we droop onto the couch beside Ari.

"I know it's been a long night," Seeker Larus says, settling into his armchair, "so let's try to keep this brief, but there are some urgent matters that we must attend to. First, has the cure been administered to all of the creatures?"

"Yes," I say. "Runa and I gave it to all of the sick gyr-puffs we could find. But there might be more we were unaware of. I'd suggest doing a full sweep of the area tomorrow—er, today—to check for any others."

Seeker Larus nods. "And the icefoxes?"

Ari straightens. "All taken care of," he says. "The mama and her cubs recovered right away." He looks like he's about to say something else, but then Seeker Freyr cuts in impatiently.

"We need a decision about the Vondur, Larus. This cannot be allowed to continue. We were lenient last time, against my better judgment, you may recall, and look what has happened."

Seeker Larus doesn't look surprised at this outburst. "You're right. Stronger action must be taken, now that they have ignored our warning. But what would you suggest? We don't have the means to imprison them here. If we exile them again, how do we prevent them from returning?"

"This is the same discussion we had before," Seeker Ludvik says, gripping his mug. "We have no other option than to banish them and strengthen our guard of the island."

"But we tried that before, and clearly it *didn't work*," says Seeker Freyr.

"I have a question," I say, trying to cut into the argument.

"Freyr, what do you propose—" Seeker Ludvik says, not hearing me.

I set down my mug and rise to my feet, clearing my throat loudly. Finally, I have their attention. "Excuse me," I say, "but can I ask how, exactly, Agnar and the Vondur came back? I don't think we can debate how to prevent them from returning if we don't understand how they did it in the first place."

A beat of silence fills the hut, and heat floods my cheeks. I sit down abruptly, but then Seeker Larus nods. "An excellent point, Seeker," he says. "I had the same thought myself. While you were administering the cure to the gyrpuffs, I questioned the Vondur and asked the same thing. Most were reluctant to speak to me, but I believe I convinced a few of them to tell me the truth, and their story makes sense."

"That dragon," Seeker Ludvik says. "Where did it come from?"

Seeker Larus leans back in his armchair. "It seems we made one critical error last time. We saw them fly into the Realm on Vin before, and we assumed that they had successfully stolen a dragon egg with the help of former Seeker Agnar. What we did not think to ask was whether that was the *only* egg they had stolen."

"Agnar tried to take Lilja's egg first, but Ari stopped him . . . ," I say slowly.

Seeker Larus nods. "When Agnar failed to steal Lilja's egg, he tried again with Vin—and again, with this green dragon. The green one was not old enough at the time of the third trial to fly them to the Realm, so they left him on the mainland and used Vin alone. We didn't think to wonder whether Vin was the only baby dragon in their possession."

"Agnar said something about that last time," I say,

remembering the conversation. "He said the reason he sabotaged the second trial was to delay the competition—because the dragon wasn't ready yet. We thought he meant Vin, but maybe he was thinking of this dragon too. He tried to delay the competition so that both of them would be ready."

"So when their first attack failed," Seeker Ludvik muses, "they retreated to the mainland *with Agnar*, who we exiled and who could teach them everything they needed to know about training the green dragon for a second attempt on the Realm."

"That's why this one was better trained," I say. "Vin was in chains when they brought him to the island, and injured and underfed. I didn't notice any of that with the green dragon, and one of the Vondur was riding him successfully at one point, while Agnar was following me on the ground. Agnar must have taught them how to fly."

"And when the dragon was ready," Seeker Freyr says gravely, "they tried a second attack. Without a competition to distract us this time, they simply tried to sneak into the Realm at night, when we would be unaware. Agnar knew the Realm well enough to move around without detection."

"*Mostly* without detection," I mutter. I haven't forgotten how the other Seekers dismissed me when I said the Vondur were on the island.

"Excuse me," Runa says quietly. Every head in the room swivels in her direction; it's the first time she's spoken since we arrived. "But what about the plague? Bryn told me it came from Vondur magic. But why would the Vondur want to infect the Realm and kill the creatures? I thought they wanted to claim it for themselves?"

"They do," Seeker Larus explains, "but they have never cared about taking the Realm's creatures *alive*. They have no magic of their own. Their spellwork relies on extracting the magic from objects like, say, unicorn horns or dragon scales. And those items are generally much easier to collect if the creatures they come from are dead."

Runa shudders. "So they caused the plague to kill the Realm, and then planned to fly in on the green dragon and collect their parts?"

"It appears that way," Seeker Ludvik says. "Perhaps the Vondur were somehow responsible for the original plague, all those years ago. They used to trade here, and could have planted something."

"Seems likely," Seeker Larus agrees.

"But I have to wonder . . . ," Seeker Ludvik continues. "Why were they here tonight? The plague hadn't killed any of the creatures yet, and it may have traveled even farther and infected more creatures if they had waited. Our quarantines were failing to contain the spread."

"And how did they manage to introduce the plague into the Realm in the first place?" Seeker Freyr asks.

"Um," I say, "I might know the answer to both those questions." Quickly, I recount how I found Vondur magic in the glacier hidden in the southern cliffs and the mysterious figure I saw in the Realm and tried to pursue before Lilja got sick, who turned out to be Agnar. Then I relay what Agnar said to me after I found the Fairy's Gold.

"In other words," I conclude, "this wasn't their first time in the Realm. I think they've been sneaking in for a while. Agnar or some of the others must have come here to plant the plague in the water, and they've been secretly returning at night to watch the plague spread, see how many creatures have been infected, and watch *us* to see if we had found the cure. That way they could make sure the plague was working and plan their attack."

"So why did they plan it tonight, before the plague had a chance to spread further?" Seeker Freyr asks abruptly.

I try to ignore the interruption. "After I realized that Lilja was sick," I say, "I convinced Runa to come with me into the Realm to find Fairy's Gold. I suspected that it was the missing ingredient from her potion, which could cure the plague. She didn't want to break the rules, but I talked her into coming with me. We found the Fairy's Gold together, and Agnar saw us. He knew we had the cure, and he knew that he had to act before we were able to give it to the infected creatures."

To my surprise, the room has fallen strangely silent, and it takes me a moment to realize why. The Fairy's Gold.

"You're certain that's what you found?" Seeker Ludvik asks after a moment. "Not simply a yellow flower, but one made of gold? Like the legend?"

Seeker Freyr scoffs. "Obviously not like the legend," he says. "It's a fairy tale for children."

"It *was* Fairy's Gold, and it was exactly like the legend," I say. "I found it in the heart of the Realm, and it cured the plague."

"Just because it turned out to be the right cure doesn't mean—" Seeker Freyr starts.

Ari clears his throat so abruptly that Seeker Ludvik jumps and nearly spills his tea. "Seeker Bryn is a naturalist. She knows magical plants better than any of us, and she knows the Realm. If she says it was Fairy's Gold, then I believe her."

"I saw it too," Runa chimes in. "It really was Fairy's Gold."

After a moment, it's Seeker Larus who breaks the silence. "All right," he says. "So what did Agnar do after he caught you with the gold, Seeker Brynja?"

I smile. "That was when Runa and I got away from them and went to put the Fairy's Gold into the potion, so that we could begin curing creatures right away. And that must've been when the Vondur went for the dragons in the Valley of Ash. It was plan B. They knew none of the creatures had died from the plague yet, because they've been monitoring the Realm. So they decided to cut their losses and go after the biggest prize they could, as quickly as they could. They went for the dragons and introduced the plague to their water."

"But how would that work?" Seeker Freyr asks. "It would

have taken days for the plague to kill those dragons, even if they got them to drink the water right away."

"Maybe there was a larger dose in that water that would've killed them quicker?" I suggest.

"Or," Ari says, "maybe they didn't care how long it would take for the dragons to die, as long as they were infected before we could get enough of the cure to save them all."

"And Agnar mentioned something about getting the cure and offering it to us in exchange for something," I add. "I think he thought he could blackmail us into letting him back onto the island or something. Maybe he thought that once all the dragons were sick, we'd agree to his terms in exchange for the cure."

Seeker Larus sits forward. "Regardless of what they were planning," he says, "it is thanks to everyone in this room that they did not succeed. This was a much closer call than any of us would have liked, but I am proud to know that our young Seekers were able to act quickly to prevent catastrophe. Even if one of them does have a penchant for rule-breaking."

He looks directly at me, and I gulp. "I'm sorry I didn't follow the rules. I didn't agree with them, so I thought that made it okay to do what I wanted, but I was wrong. And I'm sorry I brought Runa into the Realm. I know I shouldn't have. But I didn't know how else to cure the plague, and Lilja didn't have time for me to wait for approval. It was all my idea, not Runa's. She's the one who created the cure. The creatures are all safe thanks to her."

The older Seekers exchange glances. "Under ordinary circumstances," Seeker Larus says, "I would consider allowing outsiders into the Realm to be a grave offense, one that might necessitate removal from the Council of Seekers. But these were certainly not ordinary circumstances, and no one can deny the results. Besides, it is clear that the rest of this Council owes you an apology as well; you tried to tell us about the Vondur before, and we didn't listen. We must all endeavor to improve our teamwork in the future. Therefore, if my fellow Council members are in agreement, I am prepared to overlook the infraction—*this time*. But going forward, there will be no more rule-breaking. Are we all in agreement?"

Seeker Ludvik smiles. Seeker Freyr hesitates before giving me a gruff nod.

I turn back to Seeker Larus. "No more breaking the rules," I say. "I promise."

"And, Runa," Seeker Larus says, turning to her, "I believe we are all deeply in your debt. You have managed to create a cure that many Seekers tried and failed to find. I do not know how we can repay you, but if there is anything—anything at all—that we can do for you, please let us know."

Runa blushes. "Thank you, Seeker," she squeaks.

I give her a sharp nudge with my elbow. "Runa wants to be a doctor," I say loudly. "She's an apprentice to the herbalist to learn about medicines, but only because she isn't allowed to apprentice for the doctor. Which is ridiculous, because as you can see, she's the best healer in the village."

"Is that so?" Seeker Larus says. "Well, we can't have the best healer in the village kept out of work. I will speak to Dr. Baldur on your behalf, Runa."

"Thank you, Seeker," Runa says. "But don't waste your time on my behalf. Dr. Baldur has never taken a female apprentice."

Seeker Larus smiles at her. "I will speak to him nonetheless," he says. "And besides, how could he refuse to employ the Council's appointed Healer of the Realm?"

Runa stiffens. "What?"

Seeker Larus exchanges a smile with Seeker Ludvik. "I've been thinking for some time that we needed to appoint someone to a special position," he says. "Seeker Freyr is certainly a skilled healer, and the two of us are able to handle the day-to-day needs of the Realm's creatures. But when there is a widespread illness, like we've seen with this plague, it would help to have someone else we can call on. Someone who is not only a skilled healer but also quite familiar with the Realm, and who has already demonstrated an ability to heal magical creatures."

"You mean . . . ?" Runa's voice trails off in wonder.

"I call an official vote," Seeker Larus says, using his formal voice. "All in favor of appointing Runa, daughter of Benedikt, as the Healer of the Realm?"

My hand shoots into the air immediately, and so does Ari's.

"Aye," Seeker Ludvik says, raising his mug toward Runa in a toast.

"A wise choice," Seeker Freyr says firmly.

"It's settled, then," Seeker Larus says, turning back to Runa. "Assuming you accept the appointment, of course?"

"Of—of course I do," Runa says. "I mean, thank you, everyone. I'm honored."

Seeker Larus claps his hands. "You'll have to forgive us if we postpone the discussion about your official duties in this appointment for another day. I believe it's been a long night, and there are other concerns to attend to first."

Runa nods fervently as Seeker Freyr sits forward. "The *most* pressing concern," he says, "is what we're going to do about Agnar and the Vondur. We can hardly leave them trapped behind a boundary spell forever."

"I have an idea," I say, but before I can continue, Seeker Freyr speaks again.

"And who's to say there aren't even more dragons where this one came from? Who's to say how many eggs or other materials Agnar managed to pilfer before we caught him? We could be dealing with this problem for a long time, unless we take firmer action. I propose—"

Ari clears his throat again. "Sorry, Seeker Freyr," he says, "but I think you interrupted Seeker Bryn. She said she had an idea."

Everyone turns to me, including Ari, who smiles encouragingly.

"I was thinking . . . ," I say. "So we don't have any way to imprison them on the island, and exiling them without imprisoning them doesn't work. But couldn't they be imprisoned on the mainland? The Vondur have been trying to steal land from their neighbors, the Laekens, for a long time, right? They're our trading partners, and they have a court and prison system on the mainland, don't they? So all we have to do is hold the Vondur until the next trading day, and then we can ask the Laekens to take them back to the mainland themselves. I don't think they'd object to imprisoning the very same Vondur they've been trying to capture for years."

The room is quiet for a moment. "I'm not sure I like the idea of relying on others to implement justice," Seeker Ludvik says. "How do we know that the Laekens will treat them fairly and humanely? I won't agree to sending the Vondur to be executed."

Seeker Larus looks thoughtful. "Ordinarily, I'd agree with you, Seeker," he says to Ludvik. "But perhaps we could work out an agreement and make sure the Laekens accept our terms. In all our interactions with them before, they have proven themselves to be trustworthy and have always honored our agreements. I'm not certain they'd be willing, and I'm also unsure whether they have facilities capable of holding someone with Agnar's magical gift. But I think it's worth discussing with them, at the very least. Does everyone agree?"

The rest of us murmur our assent. "Good," Seeker Larus says. "The next question, then, is what to do about the water."

The room falls silent as the meaning of his words sinks in.

"It's all still contaminated," Seeker Freyr says. "The glacier, the stream, the pool in the Valley of Ash. We can set boundary spells to prevent creatures from drinking in those locations, but what if the spells fail? What if the water spreads to other areas? We have no means of combating Vondur magic."

"Actually," Ari says quietly, "I think we still do."

Everyone stares at him, and he shifts uncomfortably in his seat. Seeker Larus says, "Please continue, Seeker Ari."

Wordlessly, Ari reaches into his pocket and withdraws a small vial. Gold glimmers within it. Runa gasps softly.

"It didn't take much of the potion Runa made to cure the icefoxes," Ari says. "I still have plenty of it left over here. I'm not sure if it will still work after dawn, given the legends about Fairy's Gold, but . . . well, it still looks the same, and it hasn't vanished completely, so it might be worth a shot."

The room is suddenly full of energy. Seeker Larus leaps to his feet. "Worth a shot indeed," he says. "I think we should move at once. Seeker Ludvik, could you be prepared to remove the boundary spells around the quarantines if this works?"

Seeker Ludvik rises and sets down his empty mug. "Of course," he says. "I'll fetch Snorri at once."

Seeker Larus turns to me. "Could you return to the glacier where you found the Vondur magic, Seeker Bryn?"

"Yes."

"Good. Why don't you take some of the potion there?

Seeker Ari can help you. Seeker Ludvik, you can take some of the potion to the stream below it, and Seeker Freyr and I will take the remainder to the Valley of Ash. We should move at once."

The room is a flurry of activity as everyone rises and heads for the door. Runa stands back, but I grab her hand. "You're coming with us," I say. "It's your potion; you should be there to see if it works."

"But I'm not . . ."

"Healer of the Realm," I remind her with a grin. She smiles back.

We divide the remainder of the potion into several separate containers that Seeker Larus rummages from his cupboard. I hold a clay jug with a tiny shimmer of liquid gold in the bottom. Seeker Larus takes another jug, and Seeker Ludvik takes the vial with the remainder.

Together, we walk toward Dragon's Point, hoping for one more miracle.

TWENTY-SIX

Lilja is very indignant about this whole situation.

"I know you don't usually carry three people," I say impatiently, "but it's just this *one* time, Lil."

She huffs, looking from Ari to Runa to me. She was excited to see all of us when she and the other Seekers' dragons arrived at the Point, but she's had a long night and is clearly *not* enthusiastic about continuing to fly three people around the Realm.

"I can leave if you need me to," Runa says, but I shake my head.

"Don't worry about it. She's just being dramatic."

Runa bites her lip, looking unconvinced.

Little Puff chooses that exact moment to pop his head up from Runa's pocket and let out a chirp. Runa fetched him from the stable so that we could return him to the gyrpuff nests now that he'll be safe from the plague. He still hasn't shown any symptoms, so it seems likely that he isn't infected.

Lilja's eyes widen at the baby gyrpuff's sudden appearance, and for a second I wonder if she's considering eating him for a snack. Then she lowers her head and lets out a soft, warm breath, ruffling his feathers. Little Puff chirps happily.

Runa stares at Lilja with wide eyes. "Guess they're friends now?" she says.

Ari tosses Lilja a bilberry, his gift sparking around his hands. He sends soothing waves toward Lilja. She looks almost annoyed at being soothed, but she snaps up the bilberries and lowers her back, allowing the three of us—four, counting Little Puff—to climb up.

"That's a good dragon," Ari says, giving her a pat.

"A *ridiculous* dragon," I say, rolling my eyes, and Ari laughs.

Despite her protests, Lilja flies us to the cliffs at her usual speed, and in no time I'm leading Ari and Runa toward the glacier where I first spotted the Vondur magic, following the path of the stream. It looks even worse than it did last time I was here; everything growing along the banks of the stream has shriveled and died, and the water is murky and still.

"Wow," Runa says, gazing sadly at the water. "I never knew anything in the Realm could look so . . . magic-less."

"Your potion's going to fix that," I say. "This place will be full of life in no time."

"You know," Ari says, turning to me, "even if the potion works, we're going to have a lot to do to restore the Realm."

"What do you mean?"

He gestures toward the stream with one hand. "What happened to all the fish who lived in this stream? If the plague killed everything that lived here, we have to reintroduce them. Otherwise, what happens to the creatures who hunt here and rely on this stream for food? Sure, there are others in the Realm, but what if they're used to this territory? We should try to restore things to the way they were before the plague hit, or there could be more problems for the Realm."

"I hadn't thought about that," I admit. "And what about the phoenixes? They moved their nests because of the plague, but their new territory might not be well suited to them. We should make sure they migrate back to their old nests if they need to."

"Right," Ari says. "There's going to be a lot of work to do."

"Well, good thing we've got two of the best Seekers ever to handle the job," I say, grinning at him. "Next time people tell legends about Fairy's Gold, they'll tell the story about *us*."

Ari's eyebrows rise. "Did you just call me one of the best Seekers ever?"

"Of course not. I was referring to myself and Seeker Freyr."

"Very funny," Ari says dryly.

"Um, what about me?" Runa asks. "You Seekers can hardly handle anything on your own. You'll definitely need the Healer of the Realm to sort this mess out."

"That's for sure," I say, grinning at her.

"You know, I think this Healer of the Realm thing is an excellent idea," Ari says. "Now we can just call Runa to do all the hard work, and we can still get all the credit for it!"

Runa scoffs. "As if anyone would ever believe *you* could have done *my* work. I don't think so."

"I think you're onto something, Ari," I say. "Let's make Runa do all the tough chores so we can go play with the dragons every day instead."

"Seekers have chores?" Runa says, wrinkling her nose.

"Oh, sure," I say, exchanging a smile with Ari. "I mean, you've got to feed the icefoxes, defang the sea wolves, and then there's all of that dragon poop to clean up. . . . If you think mucking horse stables is bad, wait until you see all the dragon dens!"

"*Ewww,*" Runa protests. She stomps ahead of us. "That's it, I'm not doing a single favor for any Seeker ever again. Do your own chores and count me *out.*"

Ari and I burst into laughter. "You think she actually believes that?" he whispers to me.

I shrug.

"*Defang the sea wolves? Really?*"

"I was making it up as I went along."

We laugh again. Ahead of us, Runa huffs loudly.

Ari's expression grows serious, and he turns to me again. "Does this mean you're not still mad at me?"

I slow my pace, staring at him. "I thought *you* were mad at *me*."

"Oh, I was," he says. "I can't believe you put Lilja at risk like that."

I close my eyes and take a deep breath. I've been trying not to think about how sick Lilja was, about her eyes turning black. We came so close to losing her, and it was all my fault. I'll never take any risks with her again.

"I'm sorry," I say. "You were right about that. I wanted to save the Realm so badly that I didn't stop to think, and that put Lilja in danger. If we hadn't gotten the cure . . . if anything had happened to her . . . It would've been my fault. I'm sorry. I should've listened to you."

Ari nods once. "Lilja might have gotten it anyway," he acknowledges. "But neither of us should be careless about protecting her. And I could've helped you with that if you'd let me."

"You're right. I . . . I forgot that we're supposed to be a team. It's just, ever since the competition, I kind of feel like I've been on my own. Becoming a Seeker, proving I can do the job, taking care of the Realm . . . It's important to me, and I felt like I had to do it all alone. Like I didn't have anyone on my side."

"I've always been on your side," Ari says quietly. "Even during the competition, remember?"

I nod. "I'm sorry. From now on, I won't forget that we're a team. When we have big decisions to make, we make them together. And I'll never be careless when it comes to Lilja. I promise."

"And," Ari says, "I'm sorry too. You were right that sometimes the other Seekers don't listen to you and that I should've stood up for you. You were right about the Fairy's Gold, about being able to find a cure, all of it. We should've listened more."

"I appreciate what you did at the meeting," I say. "When you backed me up about the Fairy's Gold and when you pointed out that Seeker Freyr interrupted me and made them listen."

Ari nods. "You're always good at making yourself heard. But I'll always back you up when you need me to. I should've been doing that more. I guess I wanted to prove myself to the other Seekers too. That's probably why I didn't speak up before."

"We don't have to completely agree on everything in the meetings," I say. "We're going to have different opinions sometimes, and that's fine. We just need to do better at listening to each other."

"Agreed," Ari says. He offers me his hand. "Teammates?"

"Teammates," I say, and we shake.

"Hey, Seekers!" Runa calls from ahead of us. "Are you planning to chitchat all day? You have work to do!"

Ari laughs. "Why do I get the feeling we're going to regret giving Runa so much power?"

I grin. "She's going to keep us in line, that's for sure."

"Let's go, people! Move it!" Runa yells. Little Puff lets out a screech from her pocket.

We laugh and race after her.

We take a detour to the gyrpuff nests on our way to the glacier so we can say goodbye to Little Puff. When we arrive, a surprise is waiting for us.

The gyrpuff who was sick before now sits in the nest outside the cave, his feathers looking bright and healthy, his eyes gleaming orange. He's already made himself comfortable in the nest, and he lets out a happy shriek when he sees us.

"Hey, little guy," I say. "Feeling better?"

"I don't think it's us he wants to see," Runa says. She reaches into her pocket and withdraws Little Puff, who wriggles in her hands. "Is it okay to set him down?"

"Yes," I say. "Gyrpuffs are very social, and they love their babies. I have a feeling Little Puff will be safe with this one as his guardian."

Runa sets Little Puff down carefully. He takes a tentative hop forward, then another, then another.

The grown gyrpuff watches him for a moment, head tilted to the side. He lets out a series of croaking sounds, and Little Puff responds with chirps.

Runa sighs in relief as the grown gyrpuff nudges Little Puff gently with his beak and smoothly tucks him under his wing.

Ari and I grin at each other. "Looks like they're going to be the best of friends," I say.

"Bye, Little Puff," Runa calls. "Grow up nice and healthy, okay?"

Little Puff chirps happily, nestling against his new friend.

With one last goodbye, we leave the gyrpuff nests behind.

We're all out of breath by the time we finally reach the glacier. The Vondur magic is dark within it, just as I remembered.

Runa gulps. "Maybe the potion isn't strong enough for this."

"It's Fairy's Gold," I remind her. "Straight from the heart of the Realm. What could be stronger?"

"There isn't much of it left," she says. "And we don't know if it's going to work after dawn."

"We'll never know unless we try," I say.

Ari studies the glacier with a frown. "So what's the best way to do this? It's not like we can chisel through the glacier to get the magic out."

"I've been thinking about that," I say. "The thing is, the Vondur had to get the magic in there somehow, right? If they could get it in, there has to be a way to get it out."

"Like what?" Runa asks. "Looks like a pretty solid glacier to me."

"Think about it. Seeker Larus said the Vondur don't really have magic. They use magical objects. So in order to cast that spell, they had to tie it to something physical. If the object they used is still here . . ."

"Let's spread out," Ari suggests, "and search the area."

We each take off in a different direction, peering around rocks and into crevices, searching for anything unusual. I cast my gift out wide, since it's hard to pick up on much of anything with so much Vondur magic emanating from the water. But if there's one good thing about the plague killing off every living thing around the stream, it's that there isn't much else to interfere with my gift, so any magical item should be easy to spot—

There. Something brushes against my gift, squeezed in the gap between two nearby rocks. It's full of Vondur magic, but there's something else, too. Something that feels like . . . like the Realm.

"Over here!" I shout, hoping Runa and Ari haven't gone too far. I crouch down and peer inside the gap, trying to get a good look at the object. Something long and dark gleams between the rocks.

"Don't touch it," Ari calls, approaching from behind me. "You never know what the Vondur magic might do."

"What do we do with it, then?" I ask.

"The potion!" Runa calls, running up to us. "Try pouring some of the potion onto it, and we'll see what happens."

"Will that work?" Ari asks skeptically.

Runa shrugs. "If this is the origin of the plague and the potion cures the plague . . . I don't know, seems worth a try."

"Let's do it," I say. "Runa, you have the bottle?"

Runa passes the potion to me. I crouch down and peer into the gap, trying to pinpoint the widest part of the mystery object. It's slender and slightly curved, and I'm afraid I'll throw away the last of our potion on the rocks instead if I don't aim *just* right.

We all hold our breath as I extend my arm, keep the bottle steady, and slowly tilt it, letting a few drops of the potion spill out. They land on the mystery object, and a golden light suddenly fills the space. I close my eyes and pour more of the potion out, just to make sure—

"Think you got it, Bryn," Ari says. "Something's happening!"

Hastily, I withdraw my arm and scramble away from the rocks. The gap between them is filled with a golden glow. The light lasts for a minute, maybe two, before suddenly winking out again. The gap between the rocks is completely dark.

"Did it work?" Runa whispers.

"Only one way to find out," I say. I let my gift flow, seeking the strange object. This time there's a strong magical sensation coming from between the rocks—but it isn't dark like Vondur magic. It feels like . . . a dragon.

"I think it worked," I whisper. I move forward and slowly stick my hand between the rocks again.

"Careful," Ari says, sounding worried.

"It's okay. I know what it is."

I pull the object from the rocks and hold it up to show him.

Ari exhales. "A dragon's claw?"

"Yep," I say. The claw rests easily in my hand, long and curved. Gold dust clings to its black surface. I surround it with my gift, but there's no trace of Vondur magic anywhere.

"It's really small," Runa remarks. "Did it actually come from a dragon?"

"It must have been Vin's, or the green dragon's," Ari says. "The Vondur had them when they were only babies."

"Vin's not missing a claw, so it must be from the green one," I say. "They used its magic to cast some sort of spell. That's what created the plague."

Runa's forehead creases. "But why was it planted here instead of in the water?"

"It's light enough to float," I say, weighing it in my palm. "If they put it directly into the water, it would just get swept away, and they might have lost it. By hiding it here, they always knew where it was, and there was little chance we'd find it. I guess it doesn't have to be directly in the water for the spell to work. It just had to be in proximity to the glacier."

"Like an anchor," Ari says suddenly. "We use anchors for our gifts all the time. Their spells must be similar."

"Makes sense. They're using Realm magic too." I hold up the claw. "They got all their power from this."

"So did this really stop the plague? Is the water clean now?" Runa asks.

"I guess we'll know soon," Ari says.

Together, we walk back to the glacier. When it comes

into view, Runa gasps, and my eyes widen. Where the blackness of the Vondur magic sat before, now there is a warm, golden light filling the space. It flows into the water, too, and the stream runs gold as it travels deeper into the Realm.

"We did it," Ari says slowly. "It actually worked!"

"Let's see how far it travels," I say. "Come on!"

Together, we run back to where Lilja is waiting for us. She's very disgruntled at being woken from her nap and doesn't at all share our excitement—until we bring out the bilberries, that is.

Once we're in the air, Ari and I guide her to just above Dragon's Point, where we have an amazing view of the Realm spread out below us.

"Look, you can see it," Runa says, and she's right. The golden light beams up at us, running straight through the Realm. Even as we watch, the light spreads, until it fills the horizon, reaching the farthest points of the Realm.

"And look over there!" Ari shouts, pointing. I follow his gaze to a bright halo of gold shining up from the center of the Valley of Ash.

"Seeker Larus must've put the potion in the water there, too," I say. "It worked!"

"Hear that?" Ari asks. "It sounds like . . ."

"Phoenixes!" I say. The soft, lulling melody fills the air around us. "They must be coming back to their nests."

"What's that?" Runa asks, pointing in the opposite direction, toward the southern cliffs. As we watch, another bright light shimmers in the air. But this one is violet, the color of a defender gift.

"It's Seeker Ludvik," I say. "He's removing the boundary spells. The quarantine is gone."

Ari smiles. "Guess we don't need it anymore. You did it, Bryn. You cured the plague!"

"*We* did it," I say. "As a team."

Together, flying on my favorite dragon, the three of us watch the golden light spread out below as the sun rises on the Realm.

Acknowledgments

When I first began to write a book about a plague, I had no idea that the real world would soon reflect my fictional one. Many people worked incredibly hard to create this book despite the unprecedented challenges we've all faced in 2020, and I am endlessly thankful for their support.

First, I am so grateful for my editor, Alyson Heller, who knew exactly how to develop this story and gave me the guidance I needed. I am honored to have worked with her for four books in a row.

Huge thanks to Cathleen McAllister, who created the gorgeous cover artwork, and to the entire team at Aladdin for all of their hard work.

As always, I am indebted to my agent, Victoria Doherty Munro, for all of her guidance, hard work, and support. Many thanks are also due to the foreign rights team at Writers House and to Berni Barta at CAA for their efforts on behalf of this series.

Thank you to Alexandrina Brant, who read an early draft and provided feedback and insight. I am also grateful to Rachel Done and Allison Pauli for their support and encouragement.

Many, many thanks to the amazing librarians, educators, booksellers, bloggers, and readers who have supported me and my books. Thank you for sharing Bryn's story.

ACKNOWLEDGMENTS

Thank you to Ellie, who was my constant companion as I wrote this book. I probably could have written it faster without the puppy paws on the keyboard, but I would have enjoyed it less.

Last but never least, thank you to my family: Mom, Dad, and Katie. I love you.

ABOUT THE AUTHOR

ALEXANDRA OTT writes fiction for young readers, including her debut fantasy novel, *Rules for Thieves*, and its sequel, *The Shadow Thieves*. She graduated from the University of Tulsa and is now a freelance editor. In her spare time, she eats a lot of chocolate and reads just about everything. She currently lives in Oklahoma with her tiny canine overlord. Visit her online at alexandraott.com.